To P

DON'T GO ALONE!

Watch for the clues or you will not get the ending. Good luck.

Margaret LeNoir
10-19-11

DON'T GO ALONE!

By
MARGARET LeNOIS

A Better Be Write Publisher
New Jersey

DON'T GO ALONE!

All Rights Reserved © 2006
Margaret LeNois

No part of this book may be reproduced or transmitted in any form or by any means, graphic, electronic, or mechanical, including photocopying, recording, taping, or by any information storage retrieval system, without the permission in writing from the publisher.

A Better Be Write Publisher, LLC

For information:
A Better Be Write Publisher, LLC
PO Box 1577
Millville, NJ 08332
www.abetterbewrite.com

ISBN: 978-0-9771971-3-2
ISBN: 0-9771971-3-1

Book Cover designed by Pamela Key

Printed in the United States of America

~Dedication~

This book is dedicated to my youngest son, William, who, from the course of having to travel for business, gave me the idea for this mystery thriller.

~Thank You~

  I would like to thank my friends, Cassie Mills, William Cohen (deceased), Eleanor Joy Schwank, and Judy Babb for critiquing my new book for me; to thank Ms. Patricia Moore for taking of her valuable time to not only critique my story but to find and correct all my errors and loose ends, and for her comments that leave no string unattached for the readers to find, as she is always there for me; to my husband, Tom, for all of his support, both mentally and physically, while I was writing this book; to my mother for always being there for me and although she is now ill and no longer living with me, she will always be my best friend; and to my son, Will, for the idea for this story and for having the same creative mind as his mother. I truly appreciate and love you all

"Many that live deserve death. And some die that deserve life. Can you give it to them? Then be not too eager to deal out death in the name of justice, fearing for your own safety. Even the wise cannot see all ends. "

~**J. R. R. Tolkien (1892 - 1973)**, *The Lord Of the Rings, Book Four, Chapter One*~

PROLOGUE

April 10, 2004 *Clyde-Ashville Citizen Times*, Clyde, NC Page 1:
    Tourist Found Slain In Hotel

April 14, 2004 *Greenville News,* Greer, SC Page 1:
    Desk Clerk Checks Out

May 14, 2004 *Jackson Clarion Ledger*, Louisville, MS Page 3:
    Woman Slain In Hotel

June 10, 2004 *Atlanta Journal-Constitution*, Atlanta, GA Page 1:
    Woman Found Dead At Mayor's Ball

* * * * *

Michael Bannagan sat staring at the faded green walls with the vulgar words written all over it. *How had this happened*, he wondered, tears filling his almond-shaped brown eyes. *What had happened? He barely knew that girl. He only had a few drinks and a dinner with her, for Christ's sake.*

But he had not even invited her! She had invited herself. Each and every time! He was only guilty of being nice. Ahh, but nice guys finish last, you dumb ass.

He was thirsty, but he was not sure if they would give him a drink. *Maybe they would piss in it and laugh at him behind his back. What is the protocol in these places?* he wondered. He had never been in a jail before in his life. *He had rights,* he said to himself angrily. His eyes burned with the tears of fear and he pressed the meaty palms of his hands into them, rubbing as hard as he could. The last thing he needed was for them to see him cry.

Was God punishing him for his lustfulness? For his affairs and adultery? If it was that, then he was doomed, he decided. He needed something to drink, even if there was piss in it. He could barely swallow. He also needed to take a leak, but he knew they were watching his every move. Not that them watching him take a piss bothered him. When you are male, you learn early that you have no privacy when other males were around, from school years to the military to the gym. *He would give his right arm for a scotch and water right now,* he thought running his dry tongue over already cracked lips.

And the indignities he had had to endure! The strip-search, as if he was a common criminal or a drug dealer! But then he wasn't in here for jay-walking. God, please, he prayed silently, *get me out of this mess and I swear on all that I hold dear, I will keep my dick in my pants. I will give more than ten per cent of my earnings to the church. Anything, Lord. Anything!*

He looked over at the two of them standing there talking. He had nothing to lose. He could no longer stand the thirst. He needed a drink, pissy or not. He got up and walked over to the door. "Guard."

~Chapter 1~

Michael Bannagan, Chairman of the Board and CEO of the DymoTek Corporation of Princeton, New Jersey, stretched his six foot, one inch frame as he got out of his leased Lexus. He listened to the cracking of his bones as he stretched his long arms up over his head, twisting his neck and head from side to side. He glanced up at the high rise named the Broadmoor Hotel and sighed. *The wonderful world of Boston*, he thought wryly. He was happy that Princeton was a classier town, with its dimensions of school architecture and students with backpacks walking aimlessly to their next class, to old-world and modern store-front mixtures featuring everything you could think of, along with its bistros for flavor. Boston was a busier, more shaded way of life where everybody and everything was in a hurry to be someplace else, even though it also had colleges. Somehow its students seemed to always be late for their next class or outing, and there seemed no need for many bistros where people sat and watched the world passing by and enjoying meeting the people at the next table. Bostonians knew all the people that they wanted to know and cared to not take the time to meet any others.

Bannagan was tired of traveling day in and day out, one state to another. *He was getting too old for it*, he decided, taking his mundane, dark brown leather luggage from the trunk. *I am as tired as this luggage that I have had forever*, he thought, smiling. His only traveling companions—one suit bag and a weekender—were both as haggard as he was.

"Good afternoon, Mr. Bannagan," the desk clerk said brightly after Michael had told her his name, her large child-like brown eyes sparkling, her wide smile genuine. "Your suite is all ready for you."

"Thank you. I am really beat." Bannagan dropped his luggage at his feet as a bellhop ran over to get them. The bellhop was the perfect image of the person to be who he was. He was probably about eighteen or nineteen, thin and wiry, his dark hair parted in the middle. He could have been any one of thousands of other teenagers anywhere in the United States. His large oval, protruding brown eyes looked at the desk clerk.

"Suite two-ten," she said, looking the bellhop in the eyes for only a second, as if looking at him for too long would make him think that he was on her level.

Bannagan nodded as he took the room card-key from the desk clerk, the name Kerri engraved in gold lettering on her nametag. "Thank you, Kerri." He looked over at the Parisian Room Lounge. He smiled to himself, and quickly stepped into the elevator with the bellhop. Before the doors had completely closed, he stuck his large hand back out the doors to block them from closing. Just before stepping out of the elevator he tipped the bellboy and instructed him to put his luggage in his room, and with long strides, he crossed the lobby to the lounge. Once inside, he let his eyes adjust to the dimness before proceeding to the long dark maple bar.

"Hello, Sir, what will it be today?" the bartender said, drying his hands with a white cotton hand towel as he approached Michael.

"Hi. Yes, I'll have a scotch and water on the rocks, please." Bannagan sat down heavily on the brown leather bar stool, folding his arms on the glazed wood surface of the bar. The bartender put a scotch and water on a cocktail napkin in front of him and his tab folded upside down in the lip of the bar. "Thanks. I really need this."

"Yes, Sir. I bet you do. Staying in the hotel, are you?" the bartender asked, wiping out a heavy beer mug, which had the Broadmoor Hotel logo etched on the side.

"Yes," Bannagan answered before swallowing a large gulp of the bitter, but cold, drink. "You must be a true Massachusetts native with that accent."

"I sure am…born and bred…but I don't ever tell anyone," he said, laughing with a heavy belly laugh. "Well, my name is Ed and if you need anything, please let me know. Excuse me," the bartender said, walking toward the other end of the bar where the waitress stood waiting, an order in her hand.

"This seat taken?"

Bannagan turned to look over his right shoulder. The soft, sexy voice belonged to a beautiful black woman whom Michael figured to be in her mid-twenties, with half-closed blue eyes, her long fake eyelashes creating an awning. "Nope," Michael answered, instinctively sucking in his stomach. "Help yourself." *Those blue eyes had to be colored contact lenses,* he thought, smiling.

"Thank you. I will," she said, sitting down next to him. She reached across the bar for an ashtray with a slim hand, her long thin fingers ending in pointed, dark red nails. She removed the Broadmoor Hotel matches from the ashtray.

Bannagan wondered why, when there were obviously lots of available stools that she could have chosen to sit on, that she had picked the one next to him. *Was she coming on to him?* he wondered, staring at her muted reflection on the silver-mirrored wall at the end of the gourmet coffee section of the bar. He took another sip of his scotch. He heard her fumbling with her pack of cigarettes. He knew that he should be a gentleman and light her cigarette for her, but he figured it wasn't his place to do so. Plus he was too tired to be polite.

"Whatcha gonna have?" the bartender asked her gruffly. He waited, watching her light her cigarette. She slowly took in a deep inhale of smoke, expanding her already full breasts. She exhaled the smoke towards the bartender, which he waved away from his face with the dishtowel.

"Let's see. How about a Mai Tai?" she said, her eyes flashing at the bartender. "With a cherry—and an umbrella!" she yelled as the bartender walked across the bar to make her drink. She chuckled softly as if someone had said something slightly amusing. "Make him earn his money."

Bannagan glanced at her and smiled. He looked across at the bartender who was staring back at them.

"Gloria," she said, leaning towards Michael, her right hand extended.

Bannagan had been aware of her perfume from the minute she sat next to him, and now she was so close to him that her warm breath was caressing his cheek and ear. He could feel his insides beginning to tighten. "Mike," he answered, shaking her extended hand, only glancing in her direction. He took another sip of his drink.

"Hi, Mike. A nice strong name. Is there a Mrs. Mike?" She watched him, fascinated by his uneasy reaction. Her gaze then shifted beyond him to settle on the slightly overweight bartender. "Hey! Barkeep! How about that drink, or are you still looking up the recipe on how to make it?" She laughed a tingly little shrill laugh. It held a tinge of bitterness.

Ed came down the bar and placed it on a napkin in front of her. "Four-fifty," he said through his teeth, again drying his hands on the same white towel.

"Run a tab," she answered between sips of her sweet drink. The bartender slowly shook his head as he walked toward the cash register.

"Yes, I'm married," Michael answered before taking another sip of his drink.

She leaned toward Bannagan, her shoulder against his, her mouth close to his face again. "So, Mike. You staying here at the hotel?"

"Yes," Bannagan answered, downing the rest of his scotch now and putting the glass back on the napkin. "Well, I have to go. It was nice to meet you, Gloria. Ed, charge this to my room, please," he said putting a dollar on the bar for the tip.

"Yeah, nice to meet you, too, Mike. Hope to see you again sometime," she said, toying with the little blue and pink umbrella in her drink. She watched him saunter out of the lounge door before turning her attention back to the bartender. "So, how's it going tonight, Ed?"

~Chapter 2~

Walking into his luxurious two-room suite, Bannagan slowly peeled off his suit jacket and tie and threw them on the arm of the plush, hunter green sofa. On the table was a beautiful bouquet of Bird-In-Paradise flowers. *Now where did they get those?* he wondered. *And why? He was no celebrity. Well, if they wanted to give him flowers that was fine with him. He liked flowers. But what's with that particular flower? It seemed lately that every hotel room he went to in all the different states, there had been a Bird-of-Paradise flower arrangement in the room. Must be the flower of the year,* he decided chuckling, *or a nation-wide sale on them.*

In the bathroom with the large mirror arched with six small spotlights held delicately in golden lamps shades, he stared at his unshaven face in the mirror, rubbing it with his left hand while the right one pointed his penis toward the toilet. *Could this face still attract beautiful women,* he wondered. *She was probably a hooker, you jerk. She wanted your wallet, not your body. What would a pretty young woman want with a beat-up, tired old man of forty-seven?* He sighed.

Going back to the sitting room, Michael picked up the room-service menu and browsed over the entrees. *Same shit as every other hotel. Why don't they ever change it?* he wondered. He was really in the mood for a slab of hot baked ham with some applesauce and mashed potatoes. He picked up the telephone, called room service and ordered the prime rib, medium-rare, baked potato with just butter, a Caesar salad, and a bottle of good Chianti.

Absently he began to unbutton his white shirt, pulling the back out of his trousers, and loosening his black leather belt. His stomach fell slightly, but he rubbed his tummy and smiled. *Comfort,* he thought smiling. *Fuck holding it in for some potential strange piece of ass.* He sat down on the overstuffed sofa, picked up the telephone and dialed his home number. Four rings and the voice mail answered it announcing that no one was available to take his call, but to please leave a message. "Hi honey. It's me. I'm here at the Broadmoor Hotel. 617-555-9000, Suite two-ten. Love you." He hung up. He felt empty. Lonely. He wondered where his wife, Barbara, was. *Probably at her mother's. Or out with her friend, Donna.* He stared at the pastel peach-colored wall without really seeing it. It was seven-thirty at night and the fading July sun cast heavy rays of final light through the windows as it slowly sank into the earth for the night.

Michael hated this time of the day when he was traveling. It was the loneliest time. During the day he could stay busy with work, and later he would sleep until he had to get up and do it all again. But the evening hours were the longest and the loneliest. He pulled himself up to a standing position, stretched the kink out of his low back, and slowly sauntered over to the sliding glass doors. He slid one side open and stepped out onto the balcony, surveying the Boston landscape of varying sized buildings, listening to the dull roar of the traffic from the streets below.

"You promised!" a woman's voice shouted. Michael looked over the balcony and saw one of the hotel maids talking to the tall pretty brunette, Gloria, from the lounge. He instinctively stepped back a pace so that they would not see him if they looked up.

"Lower your voice!" Gloria shouted back, looking around her to see who might hear them. More angry talk but Bannagan could not make it out.

"No! Now!" the older black woman screeched. Gloria said something in response, but the maid was losing control, becoming enraged. "Now, Bitch! No more waiting! You hear me? You do as I say! Now!"

Gloria struck the woman across her face. The maid quickly put her hand to her cheek, staring at Gloria in amazement. Gloria turned and started walking quickly down the street.

"You're going to pay for that! You fucking hear me? You are going to pay good for that one, Bitch!" But Gloria just kept walking, sticking her middle finger up in the air without looking back. "Big time, you fucking cunt!"

Bannagan watched Gloria until she turned the corner of the hotel and he could no longer see her. He looked down towards the maid again, but she had disappeared back into the hotel. *Wonder what that was about?* he thought, closing the balcony door behind him. *Maybe Gloria didn't leave a tip. Nah. The maid wouldn't have gotten so upset over that. Drugs maybe? A man? The maid was much older than Gloria so it couldn't be about a man—or could it?* He picked up his laptop computer and put it on the desk. He hooked up to the T1 line jack and signed on, hoping that his secret friend was waiting for him online. She was.

"Hi, there," he typed.

"Hi, yourself."

"I was hoping you were on. Waiting for me, maybe?"

"Of course. Are you in Boston now?"

"Yep. At the Broadmoor. Still on for lunch tomorrow or are you going to back out on me?" There was a knock on the door. "BRB," Michael typed before he jumped up and went to the door.

"Who is it?"

"Room service, Sir."

Bannagan opened the door and the waiter wheeled the food cart into his room. "I'll get it when I am ready. Thank you," Bannagan said, adding the tip and signing the tab the waiter handed him. "Thanks again."

"Yes, Sir," the waiter said as he departed. "Thank you, Sir."

"B," Michael typed on the keyboard letting her know that he was back.

"Company? I'm jealous."

"LOL," he typed for 'laughing out loud' in computer lingo. "Sure you are. Room service with my dinner," he explained. "So, one o'clock at the Biba Restaurant?"

"One o'clock."

"And how will I know you from every other beautiful woman there?" he asked.

"I'll be dressed in a light gray suit with matching shoes. I usually wear my hair tied up for work. Just look for a blond in a gray suit. It will be me."

"Janice? Excited about finally meeting me after all this time?" he asked her.

"Yes. And nervous. Have never done this before, Michael. You could be an axe murderer for all I know."

"LOL. Nope. Just an every day typical businessman. Besides, *you* could be the murderer. The female of all species are much better at killing than the males." He hesitated for a few seconds. "Janice?"

"Yes?"

"How about some hot chat now as an appetizer for tomorrow? Come on, Baby, talk dirty to me like you normally do." He began to rub between his legs as his groin pulsed and got hot—his dinner forgotten and getting cold.

~Chapter 3~

The morning had gone as expected and as usual at his client's company, except Bannagan had a hard time keeping focused on his work. He kept watching the clock. By twelve-thirty, he was back in his hotel room freshening up. He felt like a schoolboy setting out on his first date. His stomach was in a knot, his throat dry. He stared at himself in the mirror. His dark brown hair was streaked with more gray than brown and it had receded slightly; his brown eyes had small crow's feet lines at the outer edges, and his mouth drooped at the ends. Little frown lines creased his forehead. He stepped back from the mirror and took another look. *From here it doesn't seem that bad*, he thought with a smile on his face. *But then, had he planned to stay that far away from her? Wait! A better question, was he planning to get that close to her?*

His mind flashed to Barbara. It wasn't as if he hadn't done this before. Women had always thrown themselves at him, and he loved it. He had had several great relationships over the years. *Wendy, Cynthia, Paula. Great affairs*, he reminded himself. But Barbara always seemed to know when he was having an affair. *She was like a frigging bloodhound,* he thought angrily. He would beg her forgiveness, she'd rant and rave and cry, and he would make empty promises that he really truly meant to keep at the time he said them. But he just couldn't seem to say no to the bevy of beautiful women he met everywhere he went. Money and success spelled power, and women loved power more than the first two elements, and they made it hard for him to decline their invitations and stay faithful to his wife. But Barbara had put her foot down the last time he had been caught.

"One more time! Just one more time and I am gone forever, Michael! You better listen this time because I will not say it again!" The words bounced through his brain like an electric shock. "I can't take this anymore and I don't deserve it!"

He was suddenly consumed by guilt . . . and fear. But the thought of Janice caused the anxiety and excitement of meeting her make his heart race and his throat constrict. He had never had a blind date before so this was a whole new thrill in his sex life. *But it is just a lunch,* he reasoned. *He was not going to rush into a hotel room with a stranger he had met on the Internet, hot talk or no hot talk. He did not have anything to feel guilty about,* he reasoned. *He had lunch all the time with strange females he had just met. Of course they were business clients. But this is the same thing. Almost, anyway. He could still back out,* he told himself. *Or just not show up and that would be that. But he liked their nightly lovemaking hot chats.* He had pictured her for months now. He had pictured the many things that she was doing to him each time she typed its vivid description, and his manhood was standing to the occasion now as he remembered it all. Taking one last check in the mirror, Michael Bannagan went to meet his mystery Internet girl.

As he passed the hotel check-in counter, Michael told Kerri, "Thank you for the beautiful flowers. That was a very nice touch from the hotel."

"Oh, we had nothing to do with that, sir, I'm sorry to say. Those were dropped off for you," she responded, her pretty smile always on her young face.

"But there was no card with them, so I thought it was the hotel, . . ." He smiled at her. *That was strange, since he seemed to get the same flowers at each and every hotel he had stayed in so far this year. This time it must have been Janice,* he thought. *He would have to remember to thank her.*

* * * * *

She walked into the restaurant wearing an expensive light gray pinstriped suit with a dark gray silk blouse showing at the neck, pearl earrings, and gray shoes with a matching bag. Her well proportioned, size-ten figure, and her shiny platinum blond hair pulled up tight in a bun, gave her a taller appearance then she actually was. She was striking and all heads turned as she passed each table, but she seemed oblivious to their stares. Her gait showed confidence, assurance and power. She wore just a hint of a smile as she followed the maitre d' to Michael, acting as if she had known him all his life.

"Hi there," she said, her smile showing beautiful straight white teeth that actually shined under the lights of the restaurant.

"Janice?" He tried not to fumble when he stood up, his knees weak, but he knocked over the water glass throwing ice cubes and water everywhere. She laughed, but did not bother to make an attempt to help him clean it up. The waiters came running with towels and apologies spilling out of their mouths as if they had actually done it. Once it was all cleaned up, the maitre d' helped her with her chair. She sat down gently, as if she was made of glass.

"Do you always make a scene in restaurants or was it strictly for my benefit?" she remarked softly, still smiling.

"I'm sorry. I can be such a klutz sometimes," Michael answered, smiling sheepishly.

"By the way, thank you for the beautiful Bird-Of-Paradise bouquet."

"The what? It wasn't me, Michael. Sorry, must have been another girl. Actually, I should have thought of it. Sorry," she answered, putting her napkin on her lap. "I am the jealous type; did I tell you that before? Getting flowers from another woman? Definitely a jealousy trip." She laughed out loud now.

"This is so strange, Janice. Every hotel room I go to, no matter where, there has been a vase of Bird-of-Paradise flowers and no one seems to know where they came from or why, and there is never a note with them."

"You must have a secret admirer," she said thinly.

"I doubt that," he answered, noticing her change of mood. "I have only known one person who had an attraction for that strange flower, and they have been out of my life for a while now."

The bar waitress came over to get their drink order, and they decided on a bottle of Merlot. After ordering lunch, they sipped their wine and talked, and as she ran her shoeless foot up and down Michael's leg, two pairs of eyes watched from opposite sides of the room.

* * * *

Back at the E-Com Limited Corporation Boston office after lunch, Bannagan couldn't stop thinking about

Janice. He had struck pay dirt with this one. Not only was she intelligent, witty and gorgeous, she had a personality that made others boring by comparison—including Barbara.

He leaned back in his chair, rocking slightly back and forth, tapping his pen lightly on his front teeth. He had been very disappointed when he and Barbara, after ten years of marriage, had learned that she was unable to conceive children. She wanted to adopt, but he could not bear the thought of raising someone else's child. Now he was glad that it had worked out that way. Not that he didn't love her. He truly did. He was just bored again.

He was always bored. He craved excitement, but the only excitement he ever found was in having new affairs. There was something wonderful and powerful about that initial feeling of lust, of being infatuated with a new person in your life. The game that was created by the exchange of two people getting to know each other, testing, flirting.

Where did that fun and excitement go after marriage? Michael wondered. *Why was it you had to trade those exciting feelings and actions for the feelings of comfort and security? Why couldn't you have it all? The comfort and security of having that one person to come home to and share things with like best friends do, but also that excitement of making sure you looked great, had no bad breath, nothing stuck in your teeth from lunch? That tingle when you get close to home, knowing that special person was there waiting for you, instead of the automatic sigh of relief that you are home and can just be yourself without any pretense or work necessary to look and act your best.*

The only way to have it all, he assured himself, *was to have the wife and the girlfriends at the same time. Then all the feelings were yours at different times and on different levels of intensity. You play the game when you are out, and have the comfort when you are at home. Worked for him! The trick was keeping them separated, both physically and in your own mind. There was nothing worse than remembering a movie you had seen and saying that to your wife, when in fact you saw it with someone else; or saying another woman's name when you made love to your wife.* Michael smiled at the memories. He had done both. That was how he had been caught. He had made Babs suspicious from then on and she had starting checking it all out. And then she had not trusted him anymore so she watched him like a friggin' bloodhound on a search for a killer.

But the exciting feelings of the new game were here again. He was taking Janice Willowwood-Barton to dinner tonight, and he would make all his normal smooth moves to get her back to his room and into his bed. She had told him that she would meet him at the Sheffield's Steak House at eight. He figured she was probably just nervous about being in his car in case it didn't work out. This way she would not take the chance of being stranded without her car as a safety net. But everything had gone to Michael's satisfaction at lunch so he was not concerned about dinner.

"Mr. Bannagan? Mr. Diamond would like to talk to you in his office," the young assistant said, as Michael sat daydreaming at the desk they had given him for the week

He stood slowly, staring at her, angry that his thoughts had been interrupted.

~Chapter 4~

Bannagan got lucky and found a parking spot almost directly in front of his hotel. He whistled as he walked into the Parisian Lounge. "Hi, Ed," he said, sitting down on a stool close to the door. "Scotch and water on the rocks."

"Coming right up," Ed said, as he grabbed the good scotch.

"Well, hello again," Gloria said, sitting down next to Michael. "Want to buy a girl a drink?"

"Sure," he answered, slightly perturbed at her presence. He did not want company, did not want to buy someone a drink and certainly did not want to talk to this girl right now. He just wanted to plan his strategy on how he would handle Janice, how he would be smooth, what he would talk about that would keep her interested. He motioned to the bartender to give her a drink. Ed stared at him with cold dark eyes.

"What will it be today?" Ed asked her as he put Bannagan's drink on the bar in front of him. "Another Mai Tai?"

"No. I will have . . . a Margarita!" She smiled a wide smile at the bartender, showing large bright white teeth between two beautiful full red lips, then at Michael for approval. Bannagan smiled weakly at her.

"So, Mike, how was work today?" She asked, fishing in her purse for her cigarettes.

Bannagan moved an ashtray towards her. "It was okay. How about you? What do you do anyway?" he asked her, taking a sip of his cold drink.

"I'm an entertainer," she said, still peeking at the things in her purse.

"Yeah, right," Ed said, putting her drink in front of her. Gloria shot him a nasty look. "So that's what they're calling it these days?"

"Just ignore him, Mike. I am a dancer at the Plush Slipper Lounge right now, but I hope to be a chorus girl soon." She lit her cigarette. "I have this special friend who has a cousin who hires the show girls in Vegas, and he thinks he can get me an audition, so I am just waiting. Those guys are really busy, so it takes a while, you know. Him," she said, pointing one long finger at Ed, "he's just jealous. Got the hots for me, so he figures I am always going to be a nobody. He thinks I am a hooker because I dance at a titty bar."

"You will make it, Gloria," Bannagan said trying to build up her spirits. "Me? I have to run. I have an appointment. Enjoy your drink." He got up, nodded at the bartender to charge it to his room and left.

"Thanks again, Mike," she said quickly and a little too loudly. She watched him leave, drank her Margarita down in three or four large gulps, winked at the bartender and then sauntered out of the lounge. As she passed the front desk, Kerri looked up at her.

"Hey! We don't like your kind hanging around here," she spat at Gloria. "Get out of here or I will call Ed to throw you out!"

"Ahhh, Ed. The jack-off -of-all-trades and the doer of all the dirty work for the Broadmoor Hotel. Well, *some* people like me being around here," Gloria said, flipping her head around to watch Bannagan as he was getting into the elevator. "I'll be back. Mike and I are having dinner tonight. At the Top Of Boston! 'Anything I want,' he said."

"I'll bet!" Kerri shot back, the paper invoice in her hand now crumpled from grasping it so hard.

"Going to be a hot time at the Broadmoor tonight for me, so fuck *you*. Why don't you get a job that really pays!" she said sarcastically, walking slowly toward the counter where Kerri stood. "What's the matter, little girl? You would rather make six or seven bucks an hour and keep your twat clean? Or is the hotel manager keeping that hole full?" She stared into Kerri's horrified eyes, laughed and walked out of the hotel.

* * * * *

The evening had been very enjoyable for both Michael and Janice, starting with dinner at Sheffield's, an exclusive eatery known for its bold-tasting steaks and delicately prepared exquisite desserts. He followed dinner with a horse and buggy ride through town where they leisurely sat next to each other, hands clasped tightly, the brightly flickering stars just barely visible through the trees on the one side, and totally hidden by buildings on the other. They had decided that a stopover at the Jazz Blueroom for a nightcap would be the ideal ending to such an enlightening night between two new best friends.

Now as they lay spent side-by-side on the king-sized bed in his suite with the soft easy-listening music emanating from the living room radio and the candles still flickering in the soft breeze of the air-conditioning, he decided that everything they had done that night had just preceded and provided the perfect atmosphere for their afterglow.

Janice got out of bed, her slender body still glistening with the sweat they had generated. She walked naked into the bathroom, the candlelight casting a celestial glow on her strong back and beautiful buttocks, on her long legs. Michael lay there wondering what she was thinking, and where all this would eventually go. He glanced at the illuminated alarm clock dial. Three-ten in the morning. *I am definitely going to be tired today at work*, he mused, *but it had all been worth every second of lost sleep.*

Janice came out of the bathroom and began gathering up her clothes from where she had dropped them around the room as the thermometer of lust had begun to rise. "Where you going?" he asked, watching her.

"Home. I have to go to work tomorrow. . .today rather," she replied, pulling up her panty hose.

"Go to work from here," he said, propping himself up on one elbow, the urgency to keep her with him as long as possible showing in his voice. "Stay here until dawn at least. We'll have breakfast as the sun comes up. So what if we're late for work."

She laughed. "Easy for you to say. You're the boss. I have to be there, and I do not want to show up in the same clothes I wore yesterday. That would be like wearing a neon sign that says 'Look who got lucky last night!'" She laughed again, pulling her skirt over her slip and zipping it up.

"How about dinner again tonight, maybe take in a show?" He swung his legs over the side of the bed.

"Can't tonight, Michael. I'm busy."

"Busy? What's more important than us right now? Whatever it is, can't it wait?" He smoothed his hair back with both hands. He was trying to reason with her without feeling like a fool begging for a date. "I am only here for a week."

"Michael? Don't push, okay?" she said softly. "It was fun and I had a great time, but I do have a life and I had it long before you came along. Now that you are in my life does not mean that you can take it over, or that my old life stops in mid-air. Let's just go slow and easy." She walked over in the semi-darkness and kissed his mouth sweetly. "I had a wonderful time. Good-night."

"Are you married?" he asked brusquely, and was instantly sorry he had used that tone.

"What matters is that *you* are. Good night." And with that Janice vanished into the dark living room and out into the night.

Michael wished that he still smoked cigarettes.

* * * * *

"Hey, what's happening, Ollie?" Ed asked.

Olivia said, dropping down onto one of the bar stools, "When you grow up, Ed, don't become a maid. What's happening with you?"

He laughed his husky and hearty laugh. "Not much. Just finished closing out the money. Want a soda?"

"Sure, a cola. Thanks. I'm as beat as an old porch dog," she said, putting her feet up on another stool. "Seen Gloria around tonight, by chance?"

"Just around five-thirty. Why?"

"Was she talking to that Bannagan guy in two-ten?" She took a long drink of the cold soda, her black hand wrinkled from years of doing other people's linens and scrubbing piss stains off toilet seats.

"Yep. When he left, she left. Why are you asking all this?" He stopped and leaned on the bar in front of her, crossing his large meaty arms, his tattoo of the mermaid showing. "What's up?"

"Kerri told me that Gloria had a date tonight with that guy. That he was taking her to the Top Of Boston for dinner. Any truth in that?" She turned her large, tired brown eyes to stare into his to see if there was truth in his answer. She knew this Irishman had a taste for chocolate and for Gloria in particular.

"You kidding? And how does Kerri know that?" he answered sarcastically, wiping down the bar again as if someone had just sat there with a drink.

"Says that Gloria herself told her, and says she saw them together until he got on the elevator to go get ready. Think it's true?" she asked again. Her eyes stared questioningly at him.

"So what if it is true? Who cares besides you?"

"And you," she shot back quietly. He looked down at the bar. "Well, I went past his room about an hour ago and let me tell you, Ed, there was something going on in that suite! You think people would care about who heard what through these thin walls. So's anyway, then I goes into the vacant suite next door, and Lord, you should have heard them! Like two stray dogs in heat! Wait till I see that girl!"

"Aw, Ollie, let her alone. She's grown up now. She can do what she pleases," Ed remarked, putting one last full bottle on the serving shelf. "Besides, I have to go. I'm beat. I have to close this place up tight, so take your soda with you."

* * * * *

As soon as Bannagan left for work that morning, his bed was stripped and ready for clean sheets, the dirty glasses gathered up, and the bathroom cleaned and sterilized. By the time he entered the McCauley Building at eight-thirty, all order had been restored to his suite.

~Chapter 5~

All that day Bannagan was beside himself. He had gone on-line before he left for work that morning to see if by some chance Janice was on there looking for him. She wasn't. He had gone on several times that morning and part of the afternoon, and still she had not shown up. *How could he have been so stupid as to not even get her telephone number? Or address? Or her company?* he admonished himself. *He had no way to reach her except by computer. That was the trouble of living in the virtual world—you lose sight of real life and what was needed to live there. Depended on the computer for everything without realizing that it was not the perfect answer, didn't you, asshole?* he mentally said to himself. *Of course, that was how he had met Janice, so he just assumed . . . stupid, stupid, stupid!. He would correct that as soon as he connected with her again.*

Michael left the office at five-thirty and sped back to the Broadmoor and to his suite. He hurriedly hooked up his computer, turned on his buddy messenger list and waited. After an hour and a half had gone by, he decided to go down to the Parisian Lounge for a drink and a sandwich. As soon as he came through the doors, he spotted Gloria sitting at the bar talking to an older man dressed in a dark blue business suit. She was deeply engrossed in conversation, and the man's hand was on her knee. Michael waved to Ed, and pointing to a small table in the corner, motioned him for a drink. Within fifteen minutes, Gloria was standing in front of him.

"Mind if I sit down?" she asked, already pulling out a chair.

Bannagan looked over at the bartender who was drying glasses and watching them at the same time. "Actually, Gloria, I just came down for a quick drink and a sandwich," he said quietly, almost a whisper. "I have a lot of work to do in my room."

"Great. I'm starved, though. Buy me one, too?" she begged, whispering back. "I'm just a little tight right now, but business should be picking up by the weekend. During the week, it's always slim pickings. You wouldn't let a girl go hungry, would ya, Mike?"

He stared at her, noticing for the first time how really young she appeared under all that make-up. Her blue eyes, unusual for an African-American, were shiny and yet sad. "Sure, why not? Sit down."

"Thank you," she whispered again, sitting closer. She noticed Olivia watching her from the small window in the kitchen door, a frown on her high black forehead. Gloria felt bad about slapping her the other day, but she still felt that Olivia had had it coming. *Always in my face about something,* she told herself, ignoring the scowl on Olivia's long face.

"Good evening, Mr. Bannagan. Here is your drink, Sir," the young waitress said, ignoring Gloria and putting his scotch and water down in front of him, but giving a more disapproving look to Gloria.

"Thank you. Would you bring us some menus and a drink for the lady, please."

The waitress shot Gloria a disdainful look. "Yes, Sir. Gloria? What would the *lady* like?" she said in a crisp sarcastic voice.

"What do you think, Mike?" Gloria asked, her chin resting in her hand, her upper body leaning toward him.

"Whatever you like," he said, scanning the room and looking at the other patrons out of curiosity. Gloria ordered a Meyers and Coke. The waitress returned immediately with the drink and two menus.

Gloria and Mike talked about many things, but mostly about Gloria, her favorite subject. And he ended up feeling extremely sorry for her. She had so many dreams for her future. Unrealistic dreams. Dreams that even if Lady Luck picked her up physically and carried her, she might barely make it, but Bannagan would not have bet on it. He realized that she lived in her own world of fantasy and concluded that it was probably easier for her to cope with her life by pretending that hers was different than it really was. Some people were born to lose, almost as if it was genetically ordained at birth, and Gloria was one of them.

She told him that she had been born and raised on the south side of Boston, in the projects area, and had gotten off to a turbulent start by being raped by a teen-aged boy who was her babysitter when she was only three years old.

Before Bannagan realized it, it was almost nine o'clock. He told her that he was tired, had had a great time and politely said good night. He signed a guest check for the food and drinks, thanked Gloria for her company and headed for his suite.

A few minutes later, Gloria came out of the lounge and heading for the elevators, winked at Kerri and Olivia who were both standing behind the counter glaring at her.

Two other sets of eyes watched the beautiful young dark woman as she pushed the up button for the elevator.

* * * * *

At ten-twenty, there was a knock on the door, and Bannagan yelled from his seat at the desk, "Who is it?" There was no answer. "Who's there?" Nothing. He got up angrily and stormed to the door, pulling it open wide.

"Didn't your mother ever warn you against opening doors to strangers?"

"Janice! I was just waiting on the computer hoping that you would come on," he babbled. "Come in, come in," he said stepping back and pulling her with him. As soon as he had shut the door, his mouth covered hers. "God, I thought about you all damn day! I had no way to reach you, no idea where you live or work! So, now, tell me so I am not tied to this laptop in order to talk to you." He grabbed a pen and a complimentary hotel notepad from the desk.

"I would rather not," she said firmly, still standing where he had left her by the door.

"What? Why not?" He stood quietly waiting for an answer. She did not respond. "Janice?" He sighed, long and deep. "What is it? You're married, aren't you? Tell me. That's not fair. I told you the truth about me. I was honest and up front."

"Yes, Michael, you were, but I had never asked you to be."

"Okayyyyy," he said, drawing the word out. "Work number. I'll only contact you there."

"I am married and my father-in-law owns the company. I work for him, so he would know in a matter of minutes if someone took a call for me from a man and it would get back to my husband before we hung up. It is company policy that anyone who answers the phone needs to get the caller's name, telephone number and why he is calling so that the receptionist can be sure that the call goes to the right department. I get very few calls, so it would be suspicious right from the start."

Bannagan sat down heavily on the desk chair. He stared down at the plush dark melon carpeting. She came to him and held his head against her breast, running her slim fingers through his hair. He wrapped his big arms around her waist. "So, you are married. Now what?" he asked her softly. "You seem to be the one in total control here."

She pulled him to his feet and, still holding his hand, she walked him into the bedroom. They made wild, savage love for hours until neither had the strength to go on. Michael was sound asleep within fifteen minutes.

At two-thirty in the morning, Janice was on her feet and dressed. She tiptoed out of the bedroom and gently closed the suite door behind her. She sighed deeply, turned around, and jumped at the sight of Gloria standing behind her in the hall. She cupped her hand over her mouth so as to not scream and wake up everyone on the floor. "Christ! You scared the fuck out of me!" she hissed at Gloria.

"Bitch having to go home in the wee hours, ain't it?" Gloria responded in her normal voice, leaning against the hall wall lighting a cigarette and then throwing the burnt match on the faded carpet.

"Sshh," Janice told her, her eyes still on the match lying on the hall carpet.

"Ah, I got it! Somebody's wifey is fooling around with somebody else's ole man!" Gloria laughed loudly and with her left hand she fluffed some large curls. "That's it, ain't it, Baby!" She laughed again, taking another long drag on her cigarette and shaking her head. "All you high-scale bitches think that because you are married to money, you can pretend it is an affair, when all it is, *Mrs.* Snooty-Tootie, is just another lay. It's just that you get jewelry and furs, and I get money. But who you *think* you are is what saves you from feeling like an unwanted, unloved, and unappreciated woman. You *think* you can justify it because of your husband's cold nature. Well, Bitch, all I can say is save that bullshit for your shrink. You ain't nothing but a whore, plain and simple. A plain old whore just like me! Except I am young and you is old."

~Chapter 6~

Bannagan awoke to loud screams and angry voices out in the hall. He rolled slowly over and looked at the clock. *Four-fifteen in the damn morning!* More screams—female screams. He slowly got up, and pulling on his robe, he walked groggily and bare-footed to the front suite door. The screams continued.

Michael opened the door to find the hall crowded with police officers, EMTs from the rescue squad, and other hotel guests in varying degrees of nightclothes. The screams were coming from the older maid whom Bannagan had seen with Gloria that day in front of the hotel.

"You!" she screamed at Michael when she saw him. "That's him! He did it! He did it! I heard them!" she wailed at the top of her voice. Everyone was looking at him.

Michael didn't hear what she was saying. He stood frozen, staring down at Gloria, her bloody body staining the hallway carpeting with dark blood. "It's him, it's him," the maid cried out, sinking to the floor in a sobbing heap. One officer and a woman tried to help her up until two EMTs came over and picked the frail woman up and put her on a stretcher. She continued to point to Michael, screaming over and over "It's him! I heard them!"

Two cops came over to Michael. "What's going on?" he asked them, totally confused. "What's me?" His bleary eyes were transfixed on the body sprawled face up, her eyes staring lifelessly at the ceiling. Her spandex, black mini-skirt was up snug around her hips, and her black lace panties were slightly pulled to the right, showing Gloria's curly black pubic hair. Michael wanted to pull her skirt down to cover her. *Why don't the cops to that?* he wondered. Her shiny black hair was now matted with blood, which had streamed down the side of her face, into her ear, and had blended with a larger wound at the neck. Two broken bits of her long dark red fingernails were lying close to her right hand.

"Your name, Sir?" the shorter cop asked him.

"Michael. Michael Bannagan," he said, finally looking up at the large Italian policeman who stood in front of him, now blocking his view of Gloria. "What happened here? Who killed Gloria?"

"So you knew her? Like the maid said, you knew her?" the detective asked, reaching behind him to pull out his handcuffs from under his suit jacket.

"Yes." Michael said, looking from one cop to the other. "So? I just met her a couple of days ago down in the bar. She asked me to buy her a couple of drinks and something to eat. But that was it. Those are the only times I have ever seen her. Ask the bartender."

"Don't worry, we will. But for now I think you need to come down to the station with us and we can sort this all out there."

"Sort what out?" Michael asked, now beginning to get nervous. "I barely knew her!"

"Here you go, Sarge," a young officer said breathlessly after running up the stairs from the first floor. He handed two folded papers to the Italian cop.

"Mr. Bannagan, first, here is a search warrant for your suite," the officer said handing Michael the search warrant.

"Why?" Michael asked the cop, louder than he had intended to. "Why should you search my suite, for God's sake? I didn't do anything to this girl."

"Mr. Bannagan, are you going to come quietly?"

"No, damn it! I did nothing to that girl. I do not care what that maid had to say."

"Mr. Bannagan, you need to come with us quietly or I will have to place you under arrest for the murder of Gloria Swanson."

"What??" Michael said, dumbfounded. "Wait," he said as they pulled his arms behind his back and handcuffed him.

"You don't want to give us a hard time, Mr. Bannagan. You will only make it worse for yourself," said the short cop. "Resisting arrest will make us take stronger measures to confine you. Now you are going downtown. It is up to you whether it is done the easy way or the hard way."

"You have the right to remain silent..."

Michael began to struggle. "Stop! What are you doing? Are you crazy? I didn't kill her! I told you that I barely knew her!"

"You have the right to an attorney..."

"Please! Let me talk!" he said, trying to pull away from the two men restraining him. "You don't have the right to search my room, warrant or no warrant!" He yelled to the cops now tearing his rooms apart, "And don't touch that computer!"

"If you cannot afford one…"

"Ask that old maid! *She* had a reason to kill her!"

"Really? That *old maid*, as you call her, is the victim's mother!"

Michael pulled free of the officers, but before he knew what had happened, he felt a severe sharp pain go through his entire body, so strong that he lost his breath and he fell to his knees and then onto his stomach, his hands still handcuffed behind him. The officer who had hit him with a bolt of electricity from a stun gun began to pack it back up.

"Why do they always pick the hard way?"

~Chapter 7~

"**Gloria Swanson??**" Bennedetto said, laughing. "Didn't she die years ago?" He continued to laugh while the younger detective stared at him as if Bennedetto had lost his mind.

"No, Bennie, she was killed last night…actually, this morning, at the Broadmoor. You find that funny, do ya?" Detective Dan O'Callaghan said, his slightly broken English twirling his words, even though he was second generation Irish/American.

"No. No. Gloria Swanson was a silent film star. Way before your time, kid. Actually, before mine, too!"

"Was she black?" O'Callaghan asked seriously, his ruddy large face getting a bit flushed with anger at being laughed at.

"Black? No, kid, a blonde, I think. This Gloria Swanson was black?" Bennedetto asked absently, shuffling through a stack of old reports and bulletins, a chuckle still in his throat as he continued to think about the name.

"Gorgeous. Brown maple skin, big blue eyes, long slender legs. Not so gorgeous now lying at the morgue."

O'Callaghan sat his large burly frame into his wooden chair. He pulled an official police report from its bin on his desk. "And stop calling me kid! How many times I have to tell you that? I am almost as old as you!"

"Blue eyes? Now that's different. Probably contacts. What happened to her?" Bennedetto asked, sitting down in his old wooden desk chair, which he figured was probably older than he was. The chair moaned and squeaked under his weight.

"Badly beat up, stabbed, and throat cut, ear to ear. Blood everywhere. She obviously crawled from one of the rooms out into the hall. It was hard to tell, there was so much blood everywhere, but there was a line of blood from room two-o-seven. Think she was hooking at the hotel. Everyone seemed to know her. Soon as the day shift comes on, we have to go check it out. Crime unit is still there now going over the place. Probably a million fingerprints, at the least, in that hotel room. They arrested one of the hotel guests, a guy named Bannagan who seemed to be screwing her. Shannon is processing him now. We have an eyewitness to the affair; a maid named Olivia Johnson. EMTs had to take her to Bellemead General to be sedated. Very distraught over the whole thing. Not that I blame her. She was the vic's mother and it was pretty gory. The mother found her, I think."

"Let's go check out the interrogation. Where they got him?"

"Room four," Detective Frank Corelli answered, following his partner, the big Italian machievo everyone called Bennie. They joined two other officers at the window.

"What's happening," Bennedetto asked the two street cops.

"Nothing. Wants his telephone calls. Wants his attorney. Just repeats it over and over," Officer Larsen said, leaning against the edge of the one-way window. "To look at him and his bathrobe and jammies, you would never figure him for a murderer. Strictly the businessman type. Lives in Princeton, New Jersey. Just here for a business trip. Staying at the Broadmoor according to the desk clerk. Some big CEO from a large technology company or something. This should bring his company's stock down a few points!"

* * * * *

The telephone rang and rang. After the voice mail said its usual message, Bannagan barked, "Barbara? Where the hell are you? I have been arrested and I need your help! I am at the Fourth Street Station here in Boston. Barbara, please! Call Loganthau and see if I have already talked to him. If not, tell him what I just told you and have him get his ass up here as soon as possible. I am going to try calling him next." He hung up, hearing his own heart pounding in his chest as if he had just run five miles.

He then placed a call to his attorney, Arthur Loganthau. *Where the hell is Barbara at six-thirty in the fucking morning,* he asked himself. *And why did he call her first? She'd never be able to help him. Maybe she wouldn't help him at all seeing how their marriage had been going lately. This must be punishment from God—a message that I need to stop fooling around.* He wasn't sure whether he really believed that last thought or not. He did not truly believe that his God had nothing better to do than to stay up there in heaven and plot his life course, to figure out ways to screw with him every day. He was a religious man in his own right, but Bannagan was his own devil's advocate when it came to what he believed. He was like that song, ". . . not afraid of dying, hoped there was a heaven and prayed there was no hell. . . ."

"Hello," Art said in a groggy voice.

"Art. It's Mike Bannagan. I need your help now, or I would not have called so early." He looked around the large barren room to see who might be listening. There was no one except the cop that was his current guard.

"Mike? What's the matter?" the attorney asked, propping himself up on the bed pillows on one elbow and looking at the clock on the radio on the nightstand.

"I've been arrested in Boston. You have to get me out of here!" Bannagan was getting closer to hysteria. A cop walked by who eyed him up and down.

"What? You?" Art said, laughing. "What for? Jaywalking?"

"Murder." There was a deafening silence. "Did you hear me?"

"Yes. Was it a mosquito or a gnat?" More laughter.

"You think this if fucking funny, Art? Get your ass up here and I will show you just how funny it is," Bannagan snarled at him, his hand covering the phone's mouthpiece."

"What's the precinct's address? And phone number if you have it. Have they told you anything yet? Have you said *anything* to them?" Art was grabbing his robe, and then pushing his wife gently, motioned for her to please make coffee. He knew that he would not be able to get to keep this day off, but he would never have guessed that it would be something like this—and definitely not with Michael Bannagan, Mr. Straight-as-an-arrow Bannagan.

Michael gave him the precinct address and phone number. "They have only told me that they have a witness who claims it was me who killed the woman, and that all the evidence so far also points to me. I have said nothing but that I wanted an attorney and that they are crazy and so is their witness."

"Don't argue with them. Let me have a cup of coffee while I get dressed, and I will call them and see what this is all about. Oh, Mike?"

"What?"

"Who was killed?" Loganthau asked as he was putting on his suit trousers that he had worn the day before, letting a shower go for the time being until he could sort all of this out.

"A hooker. At least I *think* she was a hooker. A woman I met in the hotel bar. Black woman." He rubbed his burning eyes with his free hand. It had been a long night. *First Janice, then this,* he thought wryly.

"You knew this woman?" he asked Bannagan, trying to find his other sock that he had thrown on the floor late last night when he had dragged himself home. He had gone out with one of his partners and his legal assistant to get drunk. He had lost his case yesterday in court, a woman charged with embezzlement of her company. She was a sweet woman, pretty, who was the bookkeeper for the small company, and although he believed that she really was guilty, he had been sure that he had saved her. He had been wrong. She had three young children, was a single mother, and now would lose her kids to the state, and he had lost her case. They had had to physically pick her up and carry her out screaming and crying when she went hysterical in the courtroom after the verdict was read.

"Kind of. I mean we had a couple of drinks together, that's all. I *hardly* knew her. Call them, Art! Get me the fuck out of here!"

"Mike, I will do my damnedest, but I have to call in Jonathan Perry on this. He has much more criminal expertise and experience than I do. I will try to bring him with me. Just stay cool, and we will be there by lunch. Okay? Can you do that?"

"Yes," Bannagan said softly, his voice breaking under the stress. Loganthau hung up. Michael replaced the telephone slowly, and a cop was at his side immediately to escort him back to his cell to wait for his lawyer to show up.

* * * * *

"Has he called you lately?" the screen asked.

"No. I have been . . . out," she typed back. "Did he bite?"

"Oh, he bit alright! LOL. "I have the bruise marks to prove it. Are you sure you want out? He's a damn good guy!"

"I want out. Don't give out on me now…and stop necking with my husband. I am counting on you to get this done right. I really need out of this marriage and everything else that goes with it, but I can't do it without the finances to carry me, so that means that we have no choice but to do it this way. I do not like it either but I know what I have to do to cover myself. Don't fucking strap me down on this now. I'll be ruined without your help."

"I won't, don't worry. Babs, what if I wanted to keep him? For myself, I mean? You have a problem with that?" No words were typed for a minute. "Hello? You still there?"

"I think I do have a problem with you going with my husband after this is all over. You and I have been best friends, like forever. If you and him got together, he would eventually find out about this. He is very smart. If you slipped up, even slightly, he would catch it and it would be all over. Besides, you don't know him like I do. You wouldn't want him if you did. Please. Let's not change the script, okay? I have a detective following you and he is recording like crazy. I received the first pictures and report yesterday by FedEx. He not only got pictures of you with him, but pictures of Michael with some black broad that was probably young enough to be his daughter. I am so lucky to have a friend like you, and I really appreciate you helping me like this. I truly owe you one."

"Yes, you do. LOL I have to go. I am having lunch with him at noon at the Sheppard's Pie. He takes me to the best places. Later."

"Got it. Thanks. Bye."

The monitor screens went black almost simultaneously.

~Chapter 8~

"Mike. You're in some serious shit here," Loganthau told Bannagan, sitting down at the small table in the attorney conference room. Bannagan looked from him to Perry and back again. "It seems that Ms. Swanson was living at the hotel, kind of, in a room that was seldom ever used for patrons, and right across from your suite. They found a glass with your fingerprints on it in her room . . ."

"What? That's impossible!" he said, cutting Loganthau off. "I was never *in* her room. I did not even know she *had* a room!" Bannagan shouted, jumping up and walking to the grated window and then back to the table.

"Try to relax, Mike. Getting upset is not going to help the situation," Loganthau said, glancing behind him at the window in the door. The guard was peeking in. "There's more, Mike. The maid said that she heard you and Ms. Swanson making love, and according to her, 'it was loud enough to wake the dead.' No pun intended. Were you getting laid?"

"No. Well, at least not with Gloria," Michael said, his eyes looking down at the oak table.

"Oh, thank God! You have a witness," Perry said, finally joining the conversation. He sat up straighter, ready to take some notes.

"No, I don't." Michael felt doomed. *It was going to be my damn sex drive that's going to take my life down the toilet,* he thought. *How ironic.*

"Excuse me, you just said . . ." Perry began, totally confused now. "You mean it was a pick-up date? Did you find her in a bar?"

"I can't use her, I tell you." He ran his hands through his hair a nervous habit that anyone who knew him, knew he often performed that totally unconscious act. Art Loganthau watched that normal movement. There was nothing he could detect from it as it was done at good times as well as bad. It meant nothing.

"And why the hell not?" Loganthau asked him, astounded by Mike's attitude. "So you have trouble coming from Barbara. Better to end your marriage than to go to federal prison for twenty-five to life! Not to mention the possibility of the death penalty. You have to bring it out in the open now."

"Because, as you know," Michael started slowly and quietly, "I am married. And so is she, but that is not the only problem." Bannagan ran his large hand through his hair again. "Oh God, what am I going to do? You have to get me out of this!"

"Oh, I see. You would rather go to jail, and possibly end up facing the death penalty, than to let your wife know that you were screwing around on her. *Again.* Not to mention, you love this girl so much that you would chance prison and/or death to protect her from a divorce from her husband? How noble of you, Mike!" It was Loganthau's turn to get up and pace.

"I can not tell you how to find her because I can't find her either, except on the computer." *There it was out. He had said it.* It sounded out loud just as Michael had thought that it would, and he could feel himself blushing.

"Oh, for Christ's sake! A computer affair? You at least know her real name, right? Or do you only know her screen name?" Perry asked, pen in hand.

"Janice."

"Janice what?" Loganthau was getting disgusted with his client and friend of fifteen years.

No response. It suddenly seemed so ridiculous to Michael that he felt like laughing, that it was like some kind of sick joke that he had pulled on himself. He felt like such a jerk; a schoolboy with no sense who walked around with one hand in his pocket all the time giving himself a quick feel when he thought no one else was looking. The excitement of the affair had already changed to shame and guilt, not to mention stupidity. He could not bring himself to look at either attorney.

"For Christ's sake!! You have no idea, do you?" Michael did not answer nor even look up. "A phone number? Home address? Where she works? Anything?" Loganthau asked, with his turn to shout, sitting back down, his hands clasped in front of him on the table.

"Willowwood-Barton," Bannagan said, quietly.

"What?"

"Willowwood-Barton. That's her last name. Janice Willowwood-Barton. Lives here in Boston. With *Mister* Willowwood-Barton," Bannagan said bitterly. *But then who was he to talk?* he thought. "Just look her up in the telephone book. Doubt if she is listed though. She is not listed on the computer anywhere either. I checked every Willowwood and Barton on there trying to find out more about her because she was being so mysterious."

"Well, scratch the alibi. Okay, we will try to find this Janice Willowwood-Barton. There really is a Janice Willowwood-Barton, Mike, right? We don't have the time for a goose chase?"

Bannagan shot him a nasty look.

"Okay. I am just checking. Did she stay all night?" Perry asked, writing notes on his legal pad.

Oh, now they want the gory details, the sex part of the story for their talks with their wives that night over dinner, Michael thought bitterly. "No. She left around two-thirty, maybe almost three. I'm not sure. I was very tired. I fell right to sleep. She had left once before around three, so I guess she did the same thing again this time. I don't fucking know. She was not there when I woke up at four-fifteen."

"You are sure about the time you woke up?" Perry asked, taking his handkerchief from his back pants pocket to blow his nose, but instead he just wiped at a moist spot under his nose, leaving a small booger peeking out of one nostril.

"Yes. I looked at the alarm clock and could not believe that there was so much noise in the hallway that early in the morning. It was four-fifteen—on the nose." *Speaking of noses,* Michael thought and smiled inside at the pun. Of course, he could not help looking at the booger, even though he tried not to.

"Did you take her to dinner first? That could be proven by any witnesses who saw you two together," Perry asked.

"Well, we didn't have dinner together that night. In fact, I did not know she was even coming to see me. She just showed up at my door around ten-fifteen, ten-thirty," Bannagan said, suddenly remembering his dinner. "However, I had dinner in the Parisian Lounge and Café there in the hotel."

"And people saw you there? Did you talk to anyone?" Hope suddenly sprang up for Loganthau.

Michael hesitated, and Perry and Loganthau looked up at him. "I had dinner with the victim." He saw the two attorneys pass a look. "No, it was not like that. I went in for dinner. Gloria was at the bar, *as usual*, except she was talking to some older guy. I sat at a table. She came over to the table and just sat down. I did not ask her to sit down. I did not motion for her to come over to the table. She asked me to buy her dinner. I figured that she was hungry, and I felt sorry for her, so I had dinner with her. I paid." Another look was exchanged between Perry and Loganthau. "Look! I am telling you the truth! I left after dinner and went up to my room to wait for Janice to come on the computer, but she showed up at my door instead. I never saw Gloria after that again until —" Michael's voice trailed off.

"You know how this is going to look, don't you, Mike?" Loganthau said as calmly as possible.

"Hey! The guy she had been playing footsy with at the bar could have done it! Ed, the bartender disliked her! He could have done it! She had a big fight the other evening and slapped that maid that is accusing *me*! The maid screamed that she would get even. Maybe she did it! Anyone could have done it! Anyone but me—*I did not do it!*"

The guard looked in the room again at Michael's outburst. "What are you looking at?" Bannagan shouted at the guard. Loganthau waved the guard away.

"I know how this must all look, but it was all innocent, and so am I! So help me, God, I am telling you the truth. Why would I lie to you guys? Art, you are, and have been for a long time, my friend and my attorney. You *have* to believe me."

"I *do* believe you, Mike. I cannot believe that this is happening to you of all people. But it is and we have to deal with it. They want a sample of your hair, Mike, both from your head and your pubic area," Loganthau stated calmly, as though he did this every day with his clients..

"What?"

"And a semen specimen. They are going to check your DNA, as well as the hair and semen. The cops claim that she had sex before she was killed. If it wasn't you, this should clear you." Loganthau sat back in his chair and stared at Bannagan who was scowling back at him. "Is there anything else you can tell us before we go?"

"When am I going to be arraigned? Can you bail me out?"

"Now. You are scheduled there in a half-hour. We will meet you at the courthouse. You will probably have to post bail. You have enough for bail, yes?"

"How much you figure?"

"Can't say right now. We hope not more than a few thousand. But this is second degree murder, Mike. Might not even give you any bail. Especially since you live out of state. We will do what we can, but we are new to this state, too, so we have no political power."

"I have a call in to a friend, Mike," Perry said, putting his hand on Bannagan's shoulder. "He is a big criminal attorney here in Boston. I am hoping that he can help us with this."

"And we have hired an investigative firm, also from Boston, who will help us weed out some of the stuff that they are calling evidence, and as soon as I meet with the prosecuting attorney, I will know what they figure they have. This P.I. firm has a really great reputation for finding out stuff, and will probably be costly, but we are looking at saving your life here, so we are taking no chances. We are calling in the big guns everywhere for everything." Loganthau knocked on the door for the guard to open it. "We will see you shortly, Mike. Stay calm."

As soon as the attorneys were out of sight, two guards came through the door with chains in their hands. "What are those for?" Bannagan asked them.

"Going to visit the judge, so you need to put on your fancy-go-meetin' jewelry," the one cop said, stooping to put the leg irons on Bannagan's ankles.

"Those aren't necessary. I am not going anywhere," Bannagan told him.

"You bet. My job is to see that you don't. Hands together, please."

Michael suddenly remembered his lunch with Janice at noon. "Wait! Get my attorneys back here! I just remembered something!"

"Calm down, man! You'll see them shortly in court." They began to walk him out of the room.

"Wait! You don't understand! It will be too late by then! You have to stop my attorneys! It's *really* important!" He pulled away from them and tried to run awkwardly down the hall, until he tripped on his own feet and fell against a desk that was in the corridor.

"Damn you, man!" the cop yelled down at him. "Now look at your head! Bob, get me something to stop this bleeding and call the nurse!"

Michael Bannagan began to lose consciousness, gladly floating off into the darkness that now surrounded him.

* * * * *

"Something's gone wrong" was typed onto the screen.

"Yes. I know. He's in jail!"

"What? Why?"

"Murdered some hooker! Knew he would lose it one day. Serves him right! Anyway, this is perfect now. You can go on your merry way and go back to your normal life. I really, really appreciate your help, Bev. I could not have done this without you."

"Wait. When did this murder take place and who was killed? Tell me what happened?" Beverly typed on the computer, fear rising up to her throat.

"It happened early this morning at his hotel. Maid found her right outside his suite in the hall. I just spoke to him from some hospital and now I have to run to Boston. Just what I wanted to do today, go bail the bastard out of jail and out of the hospital. What a fuck-up he is! He even fell and cut his head wide open. The jerk!" Barbara Bannagan said on the computer, looking at her fingernails on one hand. "He needs a baby-sitter, not a wife. Anyway, it helps me."

"He couldn't have killed that girl, Babs!"

"Why not?" Barbara asked, deciding that as soon as she got back from Boston, she needed to call and make an appointment to get her nails done. *Had three weeks flown by already? Maybe she should get her pedicure done at the same time. She was going to be free soon and would need more time to do things besides primp.*

"Because I was with him until almost three this morning, and there was some hooker out in the hall. She scared me to death! But she was totally alive and well, and very smart-mouthed so I can understand someone wanting to kill the bitch, but she was alive and he was sound asleep. He *did not* kill that girl."

"What were you doing there until three in the morning? Oh, my God! You really went to bed with him? You went to bed with my *husband*?" Barbara wrote, shocked that her friend would go all the way on this.

"Wait a minute here! You told me to. Remember?"

"I told you to make a play for him. I told you to make him appear to be cheating so the detective could get his evidence and pictures. I never told you to go all the way into bed!" No words were typed onto the screen for about thirty seconds. "No matter. Never mind."

"Wait just a minute here! Why are you suddenly the poor unknowing innocent wife? We spoke about this last night. I told you then I wanted him. 'You said no way, Jose'. Now, you play the 'You fucked my husband—eek' routine? Why? Nervous that I can give him an alibi? That I can blow your divorce for you?"

"Sure, why not? You probably blew my husband, too! Besides, Bev, I do believe that if you went to the police and told them that you were with him last night, that they could probably arrest you as an accessory to murder in the first degree." The screen remained blank. "You were probably the last one to see her alive. In fact, maybe *you* are the one who actually did it! Huh! What about that, Bev? You do her? I bet you did." Nothing appeared on the screen in rebuttal. "Time for you to bow gracefully out of the picture now, wouldn't you say? Think about it, my friend. I have to go. I have to go to Boston. My poor, poor husband needs me. LOL."

The computer was turned off and Barbara was gone. Bev sat and stared at her screen before making a copy of the whole chat conversation. *Babs always has underestimated me,* she mused. *Otherwise she would have remembered what a cover-my-ass kind of girl I have always been.* She clicked her computer off.

~Chapter 9~

Bannagan regained consciousness in the hospital emergency room, his two guards and both of his attorneys standing over him.

"How you doing, Mike?" Perry asked him.

"I have a headache. Having a hell of a week, aren't I?" he said, trying to smile but even his face hurt.

"Wait till you see the shiner you have on your right eye," Loganthau said, glancing at the guards who had left the room and were now standing guard in the corridor. "Said you were trying to escape with leg irons on. Not smart, Mike."

"Fuck them. I wasn't trying to fucking escape, damn asshole cops! I was trying to get you guys before you left the jail. What time is it?" he asked, grabbing his lawyer's arm and trying to see the time on his wristwatch, but his eyes hurt.

"Four-thirty. What was so important that you needed to practically kill yourself, or worse, get shot for trying to escape?"

"Janice. I remembered I was supposed to meet Janice at the Sheppard's Pie Restaurant at noon. Wanted to tell you so one of you could get there and find her. Tell her what's happened. I know she will do the right thing and come forward. If she knew, she would."

"Shit!" Loganthau spat, eyeing the guards. "And they wouldn't stop us?"

"No. Said I would see you in court. I was trying to catch you. Damn chains. I couldn't run. Tripped and fell. Guess I hit my head." Bannagan felt his head and realized it was bound up in gauze.

"You got three staples in your head," Perry said. "When we found out, we pled you not guilty and managed to get you out on a million with conditions. You have to report every week in person to the court clerk; and you are not allowed out of the state of New Jersey except to come to Mass for the investigation and hearings, and eventually the trial—if it goes that far."

"Think you can get up?" Loganthau asked him, lowering the side rail of the hospital bed. "We have to get back to the court and get you bailed out so we can take you home. Or is Barbara coming for you?"

Barbara. He couldn't remember whether he had talked to her or not. *Maybe it was a dream.* Michael wasn't sure.

"Yes, Barbara is coming for him," she said coming through the door, a smile on her lips. "Hi, Honey." She kissed him on the mouth. "I let him go on a business trip and look what happens!" she said, laughing. No one else even smiled. "What the hell is going on up here, anyway?"

* * * * *

Bannagan was released from the hospital and then released from prison on bail. The attorneys and the court advised him not to go back to the hotel. His car had been impounded, and all his belongings in the room were confiscated as evidence.

Barbara and Michael flew back to New Jersey, taking a stretch limo home from the airport in Newark so he could lie down on the long back seat. His head hurt and he needed to rest. She had not said a word to him since they had left the attorneys. It was going to be a long story, and a longer night.

* * * * *

"Whatcha got?" Captain Forrest asked them.

"We've got a great fingerprint of Bannagan on a glass found in the victim's room. Proves he was in there having a drink, scotch. Spoke to the bartender, Ed Mahoney. Says Bannagan and the vic had dinner and drinks together in the lounge for about two hours, and then they left. Waitress corroborated the bartender's story. Bartender says all that Bannagan drinks is scotch and water," Corelli stated standing in front of the large oak desk. Bennedetto sat in a chair across from his captain.

"The maid who found the body of the vic, Olivia Johnson, said that she had seen them both come out of the lounge together, and that they then went upstairs. She also said that this had not been the first time either. She said that she occasionally has to work the night shift at the hotel to cover for the night maid when she can't come in to work. Mrs. Johnson had gone on to say that she had overheard them making love on several occasions, because they were so loud. Lab is still checking the hair and semen samples taken from the perp to match against the sheets, tub, etcetera in the victim's room." Corelli stopped and looked over at Detective Bennedetto, who was cleaning under his fingernail with a toothpick. He took a breath and continued his update for Captain Forrest. "Other guests had remarked about the loud love making also. But no one had seen her go into his suite or him into hers. She was definitely killed in that spare room, and then she had managed to crawl her way out into the hallway. She was found by the maid about 5:00 AM." He stopped, staring at the captain for a response.

"The maid, Olivia, is the vic's mother so I am not sure how her testimony will hold up. Wouldn't you like to be a fly on that perp's wall tonight when he talks to the Mrs?" Bennedetto said, and laughed loudly. Corelli snickered. The captain just smiled.

* * * * *

"Well, you wouldn't talk to me on the plane or in the car, you want to talk to me now?" Barbara asked Michael, heading for the well-stocked bar in the family room. She made herself a Seven and Seven.

"I'll take a scotch. Straight up," Michael said almost falling onto the brown overstuffed leather sofa, his head dizzy. He rubbed his aching and burning brown eyes as he laid there.

"Is that a command?" Barbara asked, getting his drink anyway.

"*Please.*" He crossed his arms over his eyes and forehead, trying to block out the sun's heavy late afternoon rays that were cascading into the room. "I am so very sorry, Barbara," he started, barely audible. "I don't know what else to say."

"How about why you were fucking her? Or maybe why you were hanging out with her in broad daylight! With a whore! A fucking prostitute! Oh sure, you were away. Who would know you?" She let the question hang in the air for emphasis. "How about John and Georgia Miller? I told you that they were going to Boston for the week to see her mother. They are staying at the Tremont Hotel just down the street from the Broadmoor. Oh, my God, what if they saw you? Or . . ." Barbara froze, two fingertips of her left hand were lightly rubbing her thin tight lips. Her pastel blue eyes that Michael Bannagan had fallen in love with, now stared at him with genuine fright. "What if they saw them take you away in handcuffs? What if it is in the newspapers up there in Boston? Or on the news? Oh my God, Michael. Oh my God! They know everyone in our circle of friends!" She began to weep into her slim hands.

Michael got up, and getting a tissue, handed it to his wife. He slowly turned her toward him, and then embraced her close to his chest while she sobbed. It was the first time that he had ever seen his wife cry, except for the small tears running down her cheeks the day they got married. *God he hated this,* he thought to himself. *Why me, Lord? What now?* He hated the feelings of guilt, remorse and shame—especially the shame. He also hated the fact that she was more worried about her standing in the community than in his welfare. *Geez, she may be drummed out of the tennis club, refused entrance into the clubhouse, thrown off the golf course,* he thought sarcastically. *Or worse! She could be shunned by the other women of their stature; laughed at behind her back, invitations to dull dinner parties politely ignoring their mailbox.*

He soothed her by lightly pushing a strand of hair away from her face. He stared at her beautiful shiny auburn hair. He had the overwhelming desire to run his hands through it, but he could not. Barbara did not like her hair messed up. She felt that any hairdo costing one hundred and twenty-five dollars should be signed and bronzed, but never touched. She wanted to get the most out of her look for the week, until the following week when it would be done again, identically the same way. Michael hated the stiffness, the altogether look of someone who is merely a statue to be admired but never touched.

Where did the young woman go that he had married? The one who ran barefoot through the grass with her long curly hair flowing in the wind with the sun putting beautiful glints of red highlights in streaks on it, and her pink cotton housedress blowing up around her? The one who squealed with laughter when you tickled her and stamped her foot at you when you left your dirty socks on the bedroom or living room floor? The one who was always hugging you around the neck, and kissing your ear lightly as if a butterfly had just landed there? The one who wore big satiny nightshirts to bed with tiny thong bikini panties? That girl—where had she gone? She had gotten lost somewhere in the forest that is between being a poor slob starting up a business, and being rich and secure. She was running around in that large maze trying to outrun the other wives who were just like her.

He brought his big hand up, the fingers spread out into a claw—a claw that wanted to grab a big handful of that hair now as his wife sat weeping on his shoulder, just because he was angry. There was no sense making things worse. He was angry at the way things had gone, of fate going one way instead of another. He was angry that his life had changed to a world he hated, one that was about to spiral downward. And he was angry that he had no control over what was happening to him, nor had he any way to stop what was about to happen to them.

Michael Bannagan was very angry and distraught. He was also terrified. The last time that he could remember being this frightened was when his dad, a big strapping man, lay weak and fragile in that hospital bed, his life draining away so quickly that Michael saw a big difference every single day when he went to the hospital to see him. Michael had sat there holding his father's hand and trying not to cry for fear that his dad would see his tears and not think him a man. But the tears had flowed and Michael had not been able to stop them. His mother had held him, telling him that it was okay to cry, that crying was not a sign that was feminine in gender; that everyone cried when they were in pain. His father had died of a massive heart attack.

Barbara pulled herself away from him, and standing up stiffly, announced that she was tired and was going to bed. She informed him that he was now sleeping in the guest room, and silently walked out of the room without looking back.

He threw his glass across the room where it hit the mirror and shattered everywhere. He listened for a comment from Barbara, but she knew better than to push it—*at least not now*. Michael poured himself another glass of scotch on the rocks… no water and no soda. He walked as if he carried the weight of the world on his shoulders, lumbering up the stairs to his office on the other side of the house. He sat down in his big black leather executive chair and made himself comfortable in front of his computer and turned it on. He sipped slowly on his drink. *He had to find her. He had to talk to her, tell her everything that had happened. She must think that she had been stood up,* he thought glumly. *Probably madder than hell. Oh*

God, what if she never comes on again? He has no way to find her. This damn machine was his only contact!

He checked his emails. There was nothing from her. He decided to read all the emails that had piled up while he had been away. He emailed her, telling her what had happened and that he needed her to come forward, to be the friend that he hoped that she was, and that without her to prove his innocence that he was a goner. He begged her, telling her how much he cared for her. He put his emotions out on the line, stripping himself bare before her and pleading for her help just as soon as possible.

He had no choice now but to wait. And to pray.

~Chapter 10~

Michael opened the *Star Ledger* newspaper, the largest New Jersey newspaper that covered the entire tri-state area. *Well, at least it is not the headline,* he thought bitterly, his stomach tied up in knots. He was sitting on his patio trying to enjoy the morning's coolness for a day in July. The sun's light morning rays were brightening up the entire backyard. He looked across his beautiful green lawn. *Was he going to lose this view? But how could he? He hadn't killed that girl. There couldn't be any proof incriminating him!* He wondered if Babs was up yet. He guessed that she would be looking for the newspaper soon. He put two teaspoons of Splenda sugar in his coffee and some French Vanilla creamer, and slowly took a sip. He went through the paper page by page, looking over each sheet carefully. Nothing about him. He sighed. *Would it be in tomorrow's paper or the next day's,* he wondered, tapping his spoon lightly on the table. The telephone rang inside the house. He could barely hear Barbara's voice, but he figured from the conversation that it was either her parents, or his mother. Silence.

    She came out of the French doors and onto the patio like she didn't have a care in the world. Her shiny auburn hair was hanging loosely on her shoulders, the curls swaying slowly in the breeze. Now he wanted once again to touch the soft curls. Where had they come from? Why had she changed her hairstyle from that sticky hard style to the one he had known back when they were younger and he had loved grabbing it. Now she had switched back. Why? There must be another man. One that she was trying to capture as she had done him. She had on a beige silk suit with a cocoa brown blouse and shoes. "Your mother wants us to go to dinner tonight," she said firmly as if they were arguing about it. She set her coffee mug down on the glass top of the wicker table, trying to get the sleeve of her blouse buttoned.

"And what did you tell her?" he asked, folding the newspaper and placing it on the corner of the table where she could reach it. An old habit between them; whoever read the paper first placed it close enough for the other to reach it. He looked at her, analyzing her mood and decided that there was no doubt that it was still bad.

"I told her that I had other plans, but that you were probably free. You better call her back and let her know what you decide." Short clipped sentences.

Michael decided to push the mood. "What plans do *you* have?" he asked, sitting back and crossing his legs. He absently pushed his spoon back and forth slowly on the table-top with his fingertips.

"Just plans." She did not look at him, nor did she sit, choosing to stand and drink her coffee as if ready to turn and flee. "Any great world shattering news?" she asked boldly, looking down at the folded newspaper. Sarcasm.

"And these plans are a secret?" he asked, ignoring her snide remark. He was getting angry at her attitude.

"I don't think I need to report to you any more, do you?" Barbara snapped back, looking at him for the first time that morning, her eyes full of fire. Challenging.

"I see," Michael said.

"Do you?" Now Barbara was going to push the issue. "I don't think you see anything that isn't in a strange skirt." There it was. Out in the open. The challenge for a full-blown fight. He wasn't into it.

Instead, Michael picked up his coffee and walked slowly back into the house. He called his mother to tell her that he would be over for lunch instead of dinner. He needed a friendly face to talk to. He heard the front door slam, then the sound of his wife's BMW. Michael pushed back the raging tears that had formed just below the surface of his eyes, causing them to burn, and his voice cracked as he told his mother that he needed to see her. *Yes*, he decided, *he needed his mother. She would make everything better.* She had always made everything better; kissing his cuts and bruises when they happened, hugging him until the monsters went away; defending him and his actions to other adults, and making him well when he was ill. She was his safety net, even when she did not approve of what he had done, she had never chastised him about it, but would always know the right words to say to make his burden lighter to carry or contend with.

He suddenly turned and ran upstairs to his computer, his head pounding from the deep cut on his head and his heart racing. *Oh, please, let Janice be there.*

~Chapter 11~

Michael had gone to his mother's for lunch and then had come home and waited in front of his computer until three o'clock in the morning, waiting for Janice to come on line as well as for Barbara to come home, and then had given up and gone to sleep in the guest room. He was awakened by the telephone at 7:00 AM.

"Hello," he said, after clearing his throat.

"Yes, is this Michael Bannagan?"

"Yes."

"Mr. Bannagan, this is John Cummings with the New Jersey Herald. I was wondering if I could come out and talk to you about what happened in Boston. We would like to get your side of the events."

"What?" Michael was coming awake quickly. "No. Please don't call again." He hung up the phone. There it was. It had hit home.

He sat on the side of the bed, rubbing the sleep out of his eyes. He wondered if Barbara had come home last night. *Was she having an affair? It appeared to be the way it was,* he thought sadly. *Did he even care anymore?* He brushed his hair back with his fingers and then rubbed his bearded face. *Fuck it! Whoever it was, if it made her happier, then she could just get the fuck out! But she would go without any money from him! He had worked hard for everything that they had. She was an educated interior decorator. They had no kids to worry about. Let her go support herself!* He made a mental note to call his accountant and personal financial advisor and get them started on covering up his assets. It would be a brutal divorce but he had known deep down that it was coming sooner or later. He had known for many years but had gone through the motions of keeping his marriage alive until he could prepare for the lifetime switch from married to single. Some of his assets had already been covered and moved to the Cayman Islands so as to not have to pay taxes on any of it and he had not told his wife about it. He did not know why he hadn't told her. *Forethought?* he wondered. *Premonition?*

The telephone rang again. "Hello."

"Mr. Bannagan, I'm with the Boston Globe . . ."

Michael hung up. He slowly got up, put on his bathrobe and slippers and went downstairs to get a cup of coffee. He would take it upstairs to his office and sit in front of his computer like a robot. Janice would come on sooner or later, and he wanted to be there when she did. He walked slowly past his master suite door, and paused momentarily to see if he could hear sounds that would tell him that his wife was home. He heard nothing. *Fuck her,* he thought, and continued walking down the hallway to his office.

* * * * *

Corelli sat looking at the lab reports he had just received. The glass definitely had Bannagan's fingerprints on them, but he just did not look like the type that would savagely kill a prostitute. *What did she do, refuse to give him a blowjob?* he wondered. He had his usual gut feeling nagging at his brain again.

He had run Bannagan through all the normal police and FBI files and came up empty. Not even a parking ticket. The man was an absolute angel. *Stress? Going over the top into the never-never land of the criminally insane? Didn't want to work anymore and make all his money, so he would take a vacation for the rest of his life in prison? Not this guy. He seemed to have it all, so why murder a stranger? And so savagely. For kicks, maybe? Rich people had strange ways of getting their kicks. Maybe she had tried to rob him and he caught her and a fight ensued and he had accidentally killed her? Yeah, right, with so many knife wounds and a slit throat. He could easily have cold-cocked her and she would have gone down. There was no need to kill her. So why did he do it? And a knife killing was usually one of passion, one that came from emotions. What emotions could he have had with a prostitute that he had probably just met?*

Corelli ran profiles through his head like a computer while he got up to get another cup of dark, burnt-tasting black coffee—data received from many years of investigation and on-the-job experience. He stopped. The man *did* fit the profile and traits of a serial murderer. *Couldn't be,* he thought. Corelli ran to the computer, typed in unsolved homicides in the past year. Way too many. He typed in Boston. That narrowed it down to thirty-eight in the area. He printed them all out. Tearing off the pages, he sat back down in his old chair and started scanning the report for similarities. There were none. Next he checked New Jersey. Still nothing that could be even considered close to being the same type of murder. Maybe Pennsylvania? Delaware? Maryland? He would find a motive. That was what he was good at. Bennedetto called him a 'fucking bloodhound.' He was right. But then that was his job and he loved it.

* * * * *

"Well, are you satisfied now?" Barbara sat glaring at him from the light oak circular table in the breakfast nook. Thunder rolled across the sky.

Why not? Michael thought, looking at the gray overcast sky out the windows behind her. *It was his new black cloud following him everywhere he went. His very own little reminder of the fact that his whole world was suddenly turning to shit.*

"Are you going to answer me or have you nothing to say?"

"I have a better question. Where the hell were you all night?" He poured his coffee into a large mug. *He needed a lot of caffeine. He was tired from waiting for this bitch to get home last night.*

She did not answer. She just sat glaring at him. *When had the look in her blue eyes turned to hate? Why had he never noticed it before? Or had it just suddenly appeared. So many questions without answers,* he thought. "I asked you a question, Barbara. Please answer it!"

"Don't use that tone with me, you…you…you murderer!" She regretted it as soon as she had said it. He turned on her with a vengeance that not only had she never seen before, but one that she would never have guessed that he even possessed.

Michael threw his hot cup of coffee across the room, shattered pieces of ceramic glass flying everywhere, coffee running down the stressed-oak cabinets. He stood to his full height and leaned across the small table until his face was so close to hers she could feel his hot breath, his brown eyes now black as coal. The veins in his neck protruded, and his face was flushed red. "I asked you a fucking question," he spoke softly but with an undertone of a threat, "and if you think I killed that whore, just what do you think I will do to the slut I married who did not come home last night?"

Barbara rose slowly and carefully, trying not to show the fear that had started to consume her. "I need time alone, without *you*, so I am going out! Don't wait for me. We are through, over, finished!" She picked up the light green leather purse on the back of her chair, matching her tailored silk suit perfectly.

He grabbed her tightly by her arm. "Yes. That is the truest statement you have made in many years!"

"Let go of me, Michael! You are hurting my arm!" She tried to pull her arm away, but his grip was steadfast.

"Okay," he said, matter-of-factly, suddenly letting go of her arm and grabbing a handful of her hair. That stiff, 'don't touch' auburn hair that he hated with a passion.

"Michael!" she screamed, now truly terrified.

"You *are* going out! Remember you wanted to go out?" he asked in a mocking tone. "Well, babycakes, out you are! Permanently! You hear me, you fucking cunt? Go to whoever it is that is fucking your stiff and lifeless ass! Let him take care of you in the manner that you are accustomed to! He is getting the pleasure of your company, he can pay for it!"

She tried to grab the hand that held her hair, scared and at the same time angry that he had mussed her hair, but he held it tight, dragging her along backwards towards the front door. "Michael!" she screamed again. "You have lost your mind!"

"Have I? Maybe I have, but I do not need some fucking two-bit tramp who signs her checks with *my* last name, standing there giving me a holier-than-thou attitude, and calling me a God-damned murderer!" She tripped and fell on her butt, one white leather high-heel falling off her foot, her skirt sliding up her thighs. He continued to drag her toward the door, and now both her hands were holding her hair. He pulled her to her feet by her arms, opened the double front doors and threw her down on the brick porch. She started to cry.

He left the open doorway and returned shortly with her shoe and purse. He took her keys from her purse and removed the house keys. He then threw the purse, shoe and car keys at her, hitting her head and face. "Now get the *fuck* off *my* property! I will have your shit sent to your mother's house! But I warn you, do not come back to this house for any reason unless you also want *your* throat cut!" He slammed the door shut. He looked down at his hand, surprised that his fingers were tangled with a chunk of her now dyed red hair that he had pulled out by the roots.

"You can't do this!" Barbara screamed at the closed door, tears causing her mascara to streak her cheeks with black, smeared lines. Her knees were bleeding and her Hanes stockings were full of holes, but she did not notice. "You hear me, Michael Bannagan? Who the fuck are *you*? A murderer, that's what! You fucking, cheating murderer! I am going to the police! I am going to testify against you, you fucking murderer!" she sobbed, picking up her purse and keys, rummaging for a tissue to wipe her nose. "This is my house, too! You can't just throw me off my own property!" Now the tears poured down her face, the phlegm from her nose running into her open mouth. She pulled a hanky from her purse and wiped her nose and mouth. She could not find her shoe through the tears until she stepped on it and tripped again. She banged her arm against the car door. "You hear me, you son-of-a-bitch?" she said in a normal tone of voice, speaking more to herself than to her husband. "Run home to your mommy like you always do! Maybe she will give you her tit to suck on again!"

She started to get into her car when she looked over at his Explorer parked close to his Lexus. She watched the front door of the house as she slowly walked toward his car. She picked up one of the heavy large rocks that surrounded the shrubbery in front of their home and threw it as hard as she could at his precious SUV, smashing the side-view mirror and the driver's side window at the same time. She turned and limped toward her car, her left foot still shoeless. "How do you like *that*, you bastard!" she yelled toward the house at the top of her lungs.

He opened the front door again, but before he could step out, she gunned her car and raced down the driveway, screeching her tires, as she turned left onto Newman Street.

~Chapter 12~

Barbara called constantly for the next few days, but Michael had not answered the telephone, having opted to let the voice mail pick up all calls. She was furious at first, saying that she had a right to be in her own house and how dare he change the locks. Then the messages were more pleading, begging to at least be allowed to get her clothes and personal belongings, and what was she supposed to do, go buy more? That had reminded him and he had notified all her charge cards that he was no longer responsible for any debts incurred by his wife, and had frozen his bank accounts from her. "Can we please sit down and discuss all this like adults?" she had asked. She swore that there was no one else. She was sorry for all the things that she had said. She had just been angry. And she told him how much she loved him. Then she went back to leaving furious messages again. "How dare you not at least answer my calls?" "What's going on? Have you lost your mind?" Michael guessed that maybe she was right on that one. He was probably losing what was left of his sanity.

He went through her office at home, searching through drawers, papers and files. There he had found a file on himself from the Sure Fire Investigative Agency. It was complete with a break-down of dates and times, along with pictures of him and Gloria, not to mention pictures of him and Janice, holding hands, eating, and kissing. *The bitch had had him followed,* he thought, anger making the veins in his neck and temples expand and protrude. *She is lucky that she is not here,* he said to himself. *I'd kill her!*

He decided to keep the file and give his new detective agency a copy. He sat in her plush leather high-backed chair, lightly rubbing his fingers across his lips. His eyes rested on her blank computer screen. Slowly he leaned forward and clicked it on. He waited until the computer was fully up. She had a colorful beach scene of some exotic island retreat as her background. *Was that where she wanted to be?* he wondered, *or was that where she was going to go with whoever she had hidden from him. Oh, he was sure that she had someone else. He was no fool, even though she seemed to think that he was.* He knew the rules of the game, having played it before many times himself—usually winning—although Barbara had caught him and won a few of the games herself. But she was no match for him. He was a pro at this game of cheating relationships. He knew the signs…the lies…the cover-ups.

A box popped up on the screen requesting a password. *Now why the hell would she have a password on her computer if she had nothing to hide from him? There was no one else in this house besides him and their housekeeper who had no knowledge of how to use a computer…so why a password? Little cunt! Tell me again there is no one else! Nothing to hide!*

He knew that he could sit there and figure out what password she had used, but he didn't want to do that at that particular moment. He had a splitting headache and needed some Advil. He decided to call Sammy, the young computer whiz he had just hired, and have Sammy go through Barbara's computer to see what was on there. *She was so fucking stupid*, he decided. *His business was computers! He had started out as a programmer and then moved on to the guts of the hard drive! There was nothing that he could not do with this damn machine. Stupid cunt!*

The telephone began to ring. Michael ignored it. Instead he slowly started up the stairs to get some pain relievers from his bathroom and then sit in front of his own computer. He did not understand why Janice had not come on anymore looking for him. He decided that she was either mad about being stood up at the Sheppard's Pie Restaurant that day, or she had heard about him being arrested as a murderer. Probably both. But he prayed that she would come on the computer and at least hear his side of the story. She was his only hope of sunshine in this stormy situation. He sighed deeply, and clicked on his computer.

Women wanted to play the game, but then they turned tail and ran when the time came that they may be backed up against the wall. They only wanted to play when it was all in their favor, Michael thought. *They figured that they had the necessary depository for men to make deposits and so that gave them the liberty to shut it down whenever they chose to. Janice was obviously no different than the rest. They were all exactly what they were— cunts. And that was all that they were. No backbones. That was why they were so easily abused by men and society in general. As long as he was spending money on them, taking them to the best places, coming up with ways to surprise them—it was always all about them. He was disgusted with all of them. He was especially disgusted with Barbara, and with Janice. It was good that his mother was different. Or were all mothers different?*

Without realizing it, Michael had fallen asleep in front of the computer, his hand still on the mouse.

* * * * *

"Holy shit!" Detective Corelli said, pushing his chair back from his desk. He grabbed up a stack of computer reports and walked quickly into his captain's office, closing the door behind him. He sat down in the soft upholstered chair reserved for visitors, a smile on his face. "Guess what?"

"What?" Captain Forrest asked, putting his pen down and sitting back in his chair. "You look like the fucking cat that ate the canary, and I am too busy for guessing games." He crossed his arms across his chest. His tie was off, and his shirtsleeves were rolled up. There was a marine insignia tattoo on his right upper arm and there were small stained circles of sweat under his arms on his blue shirt.

"What if I told you we hit the God-damned jackpot on Michael Bannagan?" He was watching his captain's slender face, the questioning look in his light-blue eyes.

Captain Forrest didn't answer. He was taking in the expression on his detective's face also. He knew that Corelli wanted him to play the 'guess what' game, but he had reports that were overdue and he had superiors who were waiting for them. He decided to take the time to play anyway. "What are you talking about? What jackpot?"

"We have collared us a serial murderer!" He sat back, crossed his arms, and smiled.

"What? Who? Bannagan? Bannagan doesn't fit the serial killer profile. He doesn't even look like someone who would have killed that hooker, either. You are supposed to be finding me a motive. And some backup proof would be nice, too." He uncrossed his arms, stretching them high over his head, stretching. After he brought them back down, he cracked his neck with a sharp turn and then clasped his hands on top of his head, pushing his gray hair flat.

"Look," Corelli said, getting up and walking behind the captain's desk. "These are printouts of any and all people who were killed in the past year at hotels across the country. And guess what else?" Before Forrest could answer, Corelli said, "Guess who just happened to be a guest in every hotel in every city at the same times that a woman was killed over the last six months?"

Forrest looked up from the printouts, looking Corelli straight in the eye. "Get outta here! How do you know? Are you sure?"

"I checked and cross-checked every possible situation looking for similar M.O.s. I found some, but they took place at hotels in different states across the country. So, I called each hotel and asked if they had a Michael Bannagan registered during each incident, and every damn hotel said yes! The murders at all of those hotels had occurred while Bannagan was in the vicinity. Coincidence? Not hardly! Looks like our perp has some big 'splaining to do, Lucy.' I also placed calls to every police station and talked to the detectives working those cases. I asked them to send us copies of all of their reports, DNA results, the whole kit-and-caboodle! Badda-bing, we hit pay dirt on this one, Cap! My gut tells me it is as good as it gets!" He put his big meaty hands on his hips.

"Nice work, Corelli. Nice work." Forrest could see how proud his detective was, his chest all puffed out, his large round ruddy face shining with excitement. *Maybe he should take him out for a drink after shift,* Forrest thought. *Break his own rules about getting too close to his own cops.*

Before Forrest had a chance to open his mouth, Bennedetto came through the door with a manila folder in his hand. "DNA reports are in on the Swanson murder, and lo and behold, they match the perp's. Surprise, surprise, surprise." He looked first at Captain Forrest and then at his partner, Corelli, and then down at the printouts. "Sorry, am I interrupting something here?"

"Wanna hear something cool, partner?" Corelli asked his partner and best friend, a smirk on his face and a twinkle in his eye. "My gut told me there was more to Bannagan than meets the eye and I was right!"

"Only thing your gut tells you is when it's time to eat again," Bennedetto said, laughing.

* * * * *

Michael had checked his calls and they were all from reporters or from Barbara, and one from his attorneys. He called the attorneys back immediately, but they were in a conference. The secretary told him that they had called to set-up an appointment for as soon as possible. Michael made an appointment for them to come to his home the next day. He told her that the reporters were now camped at his front and back doors, and getting out would be an adventure that he would rather not take on right now.

He had already told Angelica, his maid, to stop coming until further notice, but that he would mail her paychecks to her anyway. He told her to relax and hang in there, and to think of it as a paid vacation. She had thanked him profusely, but then in a more serious tone had asked what she could do to help and asked if he was doing okay. She had also wanted him to know that she knew that he had not killed that girl, could not have killed anyone. After about ten minutes of talk, they had agreed that she would buy the normal groceries and he would let her into Barbara's side of the garage. But he also made her understand that by no means was she to let Barbara, or anyone else associated with Barbara, into the house or onto the property. She was to call the police if they did come around. He made a mental note to hire some bodyguards. Things were getting out of hand outside.

He had checked his computer again. Still no word from Janice. He was getting more and more distraught and depressed. *Why wasn't she at least trying to get in touch with him,* he wondered. *Even if she was mad about being stood-up at the restaurant, she had to know by now what had happened. Maybe she was afraid of him now, or didn't want to get involved in the mess where she might get caught up in the publicity. But she must also know that she could clear him. She had to know that he would never, could never kill anyone and that she had been with him most of the night. Why would she not come forward and help him? Was she so afraid of losing her husband? Her reputation maybe? But he would have come forward for her if things were reversed. Maybe she really felt that he had had enough time to wake up and kill Gloria. She really didn't know him well enough to know whether or not he was capable of killing someone.* He sighed deeply. He did not know anything anymore.

Something else he had fucked up, he thought wryly as he wandered into the master suite. He sat down heavily on his side of the bed. *Habit*, he thought and laughed. He had the whole bed to himself, and he still went to his own side. He looked over at his wife's large pecan dresser. Getting up, he wandered over to it. There were no pictures of him and her together anywhere in the room. He had *her* picture on his nightstand, but she had none of him. *Not even in her office, now that he thought about it.*

He opened the top drawer of her dresser. Bras all folded neatly and color coordinated. He did not even know what he was looking for, but she had so many secrets that he decided to check everything. The next drawer was her matching panties. The first large drawer contained pajamas of all kinds and colors. He reached under the folded clothes and his hand touched something. He pulled it out and stared at it for a minute before slowly opening the clasp. It was a large manila envelope filled with pictures of all sizes. There were pictures of her family and classmates from grammar and high school, and some of her college classmates, most of whom he did not know. He browsed through the pictures half-heartedly until he found one that made his skin crawl. His heart beat rapidly, and he broke out in a cold sweat. He felt like he would faint. But his hand firmly held the picture of his wife Barbara as a teenager standing with her arm across the shoulders of an obvious girlfriend. That girlfriend was clearly a very young *Janice!*

~Chapter 13~

"Coffee?" Michael asked his attorneys after they had fought their way through the crowd of reporters camped on Bannagan's lawn. "I thought we would just sit in the dining room. My maid is on temporary paid layoff until this all dies down a little, so you have to bear with me on the breakfast snacks."

"I'll have coffee," Jonathan Perry said. "Mike, this is Robert Cole from Boston. He will be the lead attorney on this action." The men shook hands and proceeded to go to the large dining room with its dark mahogany table and twelve matching chairs, all lined up like soldiers at attention. Above the table hung a six-tiered Austrian crystal chandelier that Michael and Barbara had bought in Austria on their first vacation five years after he had opened his business.

"Thank you, Mike. I will have some, too. Been a busy day already. Airport was crowded as usual. It seems like Newark Airport is constantly under new construction," Cole said.

"Mike," Art Loganthau began, "what the hell have you been doing to Barbara?"

"Barbara? Why don't you ask what Barbara has been doing to me? I just put a stop to it, that's all. I can't take any more of her shit!" Michael put the coffee tray down on the dining room table. He had put out some Little Debbie snack cakes still in their individual cellophane wrappers.

"Mike," Loganthau started again, but Michael cut him off sharply, angrily.

"Look, she not only told me to my face that she believes I am a murderer, but I found a file that she had from a detective agency. She had me followed for Christ's sake! And I found this," he said, throwing the picture of Barbara and Janice on the table, as if the men would understand what the picture meant in all of this. "And she's got someone else that she is fucking on top of everything! I would never have believed her capable of having an affair, but I know that she is. When I came back from Boston, she stayed out all night and just flaunted it in front of my face! And just look at that picture!" He ran his hand through his graying brown hair.

The attorneys all looked at the picture and then at each other. "She's screwing another woman?" Loganthau asked, confusion on his face and laughter in his eyes.

"Don't you see? Look at that picture! That's Janice! Standing with *my* wife! Janice!" he repeated again, heavily tapping the picture with his forefinger as if they should understand the whole complex picture of what was going on.

"Sit down, Mike," Loganthau said gently. "Let's take this slowly and try to put everything in perspective." Michael sat down as if defeated. He looked from one attorney to the other to another.

"You all think I am losing it, don't you? Fuck, maybe I am."

"I think there is a lot going on and it is getting all mashed together. So let's take each item a piece at a time, shall we?" Perry said. "It is the only way to look at the whole picture. If you want to understand the forest, you must study each tree."

Michael automatically looked at the small picture on the table. *Janice and Barbara, together,* he thought to himself. *They had to have been friends since high school. Maybe even longer. There was no way to tell, no way of knowing. But what did it all mean? Was it coincidence?*

"Mike? Barbara got a court order ordering you to allow her to get her belongings and personal things. You have to allow her entry to pick these items up. You cannot stop her," Loganthau was saying, his coffee now getting cold in front of him.

"No! That bitch does not come back into this house! I will box up all of her shit and have it sent to her mother's. No, better yet, I will put it all on the front porch and she can come get it! Yeah, that's it! She can pick it all up in front of the reporters, with their cameras going! Perfect!"

"No, you won't." It was the first time that Cole had spoken since he had gotten his cup of coffee. He spoke deliberately, softly, and firmly, looking Michael straight in the eyes. "The last thing you need is for a spectacle put on for the media showing you as the bad guy. Your wife will then get all the compassion, and you will get the headline saying 'Murderer Throws Wife Out! News at eleven.' If you do not want her in your house, which I remind you is also still *her* house, then you can send her stuff to her mother's. And do it as quietly and as quickly as possible. She has been gone now for over a week and she does not have her own things. Take everything that is personally hers, get it packed up and have a mover come and get it. Everything."

"Do you want to file for divorce, Mike?" Loganthau asked, opening his briefcase and taking out a leather tablet, "or would you rather wait and see what she does first?"

The telephone began to ring. "I will file," Mike answered, ignoring the ringing phone.

"Aren't you going to answer your telephone?" Perry asked.

"No. It's always Barbara or the reporters," he answered. He turned back to Art Loganthau. "I think it would be better if I filed first, don't you think so, Art? That way people will blame her for not standing behind me, for having a lover and forcing me into getting a divorce, not me, don't you think?"

"Charging what? You need proof of adultery, which I believe is on her side…not yours. Am I right?" Loganthau looked up at Michael. Michael smiled sheepishly. "That's what I thought. You can go with incompatibility whereby no one is at fault. It is the no-fault way to get your divorce." Loganthau's cell phone began to ring. He answered it and listened. "Let's go to your family room and turn on your television set, Mike."

"Why?"

"That call was from my secretary who was trying to reach me here. Your wife is holding a press conference."

The four men went to the family room and clicked on the sixty-two inch TV. After flipping through a few channels Barbara's face appeared in all its glory, as big as life on the large screen.

"Yes, he threw me out physically for no reason other than that I told him that I believed that he had killed that poor girl in Boston. That sent him into a rage. He became a wild man, becoming physically and emotionally abusive. I had no choice but to run for my life! I was so afraid that I would end up like that woman, with my . . . my throat cut!" She began to weep into a small pink hankie. Her attorney consoled her until she could continue.

"That lying bitch!" Michael screamed, jumping up from the plush black leather sofa. "That . . . that lying, fucking cunt!" His face was bright red, his eyes open wide and blazing.

"Yes, my husband has had many affairs, all of which I forgave him for because I loved him so much," she answered the questioning reporter. More weeping. "I have proof that he was having an affair in Boston with the woman he killed, and still another affair with a second unknown woman besides that. Oh, my God, that other woman could have been next! Whoever she is, she better feel really lucky that my husband was caught!"

"You mean your whoring friend that you sent to me!" Michael yelled back at the television screen. Almost immediately, his face registered stunned shock. "That's it! That's it!" he said smacking his forehead, and getting more excited. "She sent Janice to set me up! Oh, my God! How fucking stupid am I?" He sank back down onto the couch...looking totally dejected. "That's why Janice hasn't called—why she hasn't been on-line—hasn't sent me an e-mail. How damned stupid am I? Oh, my God! I have been so stupid through all of this."

Loganthau shut the television off. Everyone was quiet for a few minutes, absorbing everything that had just happened. Michael's face had gone white. He sat quietly shaking, his hands clasped in his lap, his eyes downcast on the parquet flooring.

"Well, Michael, that answers what she is going to do, and she has probably already started her suit for divorce citing adultery and special circumstances," Perry said softly.

"That is not the worst part, Mike," Cole said. "We need to talk about what is happening in Boston. It is very serious." When Michael did not look up, Cole continued, "The DNA reports are back. The sample of blood, semen and hair that you gave at police headquarters are a perfect match for the hair and semen found in the victim's bed and on her body."

"That's impossible," Michael said quietly. When no one spoke, he looked up. "I'm telling you all, that's impossible! I never slept with that girl! I never touched that girl! I only had a couple of drinks with her and a supper with her, all at her insistence! I had an affair with Janice, but not with Gloria!" *Janice*, he thought bitterly, *no wonder she would not give him her phone number, work number, work email—nothing at all. She was in on everything with his wife! Everything she had said was a lie, a joke. He was the joke. He had been set-up by his wife to have an affair with Janice so that she could get physical evidence against him for a divorce! There's no fool like an old fool*, he thought, the anger and embarrassment of the reality flushing his face again.

"Mike, were you in North Carolina, South Carolina, Georgia, or Mississippi in the last six months?" Cole asked, the level tone of his voice never changing, soft and yet firm.

"Sure, I had business meetings in all of those places. Why?" Michael asked, his heart beginning to pound without knowing why.

"Did you know that a murder occurred at each of the hotels you stayed in while you were *there*?" Cole waited for the question to sink in.

Michael's eyes opened wide, and he began to run one hand through his hair absently. "You don't think . . ." He stopped talking, looking at Cole.

"Michael, your bail has been rescinded by the state of Massachusetts. I have orders to bring you back as soon as we are done, or they will come and get you."

"What?" Mike looked at each attorney again, but his eyes rested on Loganthau. "Art?"

"There is nothing we can do, Mike. They are checking the reports on each death and they want you in jail until they find out everything they need to. I am sorry, Mike. If it is of any value to you, *we* believe you."

"Mike, isn't there anyone who can corroborate your story? This woman you were seeing in Boston, maybe?" Cole asked.

Michael looked over toward the picture on the table in the other room. "That's her there. With my wife. That is what I was trying to tell you all—that is Janice in the picture with Babs! They must have been childhood friends. They must still be good friends, although I never met Janice…never even heard her name mentioned. Babs must have gotten together with Janice and they concocted this plan so Babs could get the proof she needed to get a divorce. I am such a fool," his said softly, his voice cracking as he held back the tears. "Such a fool. And now that I am going to go to jail as a serial killer. Barbara will get her divorce and everything I own. I will lose my home, my investments and my business, and I am innocent of all these charges." The tears burst through and he began to cry. He put his head down on his folded arms resting on his knees and his body was racked by the sobs he could no longer contain.

Loganthau got up and going over to the bar in the family room, he poured Michael a large glass of scotch.

As he walked back into the family room with the drink, he picked up the picture resting on the dining room table.

* * * * *

District Attorney Wallace Stewart sat listening to Detective Corelli, as they went over all the new evidence on Michael Bannagan. Stewart was a tall, very thin man in his early forties, with prematurely gray hair and crystal blue eyes masked by his round, John Lennon-style glasses. Although he gave the appearance of being an Ichabod Crane, his opponents in the courtroom knew he was no one to fool with.

"Did you get all the samples of evidence from the other states involved," he asked Corelli, his large bony hands clasped together in the air in front of him, both index fingers touching and pointing, as if a gun.

"No, not yet. Two of the states are co-operating, but two are giving us a hard time. They want us to send them *our* DNA samples so *they* can do the match. They want to prosecute him in their own states—first. I have told them that we will pass him to each state after we are done with him. Because we are the state that has put this all together and has come up with an answer and because he is our collar, I think that has resolved most of the conflict. If not, then we will have to try to take steps to amend that situation," Corelli answered, sitting back in the armchair, his leg crossed at the knee. "I should have all the samples soon, and we will start testing…ASAP."

"Good. Just don't sit on it. And make sure you all do everything by the book and to the letter. Dot your Is and cross your Ts. I don't want any errors on this one. We are going to hang this man out to dry once and for all."

Corelli stood and gathered all the papers back into the folder.

Once Corelli reached the door, Stewart said, "Great work, Detective. I am sure the department will take very good care of you for this one."

Corelli smiled at the tall man sitting in his overstuffed, high-back executive chair. "He's turning himself in sometime today with his attorneys. I'll let you know when we have him under lock and key." He turned and left the office, closing the door quietly behind him.

Stewart leaned back in his chair. He had not had a case such as this one in all his fifteen years in the DA's office. He smiled. If he won this one, there would be all kinds of offers from the top firms in the city, maybe even in the state. He had to win this case. His next career boost would depend on it. He envisioned himself with his new Jaguar, his wife looking at him with adoring eyes as she spent all his money. But he wouldn't care; he would be able to afford it now as a partner in a big law firm. He was finally going to get to the top rung on the ladder. He smiled. He would win it. He just had to.

* * * * *

Michael had packed a small bag of things that he could take to jail with him. He was numb inside. He didn't even care anymore. He had cried it all out. He had checked his computer once more, knowing full well now that Janice would not be there, and then had turned it off indefinitely. When he had looked at the back of the photo, there was the date and the words, "Me and Bev." *Her name wasn't even Janice.* The thought of them getting together to screw him over made him angry. The thought that he had made wild, passionate love to her made him feel sad and foolish…and even angrier. He could just picture the two women sitting together at a table in a restaurant somewhere, toasting, laughing, congratulating each other on their fine acting performances. His face felt hot as it flushed with shame.

Once he was back downstairs with his attorneys, he had picked up his mail that was scattered on his hardwood floor in the hallway. He scanned through it all, and only chose to open the ones he did not recognize. The first one was a hate letter, which Loganthau crumpled up and put in his pocket. Then he opened another small envelope, which had no return address on it like the other. It contained a three by five index card with the words 'Now it's your turn to sweat!' written on it by either a typewriter or a computer. It was not signed. Cole put that one in a plastic bag, which he got from the kitchen, and slipped it into his breast pocket. The last one Michael almost didn't open, but curiosity made him. It was a note.

> *I am so sorry, Michael. It is a very long story that someday I may be able to tell you. But for now, I just wanted you to know that I really did enjoy our time together, and I feel so bad about all this. Please do not hate me, and take care of yourself. I will be praying for you.*

It was also done on a computer, but this one was signed by hand—Janice. Michael wanted to keep that one but, again, Cole took it, put it in a plastic bag and put the bag in his pocket.

The last thing Michael did was to contact his tech, Sammy, and instructed him to remove both computers from the house through the garage and to put them somewhere safe.

They had walked Michael out of the front door, his head high and his lawyers around him for protection from the press. Loganthau stopped long enough to tell the reporters that Mr. Bannagan was voluntarily turning himself in to the Boston Police Department until the whole matter could be cleared up. When asked by a young reporter about Barbara, Loganthau responded, "Mr. Bannagan's wife has every right to try to cast my client in a bad light as she is looking for a divorce and has been for quite a while. The truth will prevail in this matter, too. My client is innocent on all counts, including what was said about him by his wife. What's the matter? None of you have ever gotten divorced?" Many of the reporters laughed and mumbled about their own divorces. "Need I say more? Thank you."

The ride to Boston seemed like an eternity for Michael. His attorneys continued to try to build up his spirits by telling him that it would all be resolved, that they were hiring a top detective agency to try to find Janice...or Bev...whatever her name really was. They and the detectives would find out about the charges now pending in the other states. Michael was to think hard and long about anything that he had not thought to tell them. And so it went, all the way up there. They had only stopped once at a McDonalds' drive-up to get some food into Michael before he was arrested, without people's eyes staring at him.

As Michael was getting out of Loganthau's car at the Boston Police Department, a man walking two large dogs stopped to let him pass. Michael looked at the dogs, then at the man who had them on leads. "What kind of dogs are those?" he asked the man quietly.

"Akitas," the man answered, staring at Michael, recognition in his eyes.

"And can I ask you their names?" Bannagan's attorneys stood behind him.

"Mount and Fuji," the man said smiling for the first time.

Michael smiled back. "Thank you."

"Mr. Bannagan," the man said as Michael started to turn away, "not all of us think you are guilty. These damn whores in this city deserve what they get!"

With that, Michael gave a weak smile, stood up as tall as he could, and walked up the steps and into the police station.

* * * * *

The short, thin fingers pressed the green pushpin tack into the wall, securing the newspaper article among the many others. The hazel green/brown eyes read it over and over, a sneer distorting the lips. "How does it feel, you bastard? Will all your money and connections save you now, or will they fry your fat ass?" the voice quietly asked the wall of clippings. The eyes scanned the many clippings, a glaze covering them and turning them bright. "I love it. Do you know that, Bannagan? I only hated doing the first one. The way she screamed, the blood spurting out of her neck and getting all over me. Good thing I am a quick learner. But then you know that about me, don't you, Mike!" the voice spat in a loud octave.

"Now I actually enjoy seeing the fright in their eyes, the shock as the knife scales so easily across their throats. So, see how fast I learned? You do not know all there is to know about me, though. And you never will know, asshole. Oh, and speaking of assholes, hope you get a nice boyfriend in prison!" The voice howled in laughter, the sound reverberating off the dirty walls. "Let's see how you like getting it stuck up *your* ass!"

~Chapter 14~

Michael Bannagan lay on his new bed—a bunk in the Boston jail, his arms folded across his eyes. *What the hell had happened to his life?* he wondered. *How does someone go from being on top of the world to losing it all in the blink of an eye? Maybe I shouldn't have screwed around so much. I'm bound to get fried because of that, not because I'm really guilty of murder. But to lose, not only my wife, my business, my name, and my properties, but possibly also my life? It's too high a price to pay for just fucking around. Everyone does it, not just me, so why do I have to pay so dearly for a few nights of pleasure? I have never hurt a thing in my life, let alone a woman. And five women at that? Has the world gone totally mad? Maybe this was just some awful nightmare, because what else would make sense of it?*

Janice flitted across his mind. He could feel the heat from the shame, embarrassment and anger slowly creep up his neck and into his face. "Played for a fool," he muttered to himself. *A fucking stupid old fool. The entire show set-up on his behalf, choreographed by his wife.* He pictured himself and Janice making love, her body moving under his. *Was her orgasm faked, too? Of all the stupid things to care about right now,* he admonished himself.

Bannagan had not slept all night. He was not used to the noise, and he certainly was not used to sleeping on a cot with just one flat pillow. He had not even been in the armed forces. Nor did he appreciate the fact that there was a guard outside his cell because they had him on suicide watch. *He could not even fart if he wanted to without it being a topic of conversation, ending up on the morning news: Serial Murderer Gets Gas!* He couldn't help but smile at his own wit. *Boy, was he going to get gas,* he thought. *Or did Massachusetts use needles? Or the electric chair?* Michael did not even know if Massachusetts was still a capital punishment state. He had read stories in different archives during his college years on capital punishment and there were two particular stories that had stayed with him. They were editorials about two different murderers who had been electrocuted in the 1800s in the state of Massachusetts. *Was he going to be a capital punishment statistic?* he wondered, a severe headache starting to throb behind his eyes. He began to rub his temples with the first two fingers of each hand.

Two officers brought him a tray of food, which they set down on a chair in front of him after unlocking his cell door. "If you don't eat it, you won't get lunch." The officers turned and walked out as the officer on guard duty locked the door behind them.

Michael looked at the runny scrambled eggs, the overcooked bacon and potatoes, and the cold toast, all of it thrown on a paper plate. His utensils were plastic wrapped in a cellophane package with a little packet of salt and another of pepper. He drank the small glass of orange juice that was in a plastic cup. It was warm, but wet. He stuck his finger in the Styrofoam cup that held his coffee. It wasn't very hot, but at least hot enough. When he looked up again, the guard was watching him.

"Yum," Michael said to the cop, rubbing his tummy as he said it. The guard did not say anything but his eyes went back to the newspaper that he had been reading.

"Any chance of my reading that paper when you're done?" Michael asked the guard in a pleasant voice. "Did I make the front page? Huge headline?" he asked, holding his hands wide apart for emphasis. "The funnies section? Well, it couldn't be the sports section because this is not a fucking game! It has to be in the funnies 'cause this is one damn big joke!" He took a swallow of coffee. "Hey! Look in the society section. I'm sure my throwing my bitch wife out of the house had to have made that section, at least!"

The guard never even looked up. Michael stood up and went to the metal toilet across the room in the corner, lifted the seat and emptied his full bladder. *Who's idea was it to use orange for the color of the jumpsuits?* he wondered looking down at his clothing. The telephone on the guard's desk rang and the cop folded his newspaper. "If that's for me, tell them I am locked in a conference," Michael said to the guard.

The guard spoke softly into the telephone, looking at Michael. After he had hung up he sauntered over to the cell door. "Turn around," he said gruffly to Michael, "and put your hands behind your back through the door."

"Playtime?" Michael asked sarcastically.

"Company." The guard opened the door. "Turn around and open your legs a little," the cop demanded.

"Bet you say that to all the girls, too, huh?" Michael said moving one leg to the side, watching as the leg irons were put around his ankles. "Hey, while you're down there . . ." The cop shot him a nasty look and Michael smiled. He was escorted down the corridor to the attorney visiting room.

Michael hated the leg irons, which made it almost impossible to walk straight. "What do you expect me to do? Run my way out of here? Fight off the entire fucking Boston Police Department with my little plastic fork?" The cop did not respond.

"Good morning, Mike. How are you holding up?" Robert Cole asked him while the guard removed all the chains and handcuffs.

"I've been better." Michael sat down on the gray metal chair with the dark gray padded seat.

"Wasn't sure what you liked, so I guessed," Cole said taking a steaming hot cup of coffee out of a brown paper sack and putting it down on the gray table in front of Michael. Next he pulled out two bacon, egg and cheese sandwiches, each on a hard roll, and some little milk containers and sugar packets.

Michael grabbed one of the sandwiches and took a big bite, stuffing his mouth full. He mumbled a thank you to Cole.

"You're welcome. Now, you are going to be arraigned this morning before Judge Jullienne. He's tough but fair, so let's keep our fingers crossed." Cole sat down across from Bannagan. "I am not going to build your hopes up, Mike. You are in one hell of a spot here. We have the best private detective team checking everything out, and they are trying to find your mystery woman as well as following your wife to see what she is up to. We also feel that there is something to that little card you received in the mail on the day we brought you back here to give yourself up. It could just be a prank, but then again it doesn't hurt to see what we can find.

The police have gone through everything on your laptop and in your home . . ."

"My home?" Bannagan asked, cutting off the attorney. "They have searched my home? Oh, Christ! I can imagine what it looks like now. Can't we stop this? How can they just tear my life apart like this?" Bannagan asked near hysteria. He was on his feet and pacing around the room.

"It is all procedure, Mike. They think that you have killed five women. Do you think that they are going to take that lightly? They are going to try to hang you out to dry, and then they will ship you to all the other states, one by one, to try you for the murders there, too." Cole stopped and watched all this information sink into Mike's head. Bannagan's face went white and he kept swallowing. He sat back down in a heap.

"We are trying to get to the bottom of all this, Mike, so you just have to stay as calm as possible. I know that is easy for me to say because I am not you, but you have to understand what is happening here. We are just starting the process to clear up all this mess. There are several murder charges that we have to clear, each in a different state, and we have to take them one hurdle at a time."

"Now, if the judge does not give us bail today, you may be moved to the state prison, or you may have to stay here until venue is resolved."

"Venue? What the fuck is venue?" Bannagan asked in a deadpan voice, not even bothering to look up at Cole. He started eating his second sandwich, followed by a gulp of the now warm coffee.

"Well, there are other states involved and each is claiming venue, meaning that they think that they have priority over you being tried in their states *first* as the other murders happened there before this one." Cole shuffled through papers in his black leather briefcase.

"Like dogs fighting over a piece of meat, each trying to get a piece until there is nothing left to eat." Bannagan ran his hand through his hair slowly as his mind mulled over his fate, but no matter how hard he tried to find a light in all this, his future was just pitch black. *There is that old joke*, Michael thought, *that after all the darkness you find out that the light at the end of the tunnel was New Jersey. He would settle for that—in a New York minute.*

"Look, I know things are looking really very bad at this point, but we are tracing down every aspect of what you have told us. But you have to realize that it takes time to find an invisible woman whose name is Janice or Bev, not to mention the real murderer who has killed five women at every place you have been to in the last six months." Cole stopped talking and seemed lost in thought.

"What?" Bannagan asked, finally looking at Cole across the table.

"Have you fired anyone in the last year or so? Had any cutbacks?" Cole asked tentatively. "Someone who might have a grudge to bear?"

Bannagan sat and thought. "Well, I only hire and fire the top executives. My vice presidents and the district managers under them take care of their departments and do their own hiring, firing, etcetera. Unless someone shows me personally that they have disobeyed the rules of our corporation, in which case, I take it to that department's manager and they handle it appropriately. Why? You think it might be someone we fired?" Michael's eyes took on a shine of hope.

"Okay, have you fired anyone on the top level?" Cole continued.

"No. I am happy with my vice presidents. They have been with me from the beginning, helping my company grow to where it is now. I trust all of them implicitly!"

"How about the next level down on the food chain? They are also manager level, correct?" Cole was writing in the note section of his Day-Timer, scribbling thoughts as fast as they were coming.

"Yes, department head managers, but I don't think we have gotten rid of any of them since our lay-off a year ago. You need to check with Bill Schwartz. He is my Senior Vice President and has taken over my place as President and CEO until . . ." his voice trailed off as if he could not venture to guess at his future nor how long it would take to either clear him or hang him. "He will help you. Tell him who you are and that I sent you," Bannagan said quietly.

"How about you write him a note to that effect," Cole suggested.

"Just tell him that I said John Wayne was gay." Bannagan smiled a weak smile. "It is a secret sentence to let him know it is from me. There are other wolves that creep around a company such as mine, so we set it up in case . . . you know, in case we had to use it someday."

Cole laughed, a deep, good-natured laugh. Bannagan joined him.

"Okay. Now, let's talk about Janice, or Bev, or whoever she is. You met her on the Internet. Was it a dating site, a singles site, what?" Cole asked, turning over a page in his notes.

"No. I mean I met her on the Internet, but it was in a game room. We played Dominos together one night, and then another night, and each time we talked more and more. That's why I was so shocked to see her in the picture with Barbara when they were teenagers. It has to be a coincidence!" Bannagan again ran his big hand through his graying hair. "I cannot believe that Janice would conspire with Barbara to sock it to me. I am sure that they lost contact after school and probably have no idea that I am in the middle."

"Then why no information about herself, Mike?" Cole looked him squarely in the eyes until Bannagan was forced to look down again. "I am sure in the many conversations that you say you had, that you had to have learned a lot about her. Think."

"Our talk was not really social chatter. It was more . . . sexual."

"Oh Christ! You mean it was hot chat? She talked and you got your pud cleaned?" Cole saw Bannagan's face flush. "Okay, how about when you both got together in person? What did you talk about over dinner? Tell me that wasn't sexual also."

"Of course not. I am not a total pig!" Bannagan snapped back at Cole.

"I didn't mean to insinuate . . ."

"Look, that is how it started. I am one of thousands, maybe millions, who do that! In person, we just talked. My company, my life, computers . . ."

"But not about her, right?"

Bannagan thought about it. Cole was right. "When I tried to find out anything, she would change the subject. Told me that she wanted to go slowly. Slowly—if we had gone any slower on her life and background, we would have been going backwards." He put his hands over his face and brought them back down again. "But she wasn't slow getting into my bed. Now that I think about it, it was her seducing me into my own bed, not the other way around. I guess you are probably right. She was the one who always came to me on the Internet. She always knew where I was and would show up. And of course, she used an alias instead of her own real name. Unless she has changed her name since they were in high school, or is using her middle name now."

"Still hoping that she did not play you for the fool, huh? Look, there is much to accomplish, Mike," Cole said, snapping his briefcase shut. "I will see you in the courthouse shortly. No matter what happens, keep your cool." When Bannagan didn't reply, Cole added, "Mike? You are not the first guy played for a patsy and you won't be the last."

"Want to know her screen name? 'Fool's_Gold.' Fits, huh?"

* * * * *

The large, round-shaped brown eyes gazed steadily at the large picture of Michael Bannagan pinned to the wall. There were lots of newspaper and magazine articles pinned and taped to the wall surrounding the picture. They had been cut out of newspapers and magazines, from press releases sent out across the Associated Press, to articles that Bannagan had published on "Computer Operations and Shortcuts." The entire wall was covered, but there was a circle of space around the picture, as if the picture needed to be the center of attention without anything taking away that notion by being too close to it. The eyes studied the face—his eyes, the contour of his thin nose, the fake smile put upon his face to make him appear like a compassionate, kind man.

The eyes squinted in anger as the brows frowned causing crease lines on the forehead. The hand moved quickly—so quickly that it would not have been seen had there been another person in the room. A dart hit the picture putting a pinprick in Bannagan's shoulder and then fell to the floor, landing in an upright position in the thin worn brown carpeting.

The eyes moved to an article cut from the *Greenville News*, a newspaper in Greer, South Carolina. "Desk Clerk Checks Out" was the paper's quip across the top. It had been on the front page of the newspaper, and for four days after that, as the police and reporters searched for a suspect. As time crept by, the follow-up stories went further and further back in the newspaper. But then, notoriety and fame were not the reasons for this murder—or for any of the others.

Jackie Ann Somers—a tiny, fragile wisp of a girl who weighed only about ninety-eight pounds. Jackie Ann Somers, only eighteen years old and in her first job making eight dollars an hour and who thought that she had the world by the tail with all that money. It had been her first week at work and she had planned to buy her first car—a red, 1995 Toyota Corolla. The dealer was holding it for her until she received her first paycheck from the Fountainhead Motel. She had been easy to kill—just a call to the front desk for more towels to be brought to the wrong room—an empty room.

Getting into the room had been chancy—but easy. Had the young girl checked the registration-in list, she would have known that there was no one scheduled to be *in* that room. But Jackie had been so busy getting the new arrivals registered...tired, aggravated people who had finally arrived and wanted nothing more than to get into their rooms and freshen up, or to go get some dinner or a drink. They always took their frustrations out on the desk clerks, who were also tired and aggravated. Jackie Ann Somers who had her mind on her new car, visions of herself driving around town with her best friend, Tara, scoping out the looks from the guys passing them in their own cars, filled her thoughts instead of the hotel policy and procedures that the guest could come down and get the towels or that she was to send a maid or bellhop to deliver them to the room.

Jackie had knocked on the door and when the door opened, had stepped inside. The bat made a cracking sound as it hit the side of her head, blood squirting everywhere, running down over her like a bright red lace cape, soaking her long, straight blond hair. She had fallen in a small heap on the carpet, her eyes staring straight ahead and a sweet look still on her face. It had happened so fast that she had never even seen her attacker nor the bat. She never felt the slice of the knife across her throat. Her face had not had time to change from sweetness to shock or horror. The clean towels lay in a stack on the floor beside her as if laid there gently; another towel, slightly damp, was dropped by her hand. Jackie Ann Somers, the new desk clerk, had made her first mistake at work. But she had not been the attacker's first.

Now thinking back to that day, the thin mouth smiled sideways to the left side of the face as the memory faded once more, the eyes again glancing over the wall that had become the tribute to Michael Bannagan.

* * * * *

Michael Bannagan had luck on his side that day. Above the District Attorney's heated objections, the judge had determined that bail be awarded of another one million dollars, cash or bond. The eyes watched the proceedings from the back of the large room, and the mouth smiled when Bannagan was arraigned and he had to tie up more of his money.

As soon as he was released, Michael and his attorneys stopped at a restaurant and had a huge lunch before racing home so Michael could see what damage the police had done to his home and his belongings.

~Chapter 15~

Michael stood just inside his doorway, his brown eyes scanning the rooms in a panoramic view, from the library, to the long hallway that led to the family room and kitchen, up the stairs and down again, and finally coming to rest with a long stare into the living room. He turned slowly to his left and walked as if in a trance to the doorway of his library. The books had all been removed from the wall-to-wall built-in mahogany shelves and thrown into a large pile in the middle of his once comfortable reading room, as if the police had been planning to start a large bonfire. He bent down to slowly pick up some of the very expensive and rare first edition books that he had collected for so many years and that his father had collected before him, which now lay open on the top of the pile, their spines broken. He set the few books he had picked up in a neat pile on the thick Persian carpet. He needed to check the rest of the house before he started cleaning up the mess—no more damage could be done by just letting the books stay that way a little while longer.

He walked into the living room to find it in the same disarray as the library. There was not much in this room that they could damage. The cushions on the Queen Anne couches and chairs were thrown around the room. The logs that had been stacked neatly in the solid brass bin next to the fireplace had also been thrown around and wood chips were scattered everywhere on the large green, beige and brown Persian carpet that partially covered the highly polished oak floor. His eyes glanced into the dining room. From where he stood, nothing in that room appeared to be out of place. He guessed that it had not been touched at all. *What could they possibly do to damage a table, chairs, teacart and hutch?*

He walked into the dining room on his way to the kitchen and family room. Everything in the hutch had been placed neatly on the dining table except for one lone china teacup that lay broken on the floor. Someone had pushed the broken pieces into a small pile and left it there.

A foul odor emanating from the kitchen made his eyes water and his stomach began to churn. He took a deep breath and choked. Michael stared at the door that closed the dining room off from the kitchen…he did not want to open it, but he knew that he had to find out what was causing that awful smell of death. He took out his handkerchief and covered his nose and mouth with it, and then reached out and pushed open the door. The smell hit him like a two-by-four plank across the face. Walking into the kitchen holding the kerchief over his nose as best he could, his resolve to everything that had happened to him vanished and anger filled the void.

Everything from his refrigerator and his freezer had been taken out and thrown onto the counters, the tile floor and into the triple stainless steel sinks. Blood from defrosted meats had dripped from the packages, causing puddles and splatters everywhere. He gagged from the smell of the rotting meat. Pots, pans, appliances, dishes, glasses, and all else that had been neatly stored in the cabinets were now scattered everywhere. Even the garbage can had been turned upside-down and gone through, then left scattered on the kitchen floor. It was as if they had left everything this way out of pure meanness.

Michael ran for the bathroom off the family room, gagging into his handkerchief as he ran.

* * * * *

The thin fingers delicately traced Michael Bannagan's finely detailed facial features in the picture pinned to the wall; the long thin nose, the almond-shaped bedroom eyes, the thin lips and angled jaw. The fingers moved to a newspaper clipping. Page one of the *Clyde-Ashville Citizen Times* dated April 10, 2004. The first one. Nerves had been stretched raw for over three days before it had actually happened, and then the day arrived. Everything was ready…the waiting was over. Once at the hotel, it had been easier to do than expected.

It had just been a matter of riding up and down on the elevator until the right person got on. The elevator's stop button was pushed and before the slender woman, Harriet Whaller, knew what was happening, she had been stabbed in the chest, the knife turning slowly, first to the right and then to the left. All in the blink of an eye. Her eyes had gone very wide in disbelief, her purse and the bag of Kentucky Fried Chicken that she had just picked up on her way back to the hotel, falling to the floor. The bloody knife was then extracted and quickly dragged across her throat so that she could not scream once the initial shock of the attack wore off. She slumped slowly to the floor, her hands covering the gaping slit in her throat, her back sliding down the cold steel elevator wall and her body coming to rest in an awkward sitting position in the corner of the elevator. Her skirt had yanked up high on her long, slender and well-shaped legs as she had slid down, one leg ending up tucked under the weight of her body. She did not feel any pain from that leg. She felt nothing as her eyes stared questioningly at the person who had attacked her until her blue eyes no longer showed any depth in them. Just a superficial stare.

The knife had then been closed and put into the deep pants pocket of the sweat suit. The bloody gloves on the hands were pulled off and also put into the pocket. One hand withdrew into the long sleeve of the bulky sweat shirt in order to cover and use the index finger to start the elevator's decline to the next floor below. So careful not to leave a fingerprint anywhere. The trickiest part was getting out of the elevator without being seen. But Plan B was ready to go, in case someone started to get on the elevator when it stopped or all would be lost with a dead body lying in a heap in the corner of the elevator. How does someone come up with an excuse for being in an elevator with a dead woman covered with blood? But an excuse had been prepared, a reason for how it had all happened and why only the woman had been touched. It was easy—the body had been in the elevator when they had gotten on and they were coming for help. *Why didn't you use the elevator telephone? I was so scared, I never thought about it, I was just in a hurry to get downstairs.*

The doors opened onto the sixth floor. The long hallway was empty, both ways. The finger pressed the

Close button and the elevator door shut. Although it had taken only a few moments to get back into the room chosen beforehand and then requested at check-in, time seemed to be moving in slow motion.

The bloody clothes were then removed and discarded on the bathroom's tiled floor, just as the bile and vomit rose into the throat. It was the only time after a killing that vomiting occurred.

But it had really all been easy—too easy. "What are *you* doing today, *Mr.* Michael Bannagan?" The fingers started to again gently trace the photo. Swiftly without any warning, the first two fingers stabbed at the eyes in the picture. "Your turn to suffer, asshole!"

* * * * *

After Michael had called her to please come help him clean-up his house, Angelica arrived and stood surveying the mess in the kitchen. She had found Michael with a towel tied over his nose and mouth, trying to clean up the garbage on the floor. She had then sent her boss to his room to lie down. Cleaning was her job and she would take care of it. She had opened the kitchen and family room windows, as well as the sliding glass doors leading from the family room out onto the screened porch. As if on cue, the reporters flocked to the open windows and doors, questions flying in the air like mosquitoes. She ignored them as if they were not there, and pulled the vertical blinds closed, leaving just enough space to get some air ventilation. She turned on the ceiling fans to circulate the air and pull in fresh air from outside, and then turned on the radio to loudly play music, drowning out the reporters' calls and questions.

Next she went upstairs and turned on the large attic fan to pull the smell out of the house, and had turned the air-conditioning on high. She then went to his medicine cabinet and scrounged through everything until she found what she needed. Expertly she applied Vicks ointment to the small area beneath her nostrils as she had seen done by the FBI in the movie *Silence of The Lambs* when the characters had not wanted to smell the remains of a body. She smiled. It worked. She could smell nothing but the menthol of the ointment. Over her nose and mouth she put one of the paper surgical masks that Mrs. Bannagan used when she was finishing old furniture so that she would not be overwhelmed by paint remover and varnish fumes, and then donned her rubber cleaning gloves. Pulling out thick garbage bags she began to throw away all the food and garbage in the kitchen.

* * * * *

"What's happening with the Bannagan case?" Captain Forrest asked detectives Corelli and Bennedetto.

"Well, it seems that so far as we can tell, there have only been five murders done at hotels throughout the United States which occurred when Bannagan was checked in at the same hotel at the same time that the killings happened, and that they were all female vics. They were all knifed—either stabbed or had their throats cut—or both. Other than that, there are no similarities. None of the vics knew each other, nor did any of them, that we can ascertain, know Bannagan before he killed them," Corelli answered. Detective Bennedetto sat in the chair next to his partner with his legs crossed at the knee and tapped his black shoe with a ballpoint pen.

Forrest watched him for a second. "Hey, Ringo Starr. Practice on your own time." Bennedetto looked up, and then put his pen in his shirt pocket. "What about all the evidence? Does it all come home to the perp?"

"So far South Carolina, Georgia and Mississippi have sent us what they have, which isn't much but it is enough. They each had hair, fingerprints, and DNA matching our perp. But that's it. No witnesses, no knife."

"Maybe he checked into other hotels under a different name or names? Maybe other murders were committed by him nationwide that you did not pick up on because they did not happen at a hotel or motel. That possible?" Forrest asked them. When there was no answer from either of them, he asked, "Hey, Bennie, how come you are so quiet? Not like you to let your pard do all the info giving."

"I have a freakin' toothache, Cap," Bennedetto answered, pointing to one side of his mouth. "The doc can't see me until four o'clock. Guess I am supposed to die until then, damn bastard!"

"Okay, I will keep searching. But I figure something went amiss with this guy, Cap," Corelli said.

"Amiss?" Bennedetto mocked questioningly, grinning.

"I think he was probably doing okay, then one day, wham! He snaps," Corelli said, snapping his fingers and ignoring his partner. "I am going to see if the D.A. can get a warrant for his office building and his accounts. Maybe he had money problems. All those damn computer companies are folding and maybe he was going down the tubes along with the rest of them. With all the people he seems to employ and the lifestyle he leads, maybe he couldn't get enough cash together to carry it all. Or maybe his old lady is seeing someone else and going to take him for a bundle, and maybe even his company assets. I figure something is suddenly pushing his buttons. Then he can't hold it anymore."

"If that is the case, then why isn't he killing off his wife? That would stop her from taking his money and his assets. He probably has her insured to the hilt," Bennedetto said, finally speaking up.

"Too up close and personal—and obvious, maybe," Corelli answered, a hint of question in the tone.

"Well, see if Stewart will get you a warrant and then take the business end apart. See what falls out," Forrest said, sitting up to let them know that the meeting was over. "And Bennie, get that damn tooth fixed. It's too quiet around here without your big mouth."

* * * * *

Michael woke at one o'clock the following morning. He was not sure where he was until it all came flooding back to him that he was at home. He forced himself to move his legs to the side of the bed and let them barely touch the floor. He wiped his face and eyes with both of his hands and then ran his fingers through his hair. He tried to clear his mind, but he seemed to not be able to think. *Had he totally shut down?* he wondered *Had a nervous breakdown? How does a person know when he has had one?* He could see the lights through the drawn drapes from the reporters and strangers who now camped on his lawn. He knew it was nighttime. He looked at his bedside clock radio. He needed to take a piss before his bladder exploded.

He walked barefoot on the thick bedroom carpet into the master bathroom. While he relieved himself of his lower discomfort, he tried to remember what had taken place before he had lain down on his bed.

He remembered Angelica coming and forcing him to his bedroom to get some rest, but that was the only thing that he could remember after reaching his bedroom. He stepped on something and jumped and then he remembered the awful mess that his bedroom was in. They had dumped the drawer contents on the bed, the floor and the tops of the bureaus. The things from the walk-in closets were just thrown everywhere and anywhere. Even the pictures on the walls were scattered. They had found his safe and damaged it until they were able to open it. He hadn't even bothered to check to see what they had taken. He didn't care. He was mentally and physically exhausted, and now even after that long sleep, he felt the same way. *Had he really slept at all?* he wondered.

Michael slowly descended the stairs in the dark. Barbara had always insisted that he put nightlights throughout the house and now he was glad that he had. If he turned on a light now, the vultures outside would know that he was awake and up. He peeked into the library. It was all back in order, his books lined up as they had been before *they* had come and wrecked his home. He sniffed the air and realized that there was just a faint hint of odor left. The family room had also been cleaned up and restored to its normal order so he assumed that Angelica had restored order to his home.

When he entered the kitchen, he was amazed that it actually sparkled with cleanliness in the small lights from the two nightlights plugged into the outlets. His stomach hurt. He could not remember the last time that he had eaten. He spotted a sheet of paper on the counter and picked it up and carried it to the nightlight. It was a note from Angelica informing him that his dinner was on the second shelf in the fridge and that all he had to do was put it in the microwave to warm it up for himself. She said that she would be there early in the morning to finish cleaning up his bedroom and bath, but that she had not wanted to waken him. He peered into the refrigerator, almost afraid to look. It also was immaculate. Angelica, in her wondrous ways, had not only cooked him his favorite tuna casserole, but had gone shopping and filled the refrigerator with fresh foods, drinks and new condiments.

As he stuffed his cheeks full of warmed tuna casserole, he reminded himself to give Angelica a hug and a raise when she got there.

~Chapter 16~

In downtown New York City, Braddock "Butch" Cassidy sat at the head of the oak conference table in the small conference room, his large Stetson cowboy hat pushed back from his forehead allowing some of his graying black hair to show. His long hair was tied in the back with a rubber band. His blue cowboy shirt had the collar open and the sleeves rolled up to the elbows and was covered by his genuine black-leather vest.

There were three men and two women seated at the table also, notebooks and tablets in front of them. All were dressed in different types and colors of jeans, all had on tee-shirts. Cassidy thumbed though a stack of papers in front of him before opening a new, crisp manila folder.

"Our next case is a new one, and one that is different in nature than what we usually get into," he began, sitting back in his comfortable leather chair that was already shaped like his body. "We have a man who is accused of killing a bunch of women in different states." He watched as his group all exchanged glances. "Now, of course, he claims to be totally innocent of all the charges, but then all the prisons are full of innocent men. We have been retained to find out what has, and is, happening, one way or another. They are hoping that what we learn is that he really *is* innocent, but I got the direct impression that if he is not, they do not want to know and that we should just disappear into the woodwork."

Everyone laughed. "You are each going to take one of the murder sites in a different state. Nose around. Find the stuff that the cops would not think to ask or look for. Talk to anyone who was in the area at the time, especially the hotel workers, like the maids and desk clerks who had the most contact with our guy and with the murdered women. Dig under every rock and see what crawls out. The smallest thing might lead you to another and another. Get a list of everyone who stayed there at the same time as our guy. See if you can find any similarities. Okay, Betty, you are off to North Carolina. Don, Georgia. And leave those peaches alone or you will have another big redneck daddy sticking his shotgun up your ass!" More laughter. Larry smacked Don on the back. Don smirked and raised his eyebrows up and down quickly, pretending to be smoking a cigar and imitating Groucho Marx, the comedian. "Jo, you get Boston and New Jersey, and no Atlantic City unless it leads you there! Tom, you are off to Mississippi."

"Damn! How do I get Mississippi? I came from there! I do not want to go back!" Tom growled in earnest.

"That's why you got the job. Hey, do it good and final and get your butt back out of there." This time everyone laughed but Tom. "Let's see if we can't just prove that this guy is being set-up for some reason. Everyone has a portfolio of details in front of them. It has the background on the poor slob under fire. Then there is all the info about his company and what they do and what he does specifically. After that, there is the information on his wife, some of his many affairs, and there have been *many*, and some helpful stuff from the attorneys as to what the police have done and come up with so far. As always, your tickets are in the back of your portfolio along with your advance expense checks. Get going and good luck."

"In New Jersey and can't even hit the casinos!" Jo picked up her things, pushing her pen into her small shoulder bag.

"Friggin' Mississippi," Tom mumbled under his breath. "I have the casinos, too, but who the hell wants to play in that state?"

"Everyone, stop your whining and get going," Cassidy said, a smile on his face.

* * * * *

"This is really taking a chance, Bev," Barbara told her friend, her eyes scanning the few patrons in the diner. "I don't know what could be so God-damned important that you could not say it over the telephone." She slid across the booth, close to the wall.

Beverly also looked around and then sat across from her long-time friend. She pushed a few strands of her long dark brown hair away from her face and put the strands behind her ear. "Who would know me now with my normal dark brown hair as a brunette?"

"Me. Besides, I am not worried about people knowing who *you* are, but who *I* am."

The waitress came over to the table and handed them each a menu. "Would either of you ladies care for something to drink while you look at the menus?" She glanced at the door as an elderly man and woman walked into the diner.

"Water with a piece of lemon," Beverly said to the waitress, looking at the woman's wrinkled face, which was covered with too much make-up, as if she could make herself look younger.

"Nothing," Barbara said without looking up.

As the waitress went back to the counter, Bev whispered, "I hope when I get that old, that I have my face done instead of trying to cover it up. That only makes it look worse."

"What the hell are you talking about?" Barbara asked her, finally looking up.

"The waitress," Bev answered in a whisper. "Look at her face."

"I better not have to be working at her age. That's the difference between the haves and the have-nots. I do not intend to be a have-not!"

"No kidding!" Beverly snapped back sarcastically. Barbara stared at her for a moment.

"Aw, Bev has a case of the guilts. That's what this is all about, isn't it?" Beverly did not answer her. "Or could it be something more?" She gave her friend a smirk, her mouth curling up on the right side.

"I . . . I miss him. I would talk to him several times a day, sometimes for hours. Whenever I needed to talk to someone, he was there waiting when no one else was."

"Then get a dog!" Barbara said, a little too loudly. She took several deep breaths. "We had an agreement, Bev! You and I! Now you are acting like a damn schoolgirl. Trust me, he is no prize package!"

The waitress came up to take their order. Beverly ordered a hamburger patty on a plate with cottage cheese and a hard-boiled egg. Barbara ordered a chef salad with oil and vinegar dressing and an iced tea.

"What the hell is the problem?" Barbara asked, whispering at her from across the table.

"I think I love him," Beverly finally said softly after a few moments of silence.

"Oh, Christ!" Barbara answered. Silence fell upon the booth.

"It was one thing to help you get your proof for you to hang him out to dry on your divorce, but it is another for this man to be locked away for the rest of his life for a murder when I can prove that he is innocent. I never agreed to that! I am not sure I could live with myself or sleep at nigh knowing I helped put an innocent guy in jail for life…or sent him to the gas chamber or the needle…whatever they do in this state."

"Maybe he did it," Barbara countered nonchalantly, picking up her glass of iced tea.

"He could not have killed that girl in Boston. I was with him until almost three in the morning. He was sound asleep when I left. And that bitch was in the hallway. And I can tell you that she was very much alive!"

"But he could have also bumped into her and killed her after you left, now isn't that possible?"

Beverly thought for a moment before answering, "Yes. It's possible, but I don't believe it. He is not like that. He is not capable of such a thing."

"If you had seen me after he physically attacked me and then threw me out of my own house, you would not be saying that. I have the pictures to prove what he is capable of. I not only had the black and blues and the cuts, but the holes in my head where there was once hair!

You have not seen that side of him, and you do not know him like I do! Get over it!"

The waitress brought out their lunch. While Barbara gracefully ate her salad, Beverly pushed her food from one side of the plate to the other.

"Just remember, Bev, we grew up together, went to the same college and are blood sorority sisters, sworn to help each other for the rest of our lives. You took an oath. Now stop playing with your food and eat your lunch. You will get over it . . . and him."

"I'm not sure that I will...but even if I do that, I still have a problem with him being found guilty and punished when I know he's innocent. Don't you have even one iota of feeling left for him? My God! He was your husband for a long time, Barbara."

"No, I do not care what happens to him."

"Oh, Jesus. You already have someone else! You are already bedding another prick and you are so cold-hearted that you will let Michael go to jail or to the gas chamber!" Bev shook her head in disbelief.

"Lower your voice, Bev. In fact, it's time for us to leave. But just remember our deal, or you may find yourself in jail with him." Barbara leaned over the table, glaring at Bev with ice in her eyes, then said laughingly, "See, I'm not so cold-hearted. I'm picking up the check."

~Chapter 17~

The eyes were filled with hatred as they stared across the room and out the window with the tattered and yellowed with age, thin lace curtains. The right hand tapped its fingers on the small, old metal kitchen table, keeping a light rhythm going. A deep frown creased the forehead. *Bannagan is still in his comfortable, plush house,* the voice in the head said in a snarl, *not in some dingy studio apartment like you. Oh, yeah, you really hurt him good, didn't you?* A tinkly laugh was heard in the ears.

"Don't laugh at me!" the voice said aloud.

Think he gives a tinker's damn about you? About whether you are comfortable, warm and cozy in your big house on the river? Or don't you miss that home? What do you look at now? A desolate street, full of depraved and indifferent people, each floating day by day by pretending that their life is okay. Just like you. Except that they sleep in boxes instead of this crappy, bug-infested room. They are just like you, you know.

"I am not like them! I still care about what happens to me."

Do you? Do you, really? And I guess your family still cares about you, too, huh?

"Shut up! Just shut the fuck up!"

* * * * *

Bill Schwartz, now the acting CEO of DymoTek Corporation, sat sipping his hot coffee from the new coffee mug that his wife had given him that had the words "Big Cheese" in bold letters across it, in his new, very big, very modern and exquisite office on the top floor of the building. He liked the way his body fit the contours of the oversized executive chair, which was placed behind the shiny, massive mahogany desk. He was glad that Michael loved mahogany furniture because he did, also.

He twirled the chair around and glanced out at the town of Princeton that was just coming alive with people on their way to work. He figured that the SUVs and the pick-up trucks belonged to blue collar workers; the small compact cars to office workers such as secretaries, assistants, and bookkeepers. The older compact cars had to belong to clerks and younger generation workers. The big cars were driven by the older generation who had grown up driving Cadillacs, Lincolns and Buicks. Of course the Jaguars and Beemers all belonged to the successful and professional movers and shakers. *People don't realize that you could sit and watch the different classes of people and know what social class they were in by the cars that they drove*, he thought to himself. A Lincoln Town Car went by. *An executive?* he wondered. *Or a boss of a smaller company?* He, himself, preferred to be ostentatious and so had a black limo with a driver.

Schwartz took another sip of his coffee. *Would Mike come back and take this all away from him again?* He wondered, a knot forming in his chest at the thought.

His wife, Paige, had been out shopping, buying up all the many things that would make their home smell of success. He liked Mike and thought he was a great CEO and boss, but he liked *being* the boss of this company more. He did not want to see Mike go to jail, but if he was guilty then he deserved to be there.

The company stock had plummeted when the story broke and the Board of Directors had jumped in and all agreed that Vice President of Finance, William Schwartz, was the best man to take over the position that Bannagan had left unattended by 'his reprehensible and immoral deeds.' The stock eventually leveled off and then, over the past few months, had again begun to climb slowly upward. That made Bill feel that the world had faith in him and his newly-acquired position, that they would invest money into the company on a quicker advance than when Bannagan had run the corporation.

He finished his coffee and smiled. *Yes*, he decided, *he deserved all this.*

* * * * *

Michael got up and peered out of the bedroom window onto the front lawn. There were only a few reporters still camped out on his doorstep like vultures waiting for a taste of his meat. He was mildly surprised that most of them had left. Was he no longer today's news? Or were they just tired of the fact that he never went outside his home? He slipped into a pair of sweat pants and an over-sized tee-shirt, and then slid his feet into his comfortable leather slippers.

He came down the large winding staircase. He could smell the coffee from the top step and knew that Angelica was already there. He greeted her as he came into the kitchen. She scurried to get his coffee for him. "Angelica, I can get my own coffee."

"No, that is my job, Mr. Michael. You need to put on the news, I think."

Michael hit the TV remote and punched in his favorite news channel. The announcer was describing the scene at a high school in California where three students had gone on a killing spree and were holding other students hostage. Now he understood where most of the reporters had gone—to a more devastating story than his. He could picture them running back to their bosses, begging for the opportunity to be the reporter sent to the scene of this new horrific headline.

Michael had always disliked the news reporters for their sensationalism in broadcasting the news, especially hated when they asked the families of victims how they were feeling. How would someone in their right mind not know how the families were feeling? He found that to be cruel and insensitive, not to mention stupid and callous on the part of the reporters who did it. He also detested the family members who stood there, only a few hours after whatever event had taken place and talked to those reporters, with only a few forced tears coming down their cheeks. Had they not loved the person who had died? Except when the victims were children; then the families were usually not seen right away, as it is so hard to take and accept the death of a child.

He sipped his coffee. Angelica was already making him bacon and eggs and toast. He wondered what Barbara was doing...if she missed him. But how could she? She had framed him with Janice or Bev or whatever her damn name was. He was lonely. He was not used to not having people around him, talking business or love, whichever the case might be.

Michael decided that this was a good day to make an appearance at his company, see what was going on in his absence and let the employees know that he was still there and overseeing everything, even if from a distance. He would catch up on everything with Bill Schwartz and see if there were any problems that he could help with. He started to call the office, but then decided to make his visit unannounced.

* * * * *

"We have this guy in the bag, Chief. Everything—DNA matches, availability, locations—everything points to Bannagan. It's a slam dunk," Bennedetto said.

"Yeah? And the motive is . . .?" Captain Forrest asked him, his hands locked together behind his head, sitting back in his chair.

D.A. Stewart walked in. "So, how's it going?"

"It's in good shape. We are still trying to line up a motive," Forrest answered him.

"Maybe he is just a wacko, a bona fide serial killer. Hates women, that kinda thing," Frank Corelli chimed in. He was leaning against the wall, his hands in his pants pockets.

"How about a psych work-up? Can you arrange it, Stewart?" Forrest asked him.

"I'll try, but his lawyers will probably fight that one. They have no reason to help us on this. They may decide to do a work up later if they change their plea to insanity, but until they do, all I can do is request it. He doesn't strike me as a serial woman killer, but then his wife has really given it to him, so he might very well be a misogamist and we just don't know it. Have you guys done any kind of investigation with his neighbors and friends and employees?"

"We *have* talked to his neighbors, or should I say, we *tried* to talk to his neighbors but they all think that the world of *Mike and Babs* is a beautiful one, and they can't believe it all, blah, blah. So we did not get too far with them. The employees were afraid to talk because of possibly losing their jobs, so they claim to know nothing, but we were able to find out from them that there was a fairly large lay-off last year and a lot of management and non-management people were let go. We are running down all the names of the people laid off that we got from personnel and will see what they all have to say about the company and him in particular," Bennedetto answered. "So far the people we have talked to about the lay-off were very angry, but they did not have seniority. The management people were the ones that were livid when it came down and they are higher up the feeding chain, so it is harder for them to get work. But most of them respected Bannagan. They did not blame him. They blamed the times, and the fact that most of the computer companies were going under. Most of them thought he was an okay guy."

"We need to find the ones that were *not* happy about it and then we will hear the real truth. Maybe he treated his female employees differently than he treated the men. That would show that he disliked women, or was just chauvinistic," Stewart said. "Anyway, I will see what we can do about getting a psych profile. I want you to also check into his background when he was a kid growing up. Talk to the people who knew him then. Do not leave anything out. Are his parents still alive? Any brothers or sisters?"

"But except for motive, we have him dead to rights," Bennedetto argued.

"Oh, yeah? Maybe he *is* being framed, maybe it is all coincidental . . ." Stewart shot back. "Too many holes. Fill them in." He turned and walked out.

"So why are you all sitting here?" Forrest asked his men.

Bennie mumbled something under his breath.

"What are you mumbling about, Bennie?" Captain Forrest asked without even looking up.

"He has a mother...father died from a stroke," came the reply. Bennedetto walked out the door without looking back.

* * * * *

The receptionist stood perfectly still when Bannagan walked into the lobby of DymoTek. "How are you, Jennifer?" he asked her, noticing her frozen stare. He continued right past her, not waiting for a reply. He walked up the thickly padded stairway, which curved around to the executive offices, making a left and walking down the corridor to the senior executive wing of the building. He greeted each person he past as they all stood frozen at his appearance. "Hi there, Suz," he said to his secretary, leaning on her half wall.

She jumped and turned around to see Bannagan standing there smiling at her. "M . . . M . . . Michael," she stammered. "It's so nice to see you. Let me tell Bill that you are here."

"No, thank you, Suz. I want to surprise him." Michael looked at the phone lines and saw that his line in his office was busy. "Who is he talking to?"

"Mr. Davids from DBR Corporation. I think we are going to pick up the account for his entire corporation," she said smiling. "We have been picking up quite a few new ones lately." She suddenly got quiet and her smile faded when she realized the implication of what she had just said.

"That's great!" Michael said to ease her. "See, I am not needed after all."

"No, Michael that is not what I meant. We *do* need you."

"Pull me the reports on the company's budget for the year, the stats, and the new company list as well as the ones we had. I also want the employee list. I'll get them when I come out. Oh, and Suz?" She looked up. "Do *not* buzz Bill." His look and tone of voice made it clear to her he was not joking. He turned and started down the hallway toward his office.

Bill Schwartz was sitting with his back to the door, his feet propped up on the credenza. Michael walked in quietly and sat down across from the desk. He listened as Schwartz confirmed a dinner engagement with the person on the telephone, telling him that he would pick him and his wife up at eight o'clock that evening and for him to look for his black limo. He turned around to replace the phone in its cradle and jumped when he saw Bannagan sitting there, his hands folded in his lap. "Mike! I didn't hear you come in." His face was turning bright red.

"Limo? The company must be really doing well, Bill, if you now ride around in a limo. Is it a stretch? I always felt that it was more personal to pick them up in my own car. I thought that was a point that we had always agreed upon, or were you just humoring me back then?"

"No, it is not a stretch. More like a Town Car. Mike, some things have changed while you have been away."

"I see that. Obviously no one figured on me coming back. I mean this is *my* company, right?" he said, cutting Schwartz off, keeping his voice low and a smile on his face.

"I just feel that it looks more professional to take clients out in a limo—more impressive. People need to feel that we are secure and successful and that they are important and deserve to be in a limo. It is just a different means to the same end."

"What else has been changed with regard to SOP?" Bannagan was struggling to keep his temper, which had grown short over the course of the last couple of months.

"Not that much has changed. Hell, I don't know exactly, Mike. No big things that I can think of right now, off the top of my head." Bill became very quiet for a moment and Bannagan let him squirm. "You think it was that easy coming into your job without warning, without any guidance on everything? I had the Board of Directors to contend with, not to mention that our stock was dropping like a boulder in a lake with the ripples spreading faster than I could cut them off. Every stockholder wanted to know why." Now he stared at Bannagan without speaking.

"But I see that you managed everything okay. Started changing things to your system instead of what I had already in place that has worked for so many years. I built this company by myself, Bill. You did not help me, the Board did not help me and neither did the God-damned stockholders. *Me!* I did it. By myself! I built it up from just me, to what it is now, so where do you get off changing it to your style? Easy to do when all the hard work is done, isn't it? A little Machiavellian, don't you think? Or do you think? Does the Board think for you, too?" He interlocked his fingers together, his knuckles turning white without his realization.

"Mike, there is no need to get hostile. And just where the hell were you when the dam broke? In jail, that's where! They offered me the position, so what did you want me to do? Turn it down and let them give it to someone else? Isn't it better that they gave it to me? At least I know the important issues to stay in line with after working with you all these years! What the hell happened here? Why are you in this position? Did you do it, Mike? Level with me. I have been your associate and your friend for almost ten years now. I had to hear it all on television like everyone else. That is what teed off the Board members."

"Fuck the Board. I didn't have time to send out an interoffice memo, now did I? You think it has been easy for me through all this? I am losing everything, Bill. Babs walked out, my income has virtually stopped, my home will soon follow, and now you control my company. But the topper to all this? I am innocent! You hear me? Innocent! I have no fucking idea what is going on with all this. I have never hurt anyone in my life, let alone kill five women. If I was ever going to kill anyone, it should be that bitch wife of mine!" He stood up quickly.

"Your *wife*?" Bill repeated.

"Forget it. She set me up. I don't know how or even why, except that she must have wanted a divorce really bad, but I know deep down that she has a hand in this mess! But I would not even kill *her*, after all she has done. So just forget what I just said about her. I am very angry right now."

"I don't know what to say."

"Forget it, Bill. I will get this all straightened out, and then you can go back to your *own* office. I still own fifty-seven per cent of this damn company. So if you want to still be able to *go* back to your office, I would suggest that you rearrange what has been changed. We understand each other, I think." He said, getting up and walking to the door. "And put my stuff back on my credenza and keep your damned shoes off of it. It's not your office yet."

As Bannagan walked past Suzie, she handed him the reports that he had asked for. He took them out of her hand, thanked her, and then stormed out the front door. Once outside, his bravado failed and his shoulders slumped, and he felt beaten—beaten by his wife, his associates, his employees and his friends.

Was he better off dead? He didn't know anymore.

~Chapter 18~

The eyes watched from the street as Barbara got into her BMW, started her car, and drove out of the driveway. As she turned right onto Bridge Street, the car followed slowly behind, keeping just enough distance so as to keep her car in view. She turned left onto Route 571, heading for Route One.

The car had followed her for over two weeks now, and the person knew all of her standing appointments, knew about the affair that she was having, knew where they met and how long they were together each time. The person also knew that Bannagan really loved his wife; oh, he liked to play with other dollies, but he really did love his wife. *So now it was time to take his wife away—for good; no chance of a reconciliation. And maybe they would blame her death on him, too.* The mind played out the scenario. *Michael had reason to kill her. He really needed to kill her. It was the only way that he might survive all this, both mentally, physically and financially. She was tearing him down in the press; she was going to take him for everything that he was worth; and she was out to break him.*

So predictable, the inside voice said. Barbara was going toward her rendezvous location with that stuffed shirt, little piss of a man who now acted like he was the president of the United States instead of a fill-in for Bannagan. *Wonder what Paige Schwartz would think of her successful husband now? Took over the business* and *the wife. Not bad for a man who did not have the gumption to make it on his own. He has to take over another man's life—a man who had the backbone needed to start up and build a large corporation. More than this mealy-mouthed ass-wipe! Maybe they should both be killed—in bed together. That would shake up the system. But then they would not believe that Bannagan had done it. Of course, that might be better. Killed for having an affair behind his back. He finds out and in a jealous rage kills them both. Definitely a possibility. But she would be a hard victim to kill and there was no reason to take the chance now. There was always plenty of time to plan it and then do it another day. Today was not that day.*

* * * * *

"I am not the only one who took the lay-off badly," John Hanson said, taking a puff of his cigarette. "Some of the other District Managers got hurt worse than we did. At least my wife and I had some money set aside, plus we had my daughter's college fund. Unfortunately, we had to pull her out of college to get through it, which upset us the most, but she managed to get her own financing so that she could finish. But we needed to pull back on all the money so that we did not lose our home." He sipped his coffee.

Bennedetto asked, "Who got it worse? Do you know their names? And maybe where we can find them now?"

"Wow. Let me think for a minute. I managed to get work right away, which I didn't think that I would because of my age. But my new company saw my age as a plus. Thank goodness!"

"The names, please, Mr. Hanson."

"Well, I know that Robert Julian and Tony Divelli got hurt in that lay-off. So did Carolyn Koffee. Bob and Tony both had to sell their homes. Bob and his wife are in a small home in Jamesburg, and Tony and his wife split up and he lives in an apartment complex in Cranbury. I don't know what happened to Carolyn. I know that she and her husband split up and they sold their home, but I don't know where she is or how she is doing. And there was Wendy Westlake. I know that she and her husband also divorced, and I think she is in a small apartment someplace in the surrounding area. We were all District Managers. Tony and his wife were already separated and getting a divorce, but I think the girls' divorces came as a result of the lay-off." He lit another cigarette.

"Girls?" Corelli asked him, his pencil and notebook in his hands.

"Sorry…women…although, to me they were just girls. Young women in their twenties or thirties. Pretty young things, too. But smart? They were plenty smart. Very intelligent and highly educated women. I was surprised that as smart as they were that they were living so high, and when the lay-off came, they were destroyed. I think one or both of them had to file for bankruptcy, Chapter Seven."

Bennedetto walked around the living room, looking at pictures, checking out the names of the books on the shelves. "What do you think of Bannagan?" he asked without turning to look directly at him.

"Oh, I don't blame *him*. Poor guy sure has his troubles, doesn't he? I don't know what the others think of him, but I can't put the blame on him. He felt bad about the lay-off, but the company had to come first and we were the most dispensable of the managers. Our sections could be put back to their original spots under other managers. All of our jobs had been created with the expansion of the company, so, of course, we were the first to get laid-off. I have no problems about it, as I am over it now. Business is business and Mr. Bannagan was . . . is a good executive. He would always do what was best for the company as a whole, but he never forgot his employees either. He treated us all very fairly, so I have no complaints. He did the best that he could with the severance checks, too. I weathered the storm."

As Detectives Corelli and Bennedetto walked out, Corelli said to his partner, "I wonder who didn't survive the storm and got soaked."

* * * * *

People were gathering around now, as the EMTs and the police officers tried to push them back. "Here's her purse, Sergeant," the young officer said, handing the expensive designer handbag to his boss who was staring down at the bloody body of the pretty auburn-haired woman who had been stabbed multiple times and now lay dead in the alley of the Ramada Inn. "Who is she? Any driver's license?"

"Yes, sir. A Barbara Bannagan with a Princeton address."

Sergeant Hoffman looked up at the officer, a look of surprise on his face. He took the plastic bag, which contained the purse, from his officer. He said nothing, but went to his car to put in a call to the homicide division. The Boston group of detectives who were down from Boston and working out of the Princeton office would want to know about this immediately.

* * * * *

"Hello?"

"Mrs. Schwartz? Mrs. Paige Schwartz?"

"Yes?"

"You know, you really should be keeping an eye on your husband. He is not always at work, if you get my drift."

"Who is this? What are you talking about?" Paige Schwartz asked, her voice shaky.

"Big bosses have big affairs . . . with women with big boobs." Laughter.

"Who is this?" she demanded. The phone went dead. She looked at the ID caller box. 'Unknown Caller' it said. She dialed her husband's office. No answer on his direct line. She called the main number and got the operator. "Bill Schwartz, please."

"I'm sorry, but he is out to lunch. I can put you through to his voice mail."

Paige Schwartz hung up.

* * * * *

Michael sat on his leather sofa, his feet propped up on a hassock. He scanned through a magazine while listening to the five o'clock news on the television. Suddenly he sat upright as if someone had kicked his feet off the footrest.

"She was found in the alley of the Ramada Inn on Route One, multiple stab wounds to her chest and hands. Her face and neck have also been slashed. She was found around one-thirty this afternoon," the newscaster was saying. "Barbara Bannagan is the wife of suspected serial murderer, Michael Bannagan, accused of murdering five women at different hotels in North Carolina, Georgia, Massachusetts . . ."

Michael clicked off the television, enraged that the reporter had made it sound as if he had killed Barbara, and quickly called his attorneys.

~Chapter 19~

"**Calm down, calm** down. I just heard it myself. Where are you?" Art Loganthau asked his client and friend of many years, Michael Bannagan.

"At home. I just saw it on the news," Bannagan went on in a raised voice close to hysteria. "Who would do this? Why? I don't understand!"

"Never mind that. Where were *you* early this afternoon? The police are going to want to know."

"I went to my company for about a half hour or so and then I came home. Why would the pol..," he started and then stopped. "I did not kill my wife! Oh my God, Art, I know how this must look, but Art, I did not kill Babs! I didn't! I couldn't! You know that I couldn't!"

"Will you calm down? Please? Getting hysterical is not going to help the situation. Was there anyone at your house? Angelica?"

"No. She had gone shopping by the time I came home. Oh, sweet Jesus. I know how this looks, but it is not true. I actually missed Babs being here when I need someone the most right now. I know that sounds stupid after everything that has happened, but there is no one to talk to about all this." Tears formed above the surface of his lower lids. He cleared his throat, trying to fight them back. Michael heard car doors slam and then a bang on his door. "Hold on, Art. Someone is banging on the front door," he said as he walked to open the large front double door.

"Mr. Bannagan, please hang up and come with us," the detective said, taking the telephone away from him.

"Art, it's the cops . . ." Michael yelled into the telephone.

The detective shut off the telephone.

* * * * *

"I do not know what is happening here. I did not kill those women and I certainly did not kill my wife!" Bannagan said, running his hands through his hair.

"All these things just keep happening to poor you. That's what you want us to believe?" the black detective asked him sarcastically.

"My client is answering your questions the best that he can. There is no need for your tone of voice," Loganthau admonished. "If it keeps up, I will stop this interrogation, and my client and I are out of here. Now we are trying to help you to find out what happened, and we certainly would not be doing this if Mr. Bannagan was guilty."

"Yes, I want you to believe that because it *is* true, damn it! We have private detectives trying to help you to find your serial killer and then you will all owe me an apology and a goodly amount of money when I sue everyone involved in this comedy of errors."

"Yeah, right. And you think this is a comedy, do you? Look, Bannagan, answer us this. The Boston dicks told us that they have been watching, and checking out any and all women killed or who died at any hotel in the whole country. So how come all the murders have stopped since we caught up to you? Huh? How come since we tail your every move, is it that no one else has even died at, or close to, a hotel nationwide?"

"There!" Bannagan yelled, jumping up, knocking over the chair and startling the two detectives interrogating him, their instinctive reaction being to jump up, hands on their guns. "There you go. You said it! If you are *tailing* my every move and *know* my every move, how could I have killed my wife? Huh? I was nowhere near where Babs was killed, so how could I have done it?" He looked back and forth between the two men

They looked at him, his lawyer and each other. Bannagan knew that he had struck a nerve as neither detective said anything and the expression on their faces told more than any words could have.

"I need some coffee," the taller officer said. "We'll see what the Boston people say as soon as they get back here."

Bannagan groaned softly. It was all so useless. He couldn't take much more. They still didn't believe him. "I need to go to the morgue and see my wife's body."

"Why? Want to make sure that she 's really dead?"

* * * * *

What the hell? What killed that bitch was her always being there, always in the way. That was your idea two years ago but you didn't have the balls, the voice screamed in the head.

The slim hairless fingers gently touched Bannagan's face, which was staring out into nowhere from his picture. *Ah, you are single now; a widower. That will make you all the more attractive to all the ladies, now won't it? Unless they are afraid that you will kill them. How does that feel, Michael? How does it feel to be rejected and left standing with one hand on your ass and the other with your finger up your nose? Put a dent in your ego maybe?*

"Maybe I should kill your new lady love from Boston? I know where she is, Michael. You don't, but I do," the voice said aloud. "That might hurt you a blow now, huh? Your new one, crushed and dead and you become responsible along with the rest of the dead ladies? It's just not your year, is it?"

A loud laugh reverberated off the walls. *Stop it! Someone will hear you and take this as strange behavior,* the head voice snarled. "Who the fuck cares? I am in control now."

* * * * *

After more interrogation from Bennedetto and Corelli, Bannagan was released. The officers that had been following his every move backed up his story that he was definitely at home from about one o'clock that afternoon after having visited his company. He could not have killed his wife unless he had gone out with the housekeeper, hidden in her car, which was possible but not feasible. Bannagan could not basically take a crap without them knowing about it. Maybe he should thank them for being his alibi.

Michael had gone to dinner with his attorney, and then home to have a good cry. He had truly missed his wife being around, and now she was gone forever. He had slowly killed her love over the years. Michael could not stop crying. It was all more than he could bear.

He wished that he could die, too, but he knew that he did not have the nerve. He could not kill anything, let alone a person or himself. Maybe the killer would kill him next. He hoped so.

* * * * *

As soon as Cassidy had all of his detectives on the conference call except Don who had had an appointment; he started questioning what they had found out so far. He listened as each reported their finds, which really did not add up to very much yet, until Jo started her report of the happenings in Boston and New Jersey. He was aware, as was most of the group, all except Tom who was stranded in Mississippi and far out of the loop of mainstream news, that Barbara Bannagan had been killed. What he did not know was that Jo had followed Schwartz that day to the motel.

"They were having an affair," Jo continued. "According to the motel desk clerk, Mrs. Bannagan and Schwartz checked in there at least twice a week, always the same room overlooking the pool in the back of the motel. I had gone to Dymo that day to talk to Schwartz again as he had promised me some data on people who had been laid off, fired, and so on, but as I pulled up, he was pulling out, so I followed him. I figured that I could grab him at lunch and maybe pull some info from him over a beer if he was eating alone. I had no idea that he was boffing Bannagan's wife. Imagine *my* surprise."

"Did you follow him to the room?" Cassidy asked her, making notes as fast as he could on a legal pad in front of him.

"Yep, sure did. They even let me watch!" she said and laughed. "Sorry." She cleared her throat. "I had to stay far enough behind him, and I lost him when he got to the second floor. I saw the woman coming towards me so I pretended to be staying there at the hotel. I said hello, but she did not answer me. She was dressed in jeans and a silk shirt, but she was still overdressed for the occasion, if you get my drift," she said giggling. "Any way, she went into Room two-ten and I could hear them in there, and as there was only one other car in the parking lot on that side of the building, I can only conclude that they were in there together. So I went downstairs and rented a room on the same floor where I could watch their room from my window. After about five to ten minutes later he came out and left, and then she followed soon after."

"They must have had a fight! So you saw her get killed?" He was becoming excited. He knew that this would bring in a big stash if he caught the murderer on this one. Not to mention the publicity for him and his firm. This would put his company in the big league, bigger than they already were. He would be rolling in clients and dough. There was silence on the telephone. "Jo? Did you see her get whacked?"

"I am so sorry, Butch. I was very tired from being up most of the night and as I had already paid for the room . . ." her voice trailed off.

"So you fucking blew it all off?" he said much louder than he had intended to. Jo was one of his best detectives and she was probably exhausted.

"Well, how was I supposed to know that someone was going to fucking attack her in broad daylight at a usually very busy hotel?" She cleared her throat again. "I just figured that they were each going back to their own day's activities. I really had no inclination that she was even in danger. I had planned on talking to her, if she would see me, sometime at the end of the week. Guess I should have tried to see her before now. My God, how was I to know?"

"Not your fault. You *had* no way of knowing. But that was a good bit of info. Any chance that Schwartz did it? Maybe a lover's quarrel or maybe they were splitting up and he had waited for her to come out of the room?"

"None that I am aware of. I heard nothing but soft conversation as I walked past the room. I have no idea what went on. Even the sirens from the emergency and police vehicles did not wake me up. I'm sorry, chief. I was really exhausted."

"Everyone fax me your guest lists from each hotel and your reports by tomorrow. Let's see what comes forward. Good job, people. Keep it up and there will be bonuses for all."

* * * * *

Paige Schwartz paced from room to room, downing her Meyer's Rum and Coke faster than the ice could melt. She was already on her third one when her husband's car finally pulled up to the front door. His chauffer opened the door to let him out, handing him his briefcase as he stood up. When he entered the house, he did not see his wife standing by the window, her drink in her hand. He walked into the family room and directly to the bar to make himself a scotch and water. As he put the ice into the glass he heard his wife and turned around. He guessed by the look on her face that she had heard about Babs being killed. He guessed wrong.

"Isn't that awful about Babs being killed today?" he said as nonchalantly as he could. His hands were shaking and he hoped that she did not notice.

"What?" she asked, momentarily distracted from her questions regarding the telephone call and the innuendo it had dropped on her. "Babs was killed? Where? How? I have not heard about that."

He looked at her, surprised, but then he figured that she must have been out spending more money, as usual. "She was attacked at the Ramada Inn on Route One. Someone stabbed her a bunch of times. She was dead at the scene." His knees felt weak and he thought that he would fall if he did not sit down.

"What was she doing at the Ramada, I wonder?" Paige said, going over to the bar for yet another refill on her drink.

"It's all over the radio and television news. One of my employees heard about it and told me. I thought that we might be able to catch it on CNN." He flipped the button on the remote to turn on the oversized TV set in the corner of the room.

"I had a strange phone call today, Bill," Paige said, as she fixed herself another rum and cola.

"Oh? What was it about?" He tried to keep his voice from cracking, his hands from shaking.

"It was a woman warning me about keeping a closer eye on you. Any reason that you know of that someone would feel the need to warn me like that?" She turned to face him, leaning against the glass block and brass bar, one arm across her waist, the other hand holding her drink. She sipped slowly, keeping her eyes on her husband's face.

"No, how would I know what she was talking about?" The TV reporter was talking about the death of

Barbara Bannagan, the screen showing the earlier turmoil outside the Ramada Inn that afternoon. Both of them stared at the screen. Then a picture of Barbara's pretty face appeared. Bill Schwartz's insides were shaking, and he felt nauseous. He dared not try to stand. He could not take his eyes off the screen, remembering how they had made such passionate love day after day just prior to her death. *Could they find out that he had been there with her that day?* He wondered. *Had someone already called his wife and told her and she was playing a cat and mouse game with him now?*

"Who is she, Bill?" She gently swirled the ice in her drink, watching his reaction.

"Who is who?" he asked back, keeping his eyes straight ahead and fixed on the TV screen, pretending to be interested in the news. He had to maintain his cool or it would be all over.

"I want to know who the woman is that you have been seeing on the side, and I want a truthful answer. I would rather hear it from you before I hear it from someone else."

Bill Schwartz turned to stare at his wife, not knowing whether to tell her the whole story or to keep his mouth shut and feign innocence. He finally opted for the latter. "Paige, I have had a really hard day at work, which included Michael coming to see me and him and I having some heated words, and then I find out that one of our best friends, *his* wife, has been killed. I come home looking to shut the world out and I am getting the third degree from my own wife about some stupid anonymous telephone call about me seeing another woman. What the hell is going to hit me next?"

The telephone rang and Paige answered it. "Bill, it's the Princeton police department."

* * * * *

"Thank you for coming in, Mr. Schwartz. We felt that it would be better if we talked to you here, rather than at DymoTek," Detective Corelli said, pulling out a chair for Schwartz across from the one-way mirror.

"No problem," Schwartz answered sitting down in the offered chair. "I do not know what you think I can tell you about Michael Bannagan, other than that he was a great man to work for, and is a very good friend."

"And Barbara Bannagan?" Detective Bennedetto asked, his big hands clasped on the table in front of him.

"Well, she was a friend, also." He tried not to squirm in his seat. He knew that cops watched body language as much as listened to what you said, if not more so. How you acted when you answered their questions would speak volumes more than the words themselves.

"When was the last time that you saw Barbara Bannagan?" Bennedetto asked.

"Oh. Well, let me think. I guess it was about a month before the news broke on Michael's problems. I could check with my wife for a definite date, if that would help." He knew his forehead was glistening with sweat, but he did not wipe it off...hoping they had not noticed.

"And you have not seen her since?"

"I don't think so, but as I said, I would have to check with my wife. She keeps our social calendar." He crossed his legs but refrained from crossing his arms across his chest. That would be a dead give-away that he was drawing himself inside for protection. Schwartz had taken several seminars on body language in order to help him with dealing not only the employees, but with the Board of Directors, the stockholders and the vendors that he had to deal with on a daily basis.

"Were you at the Ramada Inn yesterday?" Bennedetto asked gruffly. His demeanor was changing to a tougher attitude than he had had when Schwartz had first come in.

"No, why would I be? But I did hear that Babs . . . Barbara was killed there. Why would you think that I was there with her?" Now he was sweating profusely and was very nervous. He was sure that they had noticed by now.

"Did I say that we thought that you were there with her? It's just that someone fitting your description checked in around eleven-thirty, and Mrs. Bannagan was seen going into the same room a short time later. She had also been seen sitting in her car just prior to this man checking in. So, who do you suppose she was meeting with there?" Bennedetto was watching this man really beginning to lose it, the sweat all over his face that he was not wiping away and his total demeanor. It had to have been him. He matched the description, he knew the victim, and they had been there many times before according to the information Detective Carson had uncovered.

"How would I know? She is not my wife. I do not care what she does nor with whom. Look, I have answered your questions on this subject. I have a very busy day ahead of me and I am going to be late for my first meeting. Am I finished here? I have a board of directors meeting to attend." He began to stand up.

"Sure, no problem. We can get in touch with you if we have any more questions."

Bill Schwartz started for the door. "Oh, one more thing, Mr. Schwartz. Mrs. Bannagan had your business card in her wallet. Why would she have that card in there, do you suppose?" Corelli asked.

"I told you that we were friends. I guess that she carried it as it has my cell number on it in case of emergencies. A lot of people I know carry my card. Is that it? Are you sure you have asked all your questions now?" He was getting angry. Now he had no choice but to openly wipe the sweat from his face with his white cotton kerchief before it ran into his eyes. His glasses were already fogging up.

"Thank you, Mr. Schwartz." Bennedetto said, not moving from where he sat. He watched Schwartz leave. "Something is going on here. I think we may have just struck pay dirt."

"Man, was he sweating like a pig. It wasn't enough that he got Bannagan's job, but he had to have his wife, too. Christ! They are like vultures, except instead of waiting for the guy to die, they are eating him alive."

"They may make a hellava lot more money than the usual perp we get in here, but they are just as low. Maybe lower."

* * * * *

Paige Schwartz answered the phone. "Hello?" She pulled her slip down under her skirt and smoothed it out. She was late for her club meeting.

"So how does it feel to be married to a murderer?" the voice asked softly, almost a whisper.

"What? Who the hell *are* you? Why don't you tell me your name?" Paige said into the receiver in a loud angry voice.

"The Ramada Inn, room two-ten is where they met all the time. But fucking her wasn't enough. No, he had to kill her, too. You women in your big houses, with your fancy clothes, and beauty appointments when one strand gets out of place, do not know anything about anything. You are out of touch with reality. You think because you live in a gilded cage that you are immune from all the shit that flies out here in the real world. When will you wake up and grow up? That shit is now all over you and you don't even smell it."

"Don't call here again or I will call the police! Do you hear me, bitch?" Paige screamed into the phone.

"See? Can't even help someone when they are in need of help. Hope you sleep well from now on. If I were you, I would sleep with one eye open and on my husband..."

Paige Schwartz slammed down the receiver and stood there shaking. She went and made herself a drink, regardless of the fact that it was only ten in the morning. She picked up the telephone again and called Madeline Stone to tell her that she could not make the meeting today, as she was not feeling very well. There were other things more important than stupid flowers. *Am I out of touch with reality?* she wondered. *Was her husband really having an affair? Could he have killed Babs?* She could believe the possibility of an affair, but with Babs? And kill her? *Not Bill. That he could not do. But was he having an affair behind her back? Could he have been with Babs?* She would find out, one way or another. She had to know or the wondering would drive her crazy.

* * * * *

Loganthau hung up the telephone and sat staring down at the court cases piled high on his shiny cherry-wood desk with unseeing eyes. After a few minutes, he rubbed his forehead, where his hair had made a slow withdrawal backwards. He hit the three numbers that would connect him to his secretary, Nancy, and heard her sweet voice ask him in a whisper what she could do for him and that if it was what she thought it was, that he would have to wait until after work. Then she giggled. He chuckled and asked her to get Michael Bannagan on the line.

When she had hung up, he thought about his own affair with Nancy and what would happen if his wife found out about it. He knew what she would do—she would divorce him in a New York minute, taking as much as she could with her. Somehow he did not feel that it was fair for wives who stayed at home all day and did nothing but play tennis, who worked out at the gym and who went to flower clubs, to get more than half when they divorced their husbands. She was educated…why couldn't she have gone to work instead of just playing all day?

She no longer had a reason to just stay home and do nothing but things that she got pleasure from since their three children were grown and out on their own. Why should he be the only one that had to work? They had a live-in housekeeper and maid, so there was nothing that she needed to do at home all day. He was getting resentful over this issue but although he had hinted that maybe she should get a job for extra money to put away in their retirement funds, she had just laughed and asked him if he was joking. No, he hadn't been, but he had let it slide. One day the time would be right for him to tell her how he really felt and that he was not joking in the least.

His phone rang and it was Nancy telling him that Bannagan was on the phone. He hit the button. "Michael, how are you doing? Better, I hope." He tried to make his voice as cheery as he could under the circumstances.

"Okay, I guess. What's up?" Michael sounded like he had been woke up from a nap, and he had been.

"I just heard from my personal investigator. Are you sitting down?" He tapped his pen on the stack of folders in front of him. When Michael told him that he was sitting, Loganthau went on. "He told me that your wife was having an affair." There was no sound. "Mike? Did you hear me?"

"Yes. I heard you. I figured that she was. That was probably why she wanted the divorce. She must have just blamed it all on me when, in fact, she had her own buck fucking her behind my back. I guess she was just better at secrets than I was." The hot tears again began to surface and his eyes burned from the salt. He seemed on the verge of crying all the time now.

"Don't you want to know who it was?" Loganthau asked softly.

"Does it matter who it was now that she is dead?" Then he quickly changed his mind. "Tell me."

"Bill Schwartz." Art waited for the information to sink into Mike's brain.

"Bill? Bill Schwartz was screwing my wife behind my back? That lousy bastard! After all I did for him—and we were friends! That sneaky, piss-off son-of-a-bitch! I'm busting my balls to give that bitch everything that she could ever want and she is sucking off my Vice President of Finance! And I am paying *him* to have it done to him! No wonder he kept telling me that I needed to go here—we were losing contacts, and go there—we were losing productivity! He wanted me gone so he could fuck my wife while I was away! That . . . that rotten no-good mother-fucker!"

Loganthau let him rant and rave and get it off his chest. He could hear Mike throwing things and breaking stuff that he figured had been given to him by Barbara or that maybe she had bought. There was way too much on the poor guy's shoulders right now. He needed to let it all out. He just sat back and let Michael pitch his fit from hurt feelings, damaged ego, and overload of stress. *It was probably a good thing that Barbara was already dead,* Art thought.

~Chapter 20~

"Detective Bennedetto, please," Arthur Loganthau said into the receiver, tapping his letter opener on the thick desk pad on his desk.

The officer on the desk asked, "*Who* do you want?"

Loganthau said, "One of the detectives from Boston who is using one of your offices there? Detective Bennedetto?" He was connected to Corelli instead. "Detective, I am not quite sure how far you have gotten in your investigation, but I think I have a bit of news for you, if you would like to do a swap on info."

"A swap?" Corelli asked. "We do not swap information with lawyers, especially not with the defense attorney."

"Of course you do! You swap out with informants, other convicts and perps to get what you want, with family members who . . ."

"Okay, okay. Whatcha got?"

"How about lunch? You and your partner busy for lunch?" Loganthau had decided that he did not like this cop who had a grudge against attorneys by the way he talks to them. *Must have wanted law school instead of an academy*, he thought. They settled on a meeting at noon at a little bistro on Witherspoon Street, close to the hospital. He had to see a patient who had been hit by a speeding car and was in critical condition and who wanted to quickly do a will in case he did not make it, as well as a law suit against the other driver.

Loganthau began to make notes on what he wanted from the detectives and what he would give them in return. He doubted that they knew that Schwartz was having an affair with Bannagan's wife. Maybe Schwartz had killed her when he had been dumped like a piece of garbage. Schwartz seemed to have a little man's complex in the term of wanting to be the "Big Cheese" as his cup said, instead of the CFO. But could his client have gotten to her first? For the first time, Art Loganthau had doubts about the innocence of his friend, Mike, with regard to the killing of his wife. He had every reason to kill her; she was divorcing him and going to take him for everything that she could get her delicate little hands on and she had the proof to back-up her allegations of adultery having put the detective agency on him; and she had been having that affair with his good friend. She had called him a murderer on national television and let the world believe like she did, that he was guilty.

Guilty? Proof of adultery? Damn, damn, damn, he thought. *The detective agency!*

* * * * *

"Carolyn Koffee?" Bennedetto asked looking up and down this pretty, dark-skinned woman, with her slender body, long nails and made-up beautiful face. He wondered how anyone could divorce this looker.

"Yes? Can I help you," she asked looking from one detective to another.

"We are detectives from Boston, Mass, and we would like to talk to you," Corelli said holding out his badge and identification for her to read. She opened the door wider and let them in. "What is this all about? I have not been in Massachusetts in a very long time."

"This isn't about you, Mrs. Koffee. It's about Michael Bannagan." Corelli looked toward his partner who was already walking around the room looking at everything as if he were buying it.

"It's Ms. and I do not know what I can tell you about Michael. I have no idea what is happening with him and this awful mess that he is in. I would never have pictured him as a murderer. I hope it proves out that he is innocent. I think the world of him."

"You do?" Corelli asked, taking the liberty and sitting down on the love seat. "After you were laid-off, lost your husband, your home and your job? I do not think that I would be as kind-hearted as you if it had all happened to me. Aren't you just a little angry?"

She hesitated before answering. "My goodness, you sure have gathered a lot of information about me. Yes, I am very angry," she finally answered. "I lost almost everything and I never saw it coming. I think that he could have given us a clue—a hint that there were problems, but nothing. That lay-off knocked the breath out of us, and me especially. Oh, my husband tried. We struggled to stay afloat, but when we lost our home that broke him." She got quiet for a few seconds. "Can I give you officers some coffee? Or something cold, maybe?"

"No thank you, Ms. Koffee. So if this is how you really feel, then why are you on Bannagan's side? Why hope that he clears out of all this? I would think that this was your chance to see justice done. It must feel just a little good to you to see him going through the same things that you went through but for different reasons." He glanced over at Bennedetto again who was looking at family pictures that were on the bookcase shelves.

"I did—at first. I went from shock at hearing the news, to satisfaction of his having problems where he, too, would lose all that he has. But now that I have watched the news and followed what is happening, I feel sorry for him. I cannot believe that Michael would do something like going around killing women, especially his wife. He loved her." She stood up. "Excuse me, I need something to drink. I have diabetes and I get thirsty very easily. You sure that neither of you would like something?" When both men had again said no, she went into the kitchen.

Corelli looked around the room. It appeared to be a small Ranchette home, but she had it adorned in pastel colors and simple furniture. She must really have taken a beating on the pay loss, but she was not living in the poor house either. "Anything interesting?" he whispered to Bennedetto, who just shook his head.

"I'm sorry. Where were we?" she asked coming back into the living room. She placed her glass of water on a cork coaster on the square plain oak coffee table, and then sat down gently on the sofa.

"Your feelings about Bannagan," Corelli reminded her.

"Yes. That is partly why I am so thirsty. My sugar is out of control because of stress. I do feel really bad for him. He worked very hard to build that company, and I know that his possibly losing the business must be an awful burden to carry. The managers that were hit hard were those of us that came on-board later on and those jobs were new positions created by the growth of the company, so, of course, we were the first to be let go and our divisions reincorporated back into the divisions that originally had them. It was just good business sense on Michael's part, but unlucky for those of us that it touched. But after I thought about it all, my husband and I were already having marital problems, and we would not have been so financially ahead had I not gotten the job at DymoTek, so Michael did us a big favor when he hired me. He gave me a large sign-on bonus of cash as well as stock in the company, so even with what happened, I managed to cash in everything and although I do not live as high as I used to, I live well. That would not be the case if I had gotten a job at a different company. He was . . . is a fair man."

"Can you tell us about the other employees who also lost their jobs in that lay-off? I mean, you seem to have weathered the storm okay," Corelli said, motioning around the room.

"By the skin of my teeth. I sold our home through the divorce and managed to pull some money from the sale of that, plus I sold my stock in the company and some other stock and some bonds, and cashed in my CDs and IRAs. I put some of it into this house. I recently got a job working nights for a small company doing their computer work and some bookkeeping. Of course, I am making much less than I did at Dymo, but at least I am paying the bills. A lot of the other managers faired pretty well also."

"Do you know of any one of the managers who did *not* fair so well?"

She thought for a few minutes and then said, "No, I think everyone managed to come out of this okay. Not great, but okay. Wait. I think Wendy didn't make it so good. The last that I heard, she had gotten divorced, lost her home, and had gone bankrupt. My old secretary, Julie Adams, told me not too long ago that she had heard Wendy was living in a studio apartment in a bad section of Trenton. You know, drug area with muggings and shootings and the like. I can't picture her there. She had this beautiful big home with a pond overlooking the river in the near distance. It was a very large, two-story, all-brick Colonial home and she had so many wonderful parties there. I had a great time when I visited. She was the hostess with the mostest. I felt really bad when I heard about her. Can you picture an elegant, educated and beautiful woman living in a place like that? She must be terrified. I don't know how much is true, but Julie usually has the scoop on everyone. You know. There's always one in every company who knows everyone's business."

"Well, we appreciate your time in this matter. Do you think that Julie would have an address for Wendy? Unless you have it." Corelli asked as they were walking toward the front door.

"I don't, but I can ask Julie."

"That's okay. We will ask her. She is still at Dymo?"

* * * * *

"No shit! A gorgeous dame like her fucking that weasel-faced wimp? Go figure," Bennedetto said stuffing the last of his New York Strip steak into his mouth and wiping his full lips with his cloth napkin.

"I can't believe it either," Corelli said. He took a big swallow of his cold draft.

"Okay, boys, I gave you your info, now give me back something. Where does my guy stand on things and what have *you* found out?" Loganthau set his fork down on his plate and motioned for the waitress.

"You got anyone checking out the laid-off employees from Dymo?" Corelli asked. Loganthau shrugged. He was not sure at this point what the detective agency was doing or what they had learned since the last report.

"Yes, sir?" the waitress asked, pad and pen in hand.

"I would like some apple pie with chocolate ice cream on it and a cup of French Vanilla coffee, black," Loganthau told the young girl. "You guys want some dessert?"

As soon as the dessert order was given, Loganthau asked what was so important about the employees. Corelli answered, "Well, we seem to be narrowing in on an employee with a big grudge against Bannagan. You know those anonymous little notes that you turned over to the district attorney? Well, we do not think that they are just a crank item. We are checking out anyone who may have had a grudge, a *big* grudge, against your client. You see, we are not *against* your client, Counselor; we are simply doing our jobs by checking out anyone, I repeat *anyone*, who might have had a reason to kill those women, or who might have wanted to set up your client. We are not the type of detectives that zero in on someone and do not look elsewhere for other things. Everything is a puzzle in a case, and we are not the type that squish the pieces to fit one person, but rather we look at all the pieces to see where they fit and why." Loganthau just stared at him. "Surprises you, don't it? Well, we don't want the newspapers saying shit about us. My pard and I have been like this from the time we started together a million years ago, and we leave no stone unturned."

"Dare I ask if any one particular name falls out of the shaker?" Loganthau asked, taking another bite of his pie a la mode and ignoring the detective's sarcasm.

"A gal by the name of Wendy Westlake might be a good place to start. But we are going to try to find a location for her, so out of courtesy, we want to locate her and speak to her before you or your headhunters do. Got it? Now as long as we are trying to see what the connection might be to Bannagan, I think you can stay put and let us do our job. But after we talk to her and get all our ducks in a row, it wouldn't hurt for you to check with your client about her and see what he can add to the puzzle. You just never know what clue may pop forward. But until we get our scoop, you keep it under wraps, even with Bannagan. Deal?"

* * * * *

Bannagan went through his old office doors so hard and fast that one door banged hard against the wall, putting a hole in the sheetrock. Bill and Paige Schwartz both jumped at the sound of the impact. Before Bill who was standing behind his desk could say anything, Bannagan had stormed around the side of the desk and had him by his jacket lapels. Bannagan hit Schwartz so hard that Bill toppled back over his executive chair, his glasses flying over his head when he hit the carpeted floor. Paige screamed in fright. She had never seen Michael in such a fit of rage. Michael picked Bill up to an almost standing position and hit him in the face again, breaking his long thin nose. Blood immediately gushed from his nose with such force that it could have been a cut artery. Paige ran out of the office screaming for help and for Suzie to call 9-1-1.

Schwartz tried to cup his nose to catch the blood, and to talk to Michael at the same time, but Bannagan could not hear him over the blood that pounded in his own ears from anger. "Fuck my wife, will you?" he screamed at Bill. He hit Swartz again, making impact this time against the side of Bill's head just above his ear. Bill was now totally dazed and unable to see. He no longer worried about his nose, and it ran like an open faucet down over his mouth and chin, wetting his shirt and blue pinstriped suit jacket, some splattering on his black shoes, onto the thick carpet.

"You fucking send me on the road so you could have an affair with my wife? How long, you mother-fucker? How long have you been fucking her? I want to know! How long?" Now Bannagan was sitting on his chest pounding his head and face as if by doing so, all the anger inside him would be gone when he stopped. He took all his pain and agony out on his one time good friend, Bill Schwartz. "I gave you everything, mother-fucker, and you had to even take my wife!. It wasn't enough, you had to have her, too?"

Several of the men from the office were trying to pull Michael off of Schwartz before he killed him, if he hadn't already. Sirens could be heard in the background. Paige Schwartz stood frozen, not only because of her husband being pummeled to death, but because what she had been told on the telephone was true. Her husband and Barbara Bannagan had been having an affair. The woman on the telephone had been telling the truth. Her husband had lied to her.

The men had finally gotten Michael restrained when the police came through the door and handcuffed him. The one cop began to recite him his rights.

"Yeah, yeah, I fucking know all that! I have it memorized by now!" Bannagan said trying to pull away from their grasp, unable to calm down.

~Chapter 21~

Michael had just gotten home after being bailed out of jail by Art Loganthau who told him to go home until *that* case came up now. Art was furious at him for losing his temper like that and putting Bill Schwartz in the hospital in critical condition. Now if Bill died, Michael would really be facing murder in the first degree and there would be no getting out of it. Almost the entire group of employees from DymoTek had witnessed the brutal beating. The best he could hope for was battery in the first degree with extenuating circumstances, according to Art.

Art had also told him, in no uncertain terms, that he had really screwed up his own defense on the murder charges. But Michael just didn't care anymore. He could not take much more of anything. He was just going through the motions of living. He could care less if Bill lived or died. As far as Michael was concerned, Schwartz could just die and go to hell with Barbara and screw her down there!

Then Art had called Michael at home to tell him about the District Attorney's request for a psych work-up and that he was now approving the request because of Michael's attack on Bill Schwartz. When Art warned Michael that he had better show up for the evaluation, Michael had refused.

At that point, Art asked, "Just how much more money do you have available to keep bailing yourself out of jail? Or are you pushing for permanent jail time, complete with cot and pillow? You had better calm the fuck down and start listening to me or you can just go find yourself another attorney. When you talk to the shrink you had better level with him."

"Really?" Michael replied sarcastically. "Don't you want me to bounce off the walls and act like I'm a looney-toon?"

Art slammed the phone down in Michael's ear.

Now back in the safety of his own home, Michael poured himself a large scotch and water over ice hoping to dull the pain, and then stuck his hands in the ice bucket that Angelica kept filled, in order to cool off the pain and swelling in his hands from the beating they had done on Bill's face and head. He wondered if there were any broken bones in his fingers as he stared at them.

His doorbell rang and he started not to open it but decided that he was still very angry and that he would give it to the next one who gave him any shit. He yanked open the door and stood staring at her.

"Aren't you going to invite me in?" she asked sweetly, her dark hazel-brown eyes bright and shining.

"Oh, yes, sure. I'm sorry. How rude of me. Please. Come in. You just startled me. You were about the last person I would have guessed would be standing outside my door. Or haven't you heard? I am the black hand of death," he told her, slowly pushing her back a little onto the front porch. He leaned over and whispered, "I believe that my home is bugged, so whatever you say to me may be recorded. I just thought you should know.

He then stepped back inside the threshold, ushering her into the formal living room. He hurriedly ran his hand through his hair and smoothed it down as he followed her into the room. He motioned for her to sit down on the formal sofa. Instead, she chose to slowly walk around the room, looking at the art paintings and tapestries, which hung on the walls, the many family pictures placed lovingly in beautiful wood or silver frames and put on the mahogany furniture. She ran her slender fingers along the smooth, shiny furniture tops.

"I was just making myself a drink. I kind of lost it and got into a fighting match with an old friend," he told her, holding up his bruised and swollen hands. "Would you like a drink? Manhattans, if I remember correctly?"

"You remember correctly," she said turning around to face him. "So, whose face did you pummel to do that to your hands?"

Her smile took him by surprise. He had forgotten how beautiful she was, especially when she smiled, showing all her beautiful small straight teeth through full red lips. He brought her drink over to where she still stood looking around the room. "Here you go," he said handing it to her. "Are you going to stay standing or would you like to sit down."

She sipped her drink slowly, delicately. The alcohol slightly burned the inside of her tongue and gums, raw from an infection that she had gotten in her mouth and was having trouble getting rid of. She could not afford to go to the doctor's and hoped that maybe the alcohol would help kill the infection. The taste of the drink was a pleasure for her to have, having not had one in so long. If she was lucky enough to have a few bucks, she would buy a cheap gallon of white wine for about seven dollars. She sipped her drink again and then sat on the sofa and crossed her legs at the ankles, pulling them back and to the side.

He had forgotten how feminine she was, too. How very lady-like. *She is still slender and well-built*, he thought to himself, although her clothes showed wear and stains. He tried to remember how she had been in bed, remember the feel of her, the scent of her. He could not. *Had it been that long ago?* he wondered. Aloud he said, "Do you remember Bill Schwartz? He was my financial vice president. I had hired him in my company from the beginning of its inception as my CPA, and then moved him slowly up to the Chief Financial Officer and the Vice President of my whole corporation. He is *now* the acting President and CEO of my corporation while I am gone. Well, I just found out that running my company, having my title and pay hike, as well as the perks that I once enjoyed, wasn't enough for him. No, he had to screw my wife, too. I guess I kind of lost it. The straw that broke the programmer's back, so to speak."

"So it upset you that Barbara was screwing around on *you?*" She laughed.

"Touché. Okay, let's change the subject to a better one. So, how have you been? How's your husband? Are you working?" he asked, leaning forward toward her, his drink in his hand.

"So many questions, so little time," she said, laughing. "I am hanging in there. I am no longer married and I am not working right now. It's a tough marketplace out there, and although I have great managerial skills, as you know, I cannot even get a job as a secretary. Can you believe that?"

"Oh, I am truly sorry," he said honestly. "Are you still on Lakeside Drive?"

"No. I lost my home in the bankruptcy and divorce. Actually, Michael, I lost everything. I have been staying in a small efficiency apartment in the worst section of Trenton. You know, drive-by shootings, screams in the night, and so on and so on." Here she smiled weakly at him, her round-shaped eyes staring down at the hardwood floors.

"Is there anything that I can do?" he asked her, getting up and taking her drink to refresh it.

"You better not make me another one or I will be asleep on this couch when I am done," she said laughing, a small silky laugh that could make anyone smile.

"That would be just fine. Actually, if you do not mind hanging around the black angel of death, you could move in here for a while until we can find you a new job and jumpstart your career again. I have plenty of bedrooms and this large house all to myself, and in fact, I could use some company. I have been very lonely since all this happened. Actually, as you know, I have been very lonely even before all this started. But that is another story. So, what do you say? Let's get you out of that area and that apartment. Want to keep a murderer company?" He laughed, the booming sound making the home sound empty and hollow in the deep silence.

"I don't know, seeing as you are in a fighting mood. I have a glass jaw," she said rubbing her small pointed chin.

"Oh I would never hit you. What could ever force me to hit a lady as beautiful as you? I would truly have to be out of my mind." He laughed and she joined him.

"You sure? I would not want to trouble you or be a pest," she responded, her long dark eyelashes at half-mast from the alcohol, barely hiding her pretty eyes.

"Please. You would be doing me a big favor. I will have someone to talk to besides my housekeeper, Angelica."

You have a housekeeper? Does she live here, too?" she asked, glancing around nervously.

"Yes, I have a housekeeper but she is not a live-in, so the nights are very long. Want to take a look around before you decide?" He stood up.

"Sure, I would love to finally see your home, Michael, but I don't need to see it to make up my mind about staying here. Unless you also have drive-by shootings and screams in the night," she said laughing. "It would be wonderful to stay with you for a while until I can get a new job, and a new and fresh start would be great, too. Thank you so very much for asking me. This is very kind of you." She followed him into the dining room.

"No, the only screams in the night are mine! I can't believe this. You are not only finally in my home, but are going to move in here for a while. You will probably be a lifesaver for me. It has been one hell of a six months for me, Wendy."

Wendy Westlake just smiled.

* * * * *

"Thank you for seeing us, Ms. Adams," Corelli said to the older woman as they had followed her back into her office cubicle, while the skirmish between Bannagan and Schwartz finally began to quiet down. Corelli and Bennedetto had been on their way to DymoTek to see

Julie Adams when the call came in from there about a fight. They were shocked to find out that it had been between Bannagan and Schwartz, but they definitely understood Bannagan's thinking on this one. Had it been either one of their wives, the same would have occurred or worse. They had laughed about it to one another in hushed whispers, until they located Julie Adams among the employees standing around the executive hallway watching the ruckus, watching as Bannagan was arrested once again, and Schwartz was rushed to the hospital by ambulance.

"Now what can I do for you two?" Julie asked politely in a soft voice. She was a woman obviously in her late fifties, and had the perfect look of everybody's grandmother with her gray and black hair, round body and spectacle eyes glasses.

"Well, your old boss and friend, Carolyn Koffee, said that if we needed any knowledge about the company and its employees, that you were the person with your fingers on the pulse of DymoTek," Corelli said smiling. He noticed that Bennedetto was looking around the small work center that was her office area. He did not like cramped quarters of any kind due to claustrophobia.

"I guess that is true seeing as I have been here forever, or actually since Michael opened the company," she answered with a small light laugh. "How is Carolyn?"

"You know better than we do," Corelli said laughing.

"So what did you need to know?" She pushed her glasses up on her small straight nose.

"Let's start with the managers who were laid off this past year. We have been able to talk to all of them but a Ms. Wendy Westlake. Any idea what has happened to her, or where she might be?" Corelli glanced over at Bennie, now standing against the wall closest to the opening of the cubicle where he could see who was doing what as they walked around. Corelli knew that he was also checking out the chicks in their short skirts and tight sweaters.

". . . known address was a small apartment in Trenton," Ms. Adams was saying when Corelli turned his attention back to her. "I am not sure exactly where, but I do know that it is somewhere close to the courthouse; around the corner from there. Find the shootings and you will probably find Wendy. Why do you want her, or shouldn't I ask?"

"We understand that she took her layoff from this company exceptionally bad. Lost everything including her husband. That true?"

"Well, you see, it started over two years ago actually, *before* the lay-off, and that is probably why she took it so bad."

"I am sorry, but I don't follow you," Corelli said with his attention now totally on the older woman.

"Oh, I'm sorry. I guess you don't know that part yet. You see, Wendy and Michael had this very torrid love affair that went on for quite a while."

"And what happened?" Corelli could tell that this lady wanted the attention that she now had from them and was going to draw it out as long as she could. She was important at this moment and that was probably not something that was normal for her.

"Well, you see, I think that if they had not been married to other people, that they would have eventually gotten married. That's how intense that relationship was, ya see. In fact, at the end, I don't think that Mr. Bannagan cared who knew about it, including *Mrs.* B. He even promoted Wendy to General Manager of Administration and gave her a section of the admin staff!

A lot of people around here did a lot of talking about how she had gotten such a cushy job, if you know what I mean." Her telephone rang and she answered it and told the caller that she would have to call them back, that she was with the detectives.

"Did it end badly? I mean, is that when Ms. Westlake was terminated?"

"Oh, no. That would have been too obvious. Michael must have decided that he had too much at stake that he might lose in a divorce if he kept the relationship alive and so he terminated it. Just like that," she said, snapping her fingers for emphasis. "Wendy was crushed . . . and humiliated. I mean *everyone* in DymoTek knew about it and then some. I think that she really and truly loved him, and although he gave every appearance that he loved her back, I guess that he didn't after all. Some of the employees thought that the Mrs. found out about it and that she had put her foot down heavily on his wallet and he let go of the affair. No, Wendy was the first one terminated, but at the big layoff of managers, not before. That way it was not so obvious to everyone and it kind of brought her down easily in front of the other employees. I think he was trying to help her save face. Like I said, I really believed that he cared very much for Wendy."

"What does Ms. Westlake look like? I mean if we saw her, how would we know it was her? You wouldn't happen to have a picture of her around the office, would you?" Corelli had his fingers crossed.

"No, no picture that I can think of, but Wendy is only about five foot one, dark brown hair, big brown and green eyes, tiny little thing with a great figure. Whenever I saw her, she had kept her hair short and back when she worked here; kind of all one length, a bob kind of hairdo. She tucked the sides behind her ears. It is a habit she has. She was always tucking her hair back, even when it was okay. Kind of like an unconscious habit, ya see." She smiled sweetly at Corelli.

Corelli asked her if there was anyone that Wendy was friends with that still worked here at the company and Julie had said no, that Wendy spent all of her spare time with Mr. Bannagan. Corelli found it strange that one minute she would refer to him as Michael and then as Mr. Bannagan the next time. The detectives thanked her and got up to leave.

When they had reached the elevator, Ms. Adams came hurrying down the hall, both of her hands holding a frame. "Officers. Officers! Wait a minute. I forgot," she said, panting.

"Forgot what?" Corelli asked when she got closer to them.

"This is a picture that was taken about six months before she was terminated. It is a picture of her and her staff, for outstanding attendance by an entire group." She showed them the picture and pointed out Wendy Westlake. They asked if they could borrow the picture and she said yes, as long as the company got it back. The detectives thanked her and left. She had watched them until the elevator door closed.

"Julie? What was *that* all about?" Carole Levine asked her.

"Oh, just some work I am doing with the detectives about Michael. I can tell *you*, but you can't repeat this. Okay?"

* * * * *

"Glad to have you all back for a while," Cassidy said to his investigators. They each took a seat around the large conference room table. One by one they all gave the information they had learned while on the road, but to this point it had amounted to very little.

"I think I have something," Betty said, going through her notes from Boston in her Day-timer. "It may be nothing, I'm not sure."

"What have you got?" Cassidy asked, taking a sip of his hot coffee.

"Well, one of the maids told me that one night she was taking extra towels to a room and she saw a woman come out of the elevator and run toward a room, which the maid thought belonged to that guest. But when the maid went back downstairs, she checked the room schedule on cleaning for the next morning and that room was listed as empty and wasn't on the cleaning schedule for the morning. She told the hotel security and when they went up and checked the room, no one was in it. Nothing was out of place except in the bathroom. The towels had been used and one had something dark brown on it, but it did not look like blood but she guessed that it could have been, but seeing as everything else was in order it was left alone. She just changed the towels."

"And this was never brought up to the cops when they were investigating the death of the woman that night?" Cassidy asked.

"I guess not. But the maid thought that it was strange behavior that night and when I asked her why it was not mentioned after that, she said that she guessed that the security guy would tell them and he must have forgotten it."

"Did the maid say anything else about the woman? I mean like her hair color, her clothes, anything?" Cassidy asked Betty, who was skimming her notes.

"Just that the woman had reddish colored hair and was dressed kind of shabbily. That is what caught her eye. In an expensive hotel like the Broadmoor, that this woman could afford to stay there. That was why she checked the room when she went downstairs. She just looked too poor to be a guest staying there."

Cassidy didn't say anything for a few seconds. "Well, I have something," he started. "It seems that at each hotel that Bannagan stayed at where a murder or death occurred, that a woman by the name of Wilma White was also checked into the same hotel." He looked at his detectives as they made notes. "Anyone know anything about a Wilma White? She was registered at each hotel and paid cash for her room each time and her room was always on the same floor as Bannagan's and close by; but everyone I have spoken to so far, has no recollection of her. Just seems really strange to me, now don't it? Now the attorney called and it seems that there was some kind of big lay-off at Bannagan's company last year and some of the big bosses were let go, and most of them took it bad but have recouped one way or another, except one. Her name is Wendy Westlake, she is five foot one inches, dark hair, hazel brown eyes, and last known address is in Trenton, close by the courthouse. Actually within a block radius; a block that is in a bad section."

"Oh, yeah, that maid said that she was short. You think it might have been her? Is she the real killer?" Betty broke in.

"I don't know, but I think we are on to something here. This woman lost everything with that lay-off—husband, home, everything! She has a reason to set

Bannagan up and get even, wouldn't you all say? So, now we have a Wilma White and a Wendy Westlake, who I believe are one in the same woman. I mean it may be coincidence that both gals have names that start with Ws, but I think it is more than coincidence. I want you to get on the telephones and get back with those hotels and see what you can find on her and if anyone, absolutely *anyone,* knows or remembers anything about her. And I mean now."

Everyone stood up to go to their individual offices when Cassidy said, "This has to be kept hush-hush for the time being. Loganthau promised the cops first dibs on her, but if we can find her first, how were we to know that the attorney and the cops had a deal, right?" he said, grinning an evil grin. "So here's the deal—I will give a three thousand dollar bonus to the one who can get us the scoop on this woman first, and a collar that fits her neck and her neck only. Got it? Now go!"

~Chapter 22~

Hours rolled into days and days turned into weeks and still there was no answer when Bill Schwartz called home. He knew that his wife must be livid over what had happened and what she had heard. There was no more denying it and she now knew that he had lied that day in the family room. How would he explain that? Of course he had to find her in order to try to explain, and she was either gone or just not answering the telephone. He had left message after message for almost two weeks now and she did not return the calls, nor did she come to see him. Now he was being discharged from the hospital and his wife was nowhere to be found. He decided to call his brother, David, to come take him home. In his condition, he did not want to go home alone anyway. Paige would never make a scene in front of someone, especially one of his family members.

He guessed that his marriage was over; his job would now be over; his beautiful home and possessions would slowly disappear. He would end up like Bannagan. How could this be happening to him? What terrible thing had he done to deserve this? He had not seduced Babs—she had seduced *him*. It had started at one of the Board of Directors' formal dinners. First he noticed her smiling at him for no reason, then it went to little things that she did that he knew were for his benefit and his benefit alone such as getting butter pats for his bread or holding his glass out to the waiter for more wine. Just little things that no one else might notice, but that she had made sure that *he* had noticed.

At another function, the footsies started when she accidentally kicked him under the table, apologized and then had made it better by rubbing it with her stocking-foot up under his pant leg. Eventually she made sure that she always sat next to him at the dinner tables where she could put her hand on his thigh or lean across him to talk to his wife, keeping her hand closest to him caressing his back, as Paige would not notice because she, too, was leaning forward in front of him. She had caught him once looking down the front of her low-cut gown and had whispered, "Like what you see?" followed by a smile and a wink.

Within a few months they were bumping into each other in unusual places. He figured out that she was either following him or was calling his secretary to find out what was on his agenda for the day and perhaps pretending to be Paige in order to do so, although she did not have to pretend to be anyone, as all of the officers and their spouses were close friends. To this day he had no idea what had ever made him start taking her out, to extreme places where he knew that he would not bump into any of the people that he and Paige knew. Finally, they learned that the safest places to meet were out in the open, like in the office after hours where they would each have an excuse for being there, or in his private car with the tinted windows. He seldom ever used his large Suburban, but it was great for making love in the back seat where no one could see them while parked in a busy hotel parking lot. Once they had even done the deed in his car in the company parking lot after everyone had left, including her husband.

What he could not blame her for was the fact that he had fallen totally in love with her. He envied Bannagan. Michael had it all, including Babs who was smart, attractive and witty. He enjoyed her company and could not wait to see her every chance that they could get away. He thought he had the best of both worlds by being married to Paige and also having an affair with Babs, but falling in love with her was something that he had definitely not counted on. Finally they started going to hotel rooms and because the Ramada Inn was close to the office, but just far enough away as to be out of range of the company employees on lunch hour, they had settled on that one as their special meeting place.

Tears were coming down his cheeks as he remembered, and now she was dead and he had just told her that day that he loved her, that he wanted them to each get a divorce so that they could marry. But she had just stood there looking at him as if he were insane, and then she had laughed, saying that she could not do that, as she was divorcing Michael to marry another man. "Another man? What other man? Do I know him?" he remembered asking her. He was just like some jealous idiot.

"But what about me?" he had asked her. She repeated the question back to him and stood there waiting for an answer, while his face flushed like an embarrassed school-boy being laughed at by the prettiest girl in the class when he had asked if he could carry her books for her. Barbara had then kissed him on the cheek, said that she had enjoyed their times together but that this was to be the last time that she could see him. With Michael going to prison forever, or maybe even executed, she wanted a divorce and would come out with everything that they owned. Bannagan would not even get his fifty percent as he had caused the break-up by murdering those women. She would get it all she had told him, and she felt that she was entitled to it, as he could not give her the one thing that she had always wanted—a child. So now she planned on taking what he could give her—everything else.

Bill could not believe it. He had stood there in the middle of the hotel room, his suit jacket in his hands, feeling like a jerk; feeling used and now being dismissed from her presence. But he loved her; didn't she understand that, he had asked her. She had laughed again, patting his cheek. After she had closed the door behind her, he had sat down on the bed, crying as he was doing now. But he loved Babs with his entire being and now she was gone forever. He would gladly have given Paige everything if she would have just gone away so that he could have Babs for his wife. He openly wept now, his sobs wracking his body.

"Oh my, are you in pain, Mr. Schwartz? I will be right back with your shot," the nurse said, exiting the room as fast as she had appeared.

* * * * *

It was such a beautiful fall day that Michael and Wendy had wanted to go for a drive in the country, but getting away from the stake-out patrol would be difficult. They decided that a decoy was necessary, so they had called the limo service that Michael had always used before, requesting a stretch limo. The driver was instructed to pull up around the circular driveway, stop for a few moments and then leave and drive all over town for three hours. There was to be no stops anywhere except for red lights, and the driver was not to draw attention to himself by driving too fast or too slow. He was also to keep all the tinted windows up, including the driver partition, so that no one could see into the back of the limo. He had explained to Renne who he was and that he just wanted some privacy from any and all reporters who would follow him. He then put the fee on his charge card along with a hefty tip for the driver. The limo owner said that he understood and that they would take care of it, and also added that they had missed his service with them. Michael had thanked them.

He and Wendy had watched through the blinds, watching the limo drive up, drive away and being followed by the unmarked patrol car, which had two guys in the front seat. They had giggled like kids, running for the garage. They were free for part of the day, but had to be back before the clock struck noon or they would turn into pumpkins. They laughed again. They were on a natural high, having outsmarted the cops who held constant vigilance outside his property. That, Wendy explained, was how she had gotten in—by having the taxi pull up in front of his house. The police had pulled forward a little but were still unable to see the front of Michael's home without pulling into the driveway.

And now as they drove with the windows down on his Suburban, the radio blared rock music, and Wendy Westlake was once again seated right next to Michael Bannagan, as she had been many times before.

* * * * *

David helped his brother, Bill, out of the front seat of his Toyota Corolla and up the front steps of Bill's large Victorian home. Paige's car was in the driveway but she did not open the front door. As soon as they had walked inside, David helped Bill to the sofa in his expansive family room and then he went back outside to get his suitcase from the car. Bill looked around as if expecting to see Paige standing quietly in a corner. She was nowhere to be seen.

David placed the suitcase near the winding steps, which led to the upstairs bedrooms and went back into the family room to check on Bill. "Anything else I can do or get you before I go back to work?"

"No. Thank you, David. I appreciate all that you have done today, leaving work and all to bring me home. Want some lunch or a drink of something before you go back?" Bill asked his brother.

"No. Thanks. I really have to get back. If you need anything or if there is any kind of problem, you just call me, you got it?" he said, motioning with his eyes and head toward upstairs, surmising that that was where Paige was.

"I will. Thanks again."

"I will call you later when I get home and check up on you," David said starting back down the hallway.

"Hello, David," Paige said, coming down the spiral staircase as if making a grand entrance.

David jumped at the sound of her voice. "Hello, Paige. I just brought Bill home. If there is anything I can do to help, please just give me a holler." He continued out to his car. He did not feel like a confrontation with his sister-in-law and he knew well enough that when she lowered her voice to that sweet sing-song octave, it was time to split the scene to avoid it. He felt bad for his brother, as he knew that he was going to get it and get it good. He would call him later and make sure that he had a place to go to if she threw him out, and he was sure that she was going to do just that.

Paige walked into the family room and up to the bar to make herself her rum and cola. She did not look at her husband, but she could feel his eyes on her back. Let him sweat what was coming. She would do it in her own time. It was *her* game now. He had had his fun; now it was her turn. After she had made her drink, she looked into the mirrored wall behind the bar. Bill was staring down at the carpet, his hands clasped before him on his knees. "Have nothing to say?" she asked without taking her eyes off the mirror image of her husband.

"What is there to say?" he responded without even looking up. He picked up the remote.

"Do *not* turn on that television set!" she said sternly turning around to face him. "You will not bury yourself into that boob tube. You hear me? This is serious, Bill."

"Everything that has to do with you or what you want is always serious, but only to you, my dear," he answered softly. If he was going down, he was going down fighting. "If you want a divorce, go get it. I will not stop you."

"Oh, I want a divorce. You can count on that. Or maybe I won't get a divorce. Maybe I will just stay here to make you miserable, maybe date someone while you can watch and think about it as you sit at home and wonder what I am doing out at night. But what I want is to know why you felt that you needed to not only have an affair, but to have it with one of my best friends? Was it to humiliate me? Was it? If so, you have succeeded!"

Her voice was rising in volume. She took a big swallow of her drink.

"I believe it became necessary when you decided that you loved your booze more than you loved me. I do not want a lover or a wife who is a boozer."

"What?" she screeched. This was not the response that she had expected. "I only have a drink or two so that I can relax. How dare you accuse me of being an alcoholic!"

"I did not use that word, but if the glass fits then use it. Go ahead. I know your glass is empty and you want another one. Make another one. That's what you want to do. Don't you think that I know when you have had a drink or two and when? Don't you think I have heard all of your lies about it—'I'm sick;' 'I'm tired;' 'I need to relax;' 'I am not drunk,' 'I have had nothing to drink today.' All bullshit. Like every other alcoholic, you justify why you need that drink and you think that I am so fucking stupid that I do not know when you have had one…or two…or three! I know the signs and symptoms. You have been a cold fish for a long time now. I have seen you drink and get all over whatever man was around. Except me! And I tolerated it. But then Babs came on to me and although I stayed as far away as I could, I finally decided why not? When your house is cold, you go to the home where you know it is warm."

Paige stood there, her mouth open, her eyes wild with rage. "How dare you speak to me like that? I have stood by you for many years, even more years than your first wife! Her you gave children; me you tell, 'no more kids.' And I stood by you anyway. When you were struggling, building yourself up in your career, I am the one who did without! And now you tell me I am cold because you need an excuse for fucking another woman? You have some brass balls, you lousy mother-fucker!"

"You know what, Paige? No matter how I felt, or what had happened, or if things had been reversed, I would have come to the hospital to see if you were okay," he said softly, slowly, as if trying to make a child understand what he was saying. "I would not have left you there alone, without so much as a bathrobe or pajamas or a razor. I would have at least called you if I was not able to get up to see you, but you did nothing. You would not even answer the telephone and say, 'Go fuck yourself, Bill, but I hope you are feeling better.'

"No. You turn back into the ice-queen. Well, my dear, get your damn divorce. I want you to. I have ruined our marriage, but so have you. But you will not get this house, nor will you get more than your lousy fifty percent in assets. So let's see how much you can earn on your own without me constantly paying the bills and picking up your tabs, and we will see if you can keep yourself in the lifestyle that you are used to.

"Yes, I have balls—big brass ones that will fight you every inch of the way on this. I would never remain married to you now. There is too much water under the bridge to stop the rush of water to keep us from drowning. It is over. We are over. Now if you want to continue this awful discussion, please go do so in the mirror as I have a severe headache and need to lie down. Until one of us moves out, I will sleep in the guest suite." Bill started to stand up but his legs would not hold him. He needed one of his pain pills, but they were in his coat pocket, which was on the other chair ten feet away where David had dropped it. And then he still needed to have enough energy to get to the bar area for some water.

Paige watched her husband and knew that he was suffering, but she didn't care. She was suffering, so he might as well join her. Again he tried to stand, and again he fell back onto the couch. She couldn't watch this. Regardless of what he thought about her, she was not made of ice. "Why are you trying to stand up?"

"I need my pain medication and some water to take a pill. I am in severe pain." He tried again.

"Stay still, I will get it. Where are your pills?" He pointed to his jacket. She walked over and took the bottle of pills out of the pocket.

"Percocet. Good deal. Think I will have one, too." She popped one of the white pills into her mouth and pushed it down her throat with a large swig of her rum and cola.

Bill watched. There was nothing he could do. If she wanted to commit suicide, he could not stop her. And although he really did not want her to do it, it sure would end his upcoming problems with her. He was then sorry that he had even thought that way. What the hell was happening to him, he wondered as his wife handed him a pill and the glass of water.

* * * * *

"I told you, he left in a stretch limo and he is just riding around town," the officer told Bennedetto on the telephone. "It is the first time that he has gone out in weeks. The only person he sees is his housekeeper. But then today a limo pulls up and takes him riding. I have no idea where he is going. Maybe he just needs air, Detective." There was a long pause. His partner turned to look at him. "But we need to stop. We need a cup of coffee, a sandwich maybe, and to take a leak. We need a back up so we can take an R and R for about a half hour. Then we will catch up to pick it back up, but the car has only stopped for traffic lights. What do you want us to do, pull the car over and ask him where the hell he is going?" Another pause. "The other guys are coming up on Route One and Interstate 295 in about three minutes. How about a switch at that intersection?"

"Sure," Bennedetto told the dispatch officer on the cell phone. He looked over at his partner and rolled his eyes.

"Thank you, sir." He hung up the receiver. "Thank you, you *dick*. Has to make me beg to let us take a piss! My fuckin' kidneys are floating!"

* * * * *

Michael had taken Wendy to the boardwalk in Atlantic City instead of to the country. He decided that he wanted a foot long hot dog, greasy French fries with cheese, and a large cold beer. He was sure that there had to be at least one stand open. It was too cold and windy for October, but the sun was bright and inviting. He needed to breathe in the salt air and know that he was really alive. Now as they sat on the brown wooden bench, stuffing their wind-blown red faces with food, there seemed no reason to speak. The gulls hovered above them while others stood on the fence railing staring at them with dark eyes. Once in a while they would squawk at one another, especially if Michael threw a piece of bun or a French fry into the air. They both laughed as the birds almost killed each other to get the morsels of food he had thrown.

He looked over at Wendy who was absently and delicately wiping the cheese from her lips. When she turned to look at him, he leaned in slowly and kissed her mouth sweetly. His body was now aching for her. He wondered if she knew what she was doing to him. But how could she? It was just a kiss between friends.

But she knew. She knew more than he could ever imagine.

~Chapter 23~

Corelli and Bennedetto had circled around the Trenton Courthouse looking at the area. It appeared to be the side streets that were the problem areas, and so somewhere on one of those streets lived Ms. Wendy Westlake, but which one and where to start looking? They had checked all the usual ways to find her, such as DMV but she had no driver's license and no car; they were running her through all the different states now. She had to have some kind of ID or license in order to survive in this world. Although there are many people out there who had none. Was she one of them? Usually it was people who did not have permission to even be here—aliens. But she had worked at DymoTek for several years and so she had had a car back then but then her license had expired and she had no car and no license on file. They had even run her through all the post offices in town and the surrounding towns. It was as if she did not exist at all.

They had decided to park the car, and start knocking on doors to see what they could find out. What if Julie had been wrong and it was not right next to the court house? But they did not want to take the chance of letting it go any longer until they found her, and with some luck on their side, maybe they would. Corelli took one side of the street and Bennedetto the other. They had a hunch—a gut feeling that both had and when that had happened, Corelli and Bennedetto had learned to listen to their feelings especially when they both had the same one.

After two hours of knocking on doors and talking to people that they were afraid to turn their backs on, on a dark night, they met halfway up the street. "I had no idea that there are so many apartments in each building."

"Never mind that, Bennie, I used to have my gun out back when I walked a beat and I had to go into places like these. Not to mention I hate the fucking hostility from each person I talk to. And the ones that just yell 'Who is it?' through the doors. I mean, man, you know that there are drugs going on in there. Some didn't even open the doors for fear we would smell it, like we couldn't smell it from under the doors. You learn anything?"

"Nope. A couple of them said that they see a gal that matches the description, but when they looked at her picture, they couldn't be sure if it was her. But 'It could be her,'" he said imitating the people and rolling his big brown eyes. But some think that this might be the girl who lives behind the courthouse on Mercer Street. Maybe we should try over there?"

"Same with me, although one guy said that he thought that she lived in the middle of the block somewhere, but he was not sure which apartment house it was, but he, too, thought it was on Mercer Street. He said that he noticed her one day when he was walking his dog around the block. This girl was sitting on the steps of one of the apartment houses on Mercer, talking to herself, or rather, arguing with herself. He said that she looked like she might have been a very pretty girl when she was cleaned up and dressed up nice. He also said that he did not think that she really belonged here. He said that he sees a girl that looks a little like the girl in the picture, except that this girl was not dressed so nice, and her hair was longer and not kept as nice as the one in the picture. But just the same, he thought it could be her." Bennedetto coughed. "I need some lunch, Partner, and a cold drink. I am so dry that I have cotton mouth. I can't talk to another person. Probably got a small high from the hallways in those houses and now have cotton mouth." He laughed. "You ever do any drugs growing up?"

Corelli looked sideways at his partner and then grinned, mischievously. "Hey, man, I grew up in Little Italy in south Boston, what do *you* think, man? They can't believe I am a cop and not running with the mob. My ma is so happy that I went to the good side of the law, rather than turn out like Uncle Angelo and run numbers for the rest of my life. But Angelo ain't as big as me. I would have been a collector, ya know what I'm saying here? Just me and my bat," he said laughing. "I mean look at me—six foot three inches, two hundred thirty pounds. Me running numbers? Nah, my forté would have been collecting. Who would have argued with me? I had the chance to do that, too, ya know? My ma would have had a heart attack and I couldn't do that to her. She was the one who raised all of us kids, especially having five sons and three daughters. My old man was always drunk and out carousing around with other women, getting soused with his buddies, or both.

My mom raised us kids alone, virtually. I have a lot of respect for her, too."

"I never had the chance to get into the gang and become a good-guy. I probably would have taken them up on it. I would have also been a collector . . . or a hitter, you know?" Bennedetto said. "Same thing—my size. But it was quick money. And good fast money. I probably could have worked my way up the ladder, too. It's surprising that we never met before the academy. I mean, you're Italian and so am I, except you lived up in Boston and I lived in New Jersey. So I guess it was a good thing I never had the chance to get in or you might be looking for me. Hey, how come they call the gang 'good fellas'?"

"'Cause they are," Corelli said laughing and pushing his partner away from him. The two detectives walked up the street toward the court house looking for a place to eat that was cheap. All the eyes on the street watched the two big machievos walk toward the courthouse from behind sneering faces, yellowed curtains, or without anyone else knowing. Everyone that watched knew that they were detectives looking for one of their own, and so the detectives were hated.

Mostly the two Boston detectives saw expensive restaurants where they supposed that the lawyers probably ate. "Should we ask a few attorneys?" Corelli asked his partner.

"We could eat and pass around her picture while we are filling our stomachs," Bennedetto said. "Sounds like a winner to me. What the hell. We are on city money, not our own."

"After lunch, let's try Mercer Street and see what we get. We will start in the middle like the old man said."

* * * * *

"I'll be right back, Mike," Wendy told Michael as she was getting out of the car. She did not want him to come up to her apartment and see how she had been living. She was so embarrassed and ashamed.

"Let me park the car and I will help you," Michael said to her.

"No, no. It will only take me five minutes. Just stay double parked like you are. Everyone does it here. I will be right down. I promise, I will only be about five minutes." Wendy ran inside her building, the smell of old food, cigarettes, weed and piss hitting her in the face as she went in the door. She rubbed her nose as she started for the stairway.

"Hey, little girl, I hear from the local grapevine that two dicks are wandering around the neighborhood looking for you. Two *big* dicks, too, I hear," Mrs. Massio said snickering at her own joke, leaning on the old stairway with her meaty left arm, her big belly hanging over her pedal pusher pants, her shirt barely covering it.

"Why?" Wendy asked. Fear was beginning to grip her, causing her throat to constrict, her temples begin to pound and her heart beat loud enough so that she thought the old bitch would hear it.

"They said that they needed to talk to you about that guy that is a serial murderer. You know, his name has been in all the papers for killing women in hotels. I don't remember his name but they told folks that they thought you might have some information that would help them. So do you?"

"Do I what?" Wendy asked, bending down to look at the car to be sure that Michael was still in it.

Mrs. Massio looked, too. "Do you have information that they need about that guy? Is that him?" she asked, thumbing over her shoulder towards the car.

"Um, no. That's my friend, Jimmy. I have to get something out of my apartment, Mrs. Massio." She started to run up the stairs and then stopped. "Mrs. Massio?"

"Yeah?" she asked as she was going back into her apartment. She wanted to get a better look at that guy in the big car.

"What did you tell them?"

"Nothin'—yet. They have been working their way up the street but then they walked up toward the courthouse. But I am sure that they will be back. Why? What do you want me to tell them? You know something?" she asked again. She came back to the stairway and looked up.

"No, I don't know anything that would help them. When they get here, will you tell them that I have gone on a vacation? I don't want to talk to two dicks. That guy that they are looking for information on used to be my boss, and I liked him. I do not want to answer their questions. You know, they are trying to hang the guy out to dry and he is really a nice guy who couldn't possibly have killed those women. Will you do that for me?" She ran for her apartment. If she didn't hurry, Michael would come in looking for her.

"Oh, sure, little girl. I can do that. You can trust *me*." Mrs. Massio bent over again trying to get a better look at the man in the large car, but she could not really see anything other than that the guy kept looking at the building. She could not even tell what color hair he had. She hated tinted windows on anything. It blocked her sight.

A few minutes later Wendy came running down the stairs, carrying a large denim bag with a shoulder strap and the word 'Barbados' written across it in large white letters. "I had to get a few things. I will be back in a few days. Okay, you will tell them that for me?"

"Sure. You know me; I keep my mouth shut about everything, Dearie." She made like she was locking her lips closed and then putting the invisible key down in her shirt.

"Thank you, Mrs. Massio. Um, Jimmy and I will be back in a few days." She opened the front door and ran down the stairs.

"Anytime," Mrs. Massio said softly, watching Wendy jump into the big SUV. She smiled a wicked grin. "Call me an old witch, huh? Thinks I have a short memory, that little slut." She laughed a sarcastic short laugh and went back into her apartment on the ground floor to watch out the window for the two dicks. *Jimmy, huh?* she thought to herself. *Sure he was.*

* * * * *

"That's all you have?" Michael asked her, trying to talk to her and watch the road at the same time.

"I told you, Mikie. Times have been hard for me. I do not own much any more," she answered quietly.

"Well, tomorrow we will go shopping and get you some clothes. You can't get a job if you do not look the part. No job means no apartment and so on. Want to do that?" he asked her, all excited about being able to help her while being able to take the constant thoughts of his own problems away for a few hours. He had really not been fair to her back then, and he should have left Babs for her, but instead he let his wife rule the roost. He knew that Wendy had taken it hard, especially when he cut the affair off in a cruel way by simply walking away from her. Helping her to get back on her feet now would help ease the guilt that he had carried about it for so long.

"Oh yeah, with the bundles of hidden money I have in this bag?" she said looking out the window. She knew what he would say next.

"No, maybe you don't, but I do have a little tucked away for a rainy day, and I guess, although the sun is shining, that it really is a rainy day. So far I still do, I think, so it's a new make-over tomorrow morning as soon as I go to my safety deposit box at the bank." He pulled her close to him and kissed her on the forehead.

Barbara had not understood why he felt that he needed to have a safety deposit box for just a little jewelry and some insurance papers, but that was because she did not have access to it and did not know that he kept money stored in there in case something happened. His father had told him stories about the depression and how hard it had been when he was growing up, so he had warned his son to do as he had done and hide money in the box in the bank where no one knew. It was the safest place. He even had it under his mother's name with him having the power to use it.

Wendy smiled to herself and snuggled in close to him. Tomorrow would be a fun day.

* * * * *

"Yes Sir. I know her very well," Mrs. Massio told Corelli and Bennedetto after looking at the picture. "In fact, you boys just missed her."

"What? Did she tell you where she was going?" He looked at Bennedetto over the woman's shoulder. He was checking the names on the mailboxes.

"Who lives in Apartment G? There is no name on the mailbox, but there is a bunch of stuff in it," Bennedetto said pointing at the mailbox.

"*She* lives in G. Never gets any mail…that is why there is no name. It's only junk mail. The mailman has me empty it out weekly because he can't do it and it's always just newspaper flyers, and the like. Nothing with her name on it so I just throw it all away." She opened the front door and threw her cigarette butt out into the street.

"Come in, come in. Don't mind my apartment. I have been ill lately." She closed her door before continuing. "She said to tell you when you found out where she lives, that she was going on a vacation. Vacation, hah!" Mrs. Massio said smugly, looking at the two detectives.

"So you didn't believe her when she said that she was going on vacation? Do you know where she might be going or who she might be going with? Maybe she told you?"

"She tells me *everything*. She said that she was taking a vacation, ran upstairs and got a small bag of stuff and ran out the door and into *his* big car."

"*His* big car? What kind of car was it?" Corelli asked her, writing down everything that she was saying. "By big car do you mean like a Cadillac? Or like a limo?"

"No, no. One of those four-wheel-drive kind of big car. In dark green with tinted windows, so I couldn't get a good look at the man behind the wheel," she said, lighting another cigarette.

"But you are sure that it was a man?" Corelli asked.

"I'm old, Dearie, but not *that* old that I can't remember what a man looks like," she snorted, laughing.

"Are you talking about an SUV type of car?" Corelli asked.

"Yeah, I think that's it!" Mrs. Massio said, flicking a scrap of paper off her armchair and onto the carpet.

"Do you know her name?" Corelli asked her, leaning against the doorsill.

"Wendy is all I know. She doesn't say too much to too many people. Very quiet she is. Almost like she has a secret. People who are that quiet remind me of my mother who used to say, 'Still water runs deep.' And this little girl is very deep, trust me." She inhaled on her cigarette like someone smoking pot would handle a joint.

Corelli made a note, not that they were going to worry about hassling some old woman for smoking an occasional joint. He automatically made notes about lots of different things so that he would once again have a mental picture of people that he had talked to, or a place that he had been. It was his way of remembering things on each case. It might be years before a case went to trial and then he was supposed to remember each little thing. He had learned early in his career to take tons of notes. He had a file cabinet and inside were folders labeled with the years and the case, and inside were all the many little note books where he had written copious notes for each case.

"Why did she tell you to tell us that she was going on vacation?" Corelli asked.

"'Cause the word on the street was that you two were walking around looking for her and when she found out, she went white and then she looked like she was going to faint; told me that if you came asking for her that I was to tell you that she went on vacation. She said that you wanted to ask her about her old boss and that he was very nice, that he could not have killed those women and that she did not want to discuss him with *you* two. And then off she went, lickety-split out to the car that was waiting for her. I even asked her if that was him in the car, but it was her friend, Jimmy, *she* said."

"Have you ever met her friend, Jimmy?"

"Nope. Never seen her with anyone before now, although I hear stuff happening in her apartment sometimes," she said winking one knowing eye at them. "Her next door neighbor, Mrs. Martinez, says that she hears her yelling sometimes, as if there is someone else there, but Mrs. Martinez says that there is never anyone else that she can hear in there. So we all think that there is something wrong with her. You know, talking to herself and all," she said, twirling her index finger and making circles by her head to show she meant crazy.

"But as far as this guy, maybe she just met him. She ain't too bad looking, and she *is* young, so maybe she picked him up somewhere. If she would stop talking to herself and get a job full time, then she might just meet someone nice. I have to tell ya, I wouldn't mind her moving out of here." She lit another cigarette.

"Why is that, Mrs. Massio?" Bennedetto asked, looking around her apartment.

"'Cause my sister wants to live in this building, now that her husband died. She can't live on the money she gets from social security. The government don't pay nothin'…hardly enough to live on." She watched Bennedetto looking at all of her stuff in the apartment. "Don't touch anything, sonny," she said to Bennedetto who was still wandering around looking at things in her apartment. Corelli put his hand by his mouth to stifle a snicker. Bennedetto made a face, sticking out his tongue at her behind Mrs. Massio's back.

"Well, when Wendy gets back, will you give her my card and ask her to call me on my cell phone, as we are here temporarily in New Jersey?" Corelli asked, handing her his card. "And here is one for you in case you can think of anything else that you might have forgotten. Also, if you can call us when she comes back we would appreciate it."

"Is it about her old boss? Is she next to be killed or something? I watch Law and Order all the time so I know how you guys work a case."

"No, we just want to talk to her and see if she can help us. Tell her not to worry and to please call us."

Once they got outside, Corelli said, "Let's get the car and head back to the station, *Sonny*." He began to laugh.

"Shut the fuck up, *Dearie*, you're not funny one bit. Let's go see if we can get a search warrant for the broad's apartment while she's *'on vacation'*."

~Chapter 25~

"Anything I want?" Wendy asked, her pretty oval face beaming, her eyes bright with excitement.

"Anything you want and everything you need," Michael said, smiling back. "You can't go around without decent clothes. You would look great going into a fancy restaurant for dinner dressed like that. You are beautiful. You just need the trimmings." He laughed, deep and hearty.

"Sounds like 'Pygmalion,' doesn't it? We could set a new trend, Mikie. We will call it 'take your significant other out for a shopping day.' Doesn't that sound like a perfect federal holiday? That way each person gets new clothes. Except that I have no money to buy you anything," she said softly, her eyes glistening with tears.

"I don't need anything. We will start that holiday next year and then you can buy me something, okay?" He paused, staring at her in the pretty sky-blue dress, with a white yoke and cuffs on the short sleeves that she had on. He had forgotten how much he had cared for her, and with her new haircut, and standing there in that dress in front of the long mirror, she looked like she had when he was having an affair with her two years ago. "You haven't called me Mikie in . . . since . . ." She walked over to where he was patiently sitting in the straight-backed chair where all the husbands sat while the women tried on clothes, and leaned over and kissed him on the mouth. At least she could pretend that they were married.

"I think this stuff will about do it, Mike. Wanna go eat now? I am so hungry," she said, slipping her small feet into the new white leather pumps he had bought her.

"Miss, my . . . friend will wear that dress and shoes out. We have reservations for dinner and we don't want to be late. So don't forget it when you tally up our purchases." They loaded all the packages into the rented limo and the driver drove them to the restaurant. "I think I had a great idea hiring two limos this time. I hate driving," he remarked, taking her hand and sitting close to her. He took the Dom Perignon champagne from the ice bucket, put a small hand towel over the top of the bottle, and popped the cork.

"Michael? You have been so sweet to me. I cannot believe all this." She smoothed out her dress so that it would not get wrinkled. It was the first new thing that she had gotten since her divorce.

"It's the least I can do. I mean if I had not laid you off, you would not be in this predicament, now would you?" He figured that he would be able to help her get a decent job now that she had some nice clothes to wear and her hair was back to normal and she looked terrific. He had a knot in his stomach that he knew was not from hunger—at least not for food. He already had his old feelings back, just as strong as they had been back then. She had proven herself to be a survivor with everything that she had been through. But he needed to go slowly or he would scare someone as delicate as she was. He knew deep down that she was really shy and not at all pushy. He knew so much about her, yet nothing at all. He had been ready to leave Barbara back then, but Barbara had shown him just how bad off she would leave him financially and socially, if he left her for Wendy. And he knew Barbara. She always meant what she said.

Now Barbara was gone not even five weeks, and here he was with Wendy. But he had loved Wendy in a way that he had never loved Babs. She made him quiver whenever she was close to him; made his mind go blank except for thoughts of her. When they had danced together last night in his family room to the sounds of some light jazz, it was as if no one else existed, no one else was anywhere around them, no one else mattered. All of his problems disappeared for as long as he held her, swaying slowly to the soft music. Now that she was back in his life, and Barbara was gone, all the old feelings were flooding through a door that he had closed back then. And he had no life preserver to save himself. He didn't care if he drowned as long as he had her back in his arms. She was his friend, and right now he needed to hold onto her with all his might. He had been thrown to the wolves by almost everyone he knew. *Was he just using her?* he wondered. He didn't care if he was. He needed her right now and that was all that he understood.

* * * * *

"Are you sure that I can legally let you officers into her apartment?" the heavy-set black woman asked the two huge men. She was shabbily dressed, looking as if she had no idea where her next meal was coming from, but her hairdo was extraordinary and must have taken a very long time in order to get it so perfect, and her fingernails were done to perfection.

"We have a warrant, ma'am," Corelli said. "Want to read it?" He handed it to her although she did not want to take it.

"Lord, no. I have no idea what all that legal stuff is about. Just don't mess up anything and she won't even know that you were here." With that she turned and left the small room, taking the warrant with her and closing the door.

"Mess it up? How the hell can we mess it up any more than it already is?" Bennedetto said once the woman was gone. The small efficiency room had been left totally unkempt. If someone was looking for her, the detectives would have sworn that she had been robbed. The cabinet drawers were on the floor and empty, as were the kitchen cabinets. The bed linens lay on the floor in a heap.

"Look at this wall, Bennie. Looks like she had a lot of stuff pinned to this one wall. Wonder what it was," Corelli said, examining the wall full of tiny holes by running his large hand over it.

"Maybe she is hot on some star. I see nothing here. If she came in to get some stuff for a vacation, what the hell could it have been that she got? And what was on this wall that she felt it necessary to take it with her?" Corelli scratched at a pimple that had just broken out on his chin.

"Maybe those holes were there before she even took the place. It doesn't exactly look like the place has been painted in twenty years. Who the fuck knows? Could be a lot of reason for those holes. Could even have been the one place that tenants over the years put up a picture and each one made a new hole." Bennedetto slammed the last metal drawer back into the kitchen cabinet.

"Looks to me like she is totally gone. Split. There is nothing here that seems to belong to her at all. Let's get the hell out of here. At least now we know where she *did* live. Let's go talk to her neighbors. Maybe we will get lucky."

* * * * *

"So this was all that you found?" Butch Cassidy said as he thumbed through the many, many newspaper articles that Jo and Don had found when they had jimmied the door open on Wendy Westlake's apartment.

"Believe me, if there was anything else there, we would have taken it, but it looked to us like she had split. There was only these clippings and picture on the wall, and some blank index cards on the kitchen counter, and the darts that were stuck in the picture of Bannagan on the wall," Jo answered. She switched her weight to her other leg as she leaned against the back of an office chair.

"She must really have it out for him to throw darts at his picture, and the index cards were like the ones that Bannagan received with the messages on them. But there was no typewriter or computer there, right? So where did she write the messages? They weren't hand written," Don said, his thumbs locked into his belt loops as if he was proud of himself for his find.

"Did you guys put the place back the way it was?" Cassidy asked absently. He continued to thumb through the articles, stopping to read each one.

"Well, no," Jo answered. "We really didn't have time. We could hear all kinds of different voices out in the hallway, so we really wanted to get the hell out of there. I was in no mood to be arrested, or worse. You should see that neighborhood. I can't believe that a woman that was used to the finer things in life would be living in that area, and in that apartment."

"I wonder if she was cutting out these articles just to watch over what he was doing or if she kept them because she had done these people and she had these as mementoes. She must be a wacko of some kind." Cassidy pulled out a chair and sat his heavy body down into it. He pulled his long ponytail off his back so that he would not sit against it when he sat back, and then stroked it a few times distractedly as he studied the clippings.

"She would have had to have known about each murder as they happened so that she could get these clippings from the local newspapers. That means that she was in the same state and town and hotel each time that he was. She was either following him to see what he was up to, in which case, she knew that he was murdering these women and did not report it to the police nor did she try to stop it. And why not? If she was out to get him, she could have by simply going to the police and turning him in. I do not think that that is the case. I think that my other hunch is the correct one—she was doing the killings and making sure that it looked like he had done it. She was setting him up to take a huge fall like he had done to her."

"Oh, my God, that makes sense!" Jo said enthusiastically, now also taking a seat at the conference table across from her boss.

"Sure. It has to be! She took a big crash when the company, i. e. the company—*him*—had laid her off. She lost her home, her husband, her name and reputation. Maybe she had had a crush on him and that sparked it. Jo, see if you can find out from any of the employees if this bitch and Bannagan had had an affair of any kind. Don, check out the area of her apartment and see if you can find a computer or typewriter that is useable by the public. Try a library or school if there is one nearby. We will see if the type matches the cards. There is a guy here in the city that does that, matches up typewriter and computer prints. Take the picture of her that the lawyer gave us and see if anyone remembers seeing her around that area of the processors, maybe remembers some conversation. I think we have it folks. Let's keep it under our hats until we can prove it."

Don summed it all up—"We also now have to find her ass."

* * * * *

Shopping and dinner had been wonderful. It had been an invigorating change from the stress they had both been under in their own individual lives. They had fallen asleep in front of the fireplace, curled up in each other's arms.

Neither one of them could have been happier than they were this one day.

~Chapter 26~

"Okay, let's go over this again to make sure that we all have it," Captain Forrest said, speaking to Bennedetto and Corelli on the telephone by way of the room conferencing speaker. The detectives had it on one side, and Captain Forrest sat on his side, along with Prosecuting Attorneys Wallace Stewart and Janet Pennington listening. "It's looking like we have a perp that is not our man. Bannagan? That it may be a woman named Wendy Westlake, who used to work with Bannagan?"

"I know it sounds pretty much off-the-wall, but things are beginning to stack up down here, Cap," Corelli said, a little louder than he had to in order for them to hear him. He kept leaning close to the telephone microphone and talking louder than normal.

"And you base this on circumstantial evidence? You guys down there pick up some of those Italian broads and want to stay down there or something? Or are you just plain drinking?" Forrest sat back in his chair, his hands playing with a ball-point pen.

"I know that we don't have it all together yet, Cap, but we found out that this Westlake broad had asked Bannagan's secretary for his schedule for the year. She told the secretary that she and Mrs. Bannagan were planning a surprise for him, and that they were gathering information and pictures from his different trips for the party they were going to have and that they needed his travel schedule for everything that was scheduled for him. After the secretary had given it to Westlake, she was worried that she had done something wrong because she knew that Westlake no longer worked for the company and that she should not have given out her boss's schedule, but she was too afraid to tell him what she had done. Then when the secretary talks to Mrs. Bannagan on the telephone, she asks her about this surprise party and finds out that the wife knows nothing about any party and that under no circumstances would she have had Wendy Westlake help her with anything, and in fact Westlake would not even be invited if there really was one. After a while the secretary forgets all about it. She remembered it when we started asking questions of all the employees."

"Yeah, and now this Westlake chick takes a quick powder when she finds out that we are looking for her for questioning," Bennedetto pipes in, as if suddenly waking up. "We checked out her apartment and there is nothing of a personal nature in there. Zip! Nada! Zilch!"

"I got it, I got it. Speaking of a personal nature, Bennie, your wife called and wants to know when the hell you are coming home or did we send you there for good. Handle it. Don't you call home, for Christ's sake?" Captain Forrest asked him.

"I'll take care of it, chief. She's just the very jealous type." Bennedetto rolled his eyes at his partner and shook his fist in the air. "You know Italian wives."

"If that is the case, guys, and you feel that this woman may have had a hand in it, then how do you explain the DNA that was found each time?" Stewart asked them.

"We can't—yet," Corelli answered. "It's a feeling that we have after talking to everyone down here. We can't explain it all yet, but I think we are close."

"Well," Captain Forrest said, raising his voice to be heard, "we have been talking to the other states and they have nothing. They have each come to a dead end with no where to go with it. Plus that fucking...s'cuse my language, Janet... that damn detective agency seems to be one step ahead of everyone and the other precincts involved are really pissed off. They better not have evidence that we don't have or I will yank that jerk's badge and license! Not to mention putting you two back in uniform to march the streets!"

* * * * *

"Okay, so we know that Westlake had his schedule, and she was keeping the newspaper clippings as reminders of what she had done, and that she hates Bannagan as per the darts and the picture. How did she do the DNA? That is a big thing, folks. Without that, Bannagan is still going to do the time whether or not he did the crime," Cassidy told his people.

Everyone sat quietly thinking. When the telephone rang, everyone jumped. "Butch Cassidy Detective Agency, Jo speaking, may I help you?"

"Jo, it's me, Betty. Boss around?"

"It's Betty," she said to Cassidy.

"Put her on speaker phone." Once Jo had pushed the buttons, Cassidy said, "Hey, Bet, I was wondering what had happened to you. I figured you finally found a man and had eloped or was at least getting laid."

"Are you crazy or what?" she said laughing.

"What did you find out down there?" Cassidy crossed his fingers and showed everyone. Everyone else followed his lead and did the same thing with both hands.

"I have plenty. Ready for this? I think the killer is a woman." She waited for a response.

"That is what we have going up here, too. What did *you* find out?"

Betty was disappointed that she had not shocked her boss, but he was always ahead of all of them. "Well, it seems that according to one of the maids here, a Mary Hightower, she saw a new maid cleaning up Bannagan's room one day when he was staying there. Mary knew that *she* was scheduled to clean that room so she went up to the new maid and asked her what she was doing. The new maid told her that she was trying to get a job there, and that the supervisor had sent her to that room to clean it up as a test and that the supervisor would be there shortly to check out the room."

"So? What has that got to do with the price of beans in Boston?" Cassidy asked, uncrossing his fingers and sitting back in his chair. He was disappointed. He had hoped that Betty had something great to report.

"Now hold on a minute, I am not done telling you. The maid said that this woman did not look like a maid. She looked like the type that would *have* a maid, not be one. She said that the woman had a turban over her hair, but her eyebrows were perfect, her nails were perfect, and even without make-up her face was really cared for. Women notice these things. You can tell when skin has been truly cared for."

Jo nodded at Cassidy that that was a true fact. "And?" Cassidy asked her, ignoring Jo.

"This maid, Mary, then gets suspicious and goes down to see her supervisor, as normally she would have been told that there was a change made, plus no one *tries out* for a maid's job. You are either hired or you're not."

They could tell that Betty was getting excited. Her voice was getting higher and louder as she spoke. They could feel the tension.

"Mary then asks her supervisor about the new maid and the supervisor, a Mrs. Elvira Harrison, says that there is no new maid. So they both go back upstairs as fast as they can and the strangest thing—the sheets are gone and they have no idea what else is missing. They check everything and also find that there is no soap in the bathroom. So now the maids are really wondering what the hell has happened, and so they start looking for this woman and they call down to security and tell the guard what had happened. Now he is looking for this maid also.

"They don't find her but they finally find the used sheets on the floor in the upstairs women's bathroom on the second floor. So they wait until Bannagan gets back and they explain that there was a woman posing as a maid and that they were wondering if anything was missing from his room. He checks and finds nothing gone. To this day they have no idea what it was all about. But they told me that that was the only strange thing that they can think of. They found that the only room that the sheets and soap were taken from was Bannagan's room."

"Really?" Cassidy says, his mind absorbing all the information, tying it in with everything else they suspected.

"And one last thing, Boss. The front desk clerk told me that flowers were brought in to be placed in Bannagan's room."

"So? Your point is . . . ?"

"The clerk said that they were really unusual, especially for that time of the year. They were out of season, so they really had a hard time finding them.."

"Oh yeah? What kind were they?" Cassidy said, now sitting up again.

"A bouquet of Bird of Paradise flowers. She said that Bannagan had also asked about the flowers because he thought the hotel had done it."

Cassidy thanked Betty, told her to come on back home and that she had done a great job. "Okay, everyone, get on the phones. Call the hotels and find out if there were any other incidents having to do with mysterious things with the sheets, soaps, etc. Also, ask about any deliveries to Bannagan of Bird of Paradise bouquets or any other kind of flowers. And I mean now! I do not care how long it takes them to get the info, but tell them we need it now! I think we may have just found out about the DNA! It came from his sheets and soap and probably from the bathroom, anywhere in that room, and then it could be planted. Get on it!"

* * * * *

"Good morning," he whispered into her sweet smelling hair. "I have really missed you and didn't know how much until now. He gently pushed a strand of her hair away from across her eyes. He kissed her eyelids, first one then the other. She snuggled closer to him so that she was almost under him. "I should never have let Barbara break us up. She was livid when she found out about you and that I wanted a divorce so that I could marry you. Did you know that? Did I tell you that back then?"

"No, you didn't," she answered softly. "You never really told me much of anything, only that we were through and that you could not see me anymore." She did not move, but Michael could feel her body tighten.

"She threatened to take everything that I had struggled so hard to build up and then I would have had nothing to give you, Wendy. I would not have even been able to take care of you. She also threatened to be sure that the Board of Trustees made sure that I had to stay on and work for the company for a few years, but only as an acting President as she would be the CEO after she got my stock in the divorce. I panicked.

"She also threatened that she would have you fired and would blackball you in this state so that you would not be able to get a job anywhere and that she would also sue you for alienation of affection. I gave in. I am so sorry that I did not stand and fight her, but I could not bear the loss of everything—on top of that, I could not let her hurt you every way that she could, and believe me, she would have hurt you. She would have called her parents, had their attorneys get to work on both of us and then whatever was left over when they got done, we could at least have each other. I buckled. I am so sorry. I truly loved you. I still have deep feelings even now."

Wendy was sobbing quietly in his arms and he held her close, stroking her soft hair to soothe her. He felt as bad now as he had back then when it had all happened and Barbara had confronted him. "Why are you dressed already?" she asked him sitting up suddenly and pulling the bear rug around her as a chill brushed against her.

"I have an appointment with a shrink. Remember? Art told me I had to go."

"Art? Wasn't he your attorney back a few years ago?" Michael nodded, yes.

"Well...I have something to tell you, too, Michael."

* * * * *

Corelli and Bennedetto decided to go to the DymoTek Corporation to see if they could find any little thing that they did not know already. They were coming to a dead end on how to prove that this Westlake woman could be the killer. They had to come up with more—much more.

As they sat in the cafeteria watching all the employees come to work and stop in the cafeteria for their bagel and cream cheese, or a bacon, egg and cheese on a hard roll, they really studied the faces that looked at them and then hurriedly looked away.

"Think any of them know something?" Corelli asked Bennedetto.

"Yep," he answered, his mouth full of his egg sandwich.

Corelli sipped his coffee, occasionally blowing on it to cool it off. "Is that all you do is eat, Bennie?"

Bennedetto ignored him.

They watched some of the women look at them and then quickly scurry away. It was clear no one wanted to get involved, especially in a murder investigation. When Corelli spotted Julie, he motioned her over. She walked over to the table, her coffee in her hand.

"Good morning there, officers," she said politely. "What can I do for you today?"

"Do you have some time to talk right now?" Corelli asked her.

"For a few minutes. Whatcha need?" She took a sip of her coffee, blew on it, and tried another sip.

"Did you know Wendy Westlake really well?" He clasped his hands together and placed them on the table in front of him. He leaned forward toward her as if he did not want to miss a word she said.

"Sure. I guess about as good as anyone here and maybe better than some—except Michael. He knew her *really* well, if you get my drift." She took a bigger drink of her coffee.

"Were they having an affair?" Corelli asked her. He did not even know where the question had come from. It had just come out of nowhere.

"Yes. And what an affair it was," she answered, sighing. "It was the kind of affair that every woman dreams of. He made no bones about it, even though he was a married man."

"Like how? What made it so special?" Bennedetto asked, wiping his large mouth and full lips now that he had finished his breakfast.

"Oh, please. He was always by her desk…or he had her come into his office every ten minutes…or he would go into her office and close the door. We all knew that he did that so that he could kiss her. He took her to lunch every day and many times it was a very long lunch, and she stayed late with him at night after everyone else had left work for the day. Who knew what went on when no one was here? Everyone could see the way that they looked at each other—not the way that a president looks at his senior assistant, even when he has had her as his assistant for a very long time does he look at her that way, that special way that Michael looked at Wendy.

"Every few days he sent her either candy or flowers or even some little thing. Like special flowers—Bird of Paradise bouquets. It was her favorite flower and hard to find when they were out of season, but Michael didn't care how much they cost. Of course, there was no signed note on it, just words like 'I love you' or 'Until tonight,' stuff like that. But they were never signed. Everyone knew that they came from him. It was a romance like Prince Charming and Cinderella. We all enjoyed it along with them. It was wonderful to watch as they tried to maintain a façade of work as much as they were in love with each other. It was funny and sweet at the same time."

Corelli and Bennedetto could almost feel what she was trying to describe. They, too, had once been in love like that before they had married and the feelings had changed to comfort instead of romance. They each wished that they could have that feeling back once more in their lives.

What kind of candy did he send her?" Corelli asked.

"Oh, Godiva chocolates, of course; nothing but the best for her. Look, guys, if you need any more info, we need to do this at lunch time. I need to get my butt upstairs to work or I will be down at the police station asking you guys for a job."

* * * * *

"I was so mad at you for dumping me the way you did, in front of everyone, Michael, in front of *everyone*! I hated you for that! And then a few months later you had me laid off. Just like that! No warning, no nothing. You have no idea how many names I called you, how much I hated you for the humiliation you put me through! After all, *you* were the one who made no hidden thing of our affair. You didn't care if anyone and everyone in the office knew, or if my husband found out, and then you basically slapped my face by telling me that you can't see me anymore, that it was over and then I get fired a few months later? Just like that. Poof! You were gone, our affair was over, and then wham! I'm out of a job where you did not have to see me at all! How did you expect me to feel? What did you think I felt for you at that point? I hated you, Mike, I hated you! I cried and cried, and then when I thought that I could cry no more, I get fired! I sobbed until my head pounded and my chest hurt!" She began to sob again.

"Oh, God, I am so sorry," he said reaching out to hold her, but she pulled away.

"I don't know about this starting all over again, Michael. I can't go through it again. I loved you with all my heart but you let money and possessions come between us. We would have, and could have worked it all out no matter what had happened. We would have had each other. I know you can't live on love alone, but we could both have started over and still had each other, but no. You let that bitch wife of yours scare the pants off of you, but then I guess you really didn't wear the pants, did you? She did! I just don't trust you anymore, Michael after you did that."

"Wendy . . ." Just then the telephone rang and it was Art Loganthau. "I'm sorry, honey, I have to take this. It is my attorney. Good morning, Art, how are you or are you bringing me more bad news?" Michael got up, slid out of his dress slacks and pulled on his sweat pants. He turned around as Wendy got up, and covering herself with the sheet, went into the bathroom, closing the door behind her.

"Mike, do you know a woman by the name of Wendy Westlake? Used to work for you?"

"Of course, she was my senior assistant for a very long time. Why?" he asked in a lower tone, again taking a look at the closed bathroom door.

"Well, I have been getting calls from everyone today. Mike, sit down. What I am about to tell you is going to shock the shit out of you."

"I already am sitting down."

"First the detective agency called and with everything they have found out, they think that the real murderer is Wendy Westlake."

"What?" Michael said loudly. "Have you all lost your mind?" Again he glanced at the bathroom door.

"Mike, the detectives from Boston just called. They also think it is her. Did you have an affair with her? A big affair for quite a while?"

"Well, yes, but . . ." he started.

"Trust me, Mike. They have a lot of evidence and some witnesses that have enough proof adding up to the possibility that it is your old sweetie. We have to go over all of this, but right now they are all looking for her. They feel that she is very dangerous"

Wendy came out of the bathroom and Michael could tell that she had been crying, her face was puffy and her eyes were red. "I see," Michael said. Wendy slid delicately into the new silk bathrobe that he had bought her and then went out of the bedroom and down the stairs.

"Do you know where she could be, or if she has any family and where they live or anything that will help find her? We need to find her. Once the cops have all the stuff as well as her, they may be able to put it all together and you may be in the clear."

Michael did not answer.

"Mike? Do you have any information that might lead them to her family or to her? Can we meet for lunch today and I will go over everything?" Loganthau asked him again.

Michael heard the click of an extension phone being picked up. "I'll call you back, Art," he said quickly, and hung up the telephone. He sat there for a few minutes trying to understand how they could have come up with Wendy Westlake's name and why they could possibly think that she was a murderer. But then she had just told him how upset and angry she was when the break-up and lay-off had happened. Could it be the truth?

"Mikie? Coffee is ready," she called up the stairs.

~Chapter 27~

Art Loganthau met Bannagan at a private restaurant on Witherspoon Street. After they had ordered drinks, they scanned the menus.

"Why so quiet? You look upset, Mike. If you still care for this woman, I know it is hard to believe, but they have learned that a woman under the name of Wilma White has been at every hotel that you were at, at the same time. Does that not strike you as odd?"

When Michael did not answer he went on. "They checked out the information that this woman had written on her check-in ticket and none of it is real. The whole thing is phony. Then we find out that someone posing as a maid, went only into your room, took your sheets and your soaps out of the bathroom and no other room. And that happened on every occasion because after they checked all the hotels, they found that at each one this strange thing had occurred. They only saw the maid at one of the hotels, but each had the same thing happen. On top of it, didn't your ex-sweetie love Bird of Paradise flowers?"

Michael finally looked up. His eyes said that Art had finally struck a nerve. Michael had forgotten that.

"That's right, Mike. We know that you received a bouquet of those particular flowers at each hotel. When they finally found Wendy Westlake's apartment in a terrible part of downtown Trenton, they found a wall with all the newspaper clippings of the murders clipped out of each newspaper, plus a picture of you in the center with dart holes in the face. I'd say that the woman really hates you and you were definitely set up…*big* time.

She got the DNA from hair on your sheets, on the soap, probably from your hairbrush, toothbrush, and in the tub. She took glasses out of your room and put them in the murdered women's rooms…those that had rooms. The woman killed in the elevator? A few strands of your hair were on her clothes—the desk clerk?—same thing. And the others, the same. The only difference was the hooker in Boston. I think that is where she had some trouble. The hooker must have really fought for her life. There's more, Mike. We need to find her. If you know where her family is so that they can check and see if she is there, we have to do it."

"Her mother lives in New Hampshire, but she is not at her mom's house," Michael said softly. Art stared at him, waiting, but he did not continue.

"How do you know that? Do you know where she is?"

The waitress brought the food and set it on the table in front of them. "Is there anything else I can get you gentlemen?"

"Another scotch for me, please," Michael said flatly.

Art said that he would take another drink also. "Mike? What is it?"

"I owe her, Art. I know it sounds fucking stupid, but I care about her. I can't help it. I have for many years now, but Barbara screwed it up. I should have stood my ground back then but I didn't. I was too worried about losing my business, my savings, my home and my money! And I cannot believe that Wendy is capable of murder. She screams when she sees a bug."

"Mike? Where is she?" Art asked again. He was now convinced that Michael knew where she was.

"She's at my house," Michael finally said softly, taking a big swallow of his drink.

"*What?* What the fuck is she doing there? How did . . . never mind, it's not important. How long has she been there?"

"About two weeks now. Art, I care about her something awful. I was going to ask her to move in with me. Fuck, fuck, fuck!" he said and pounded the table, making the dishes rattle and people at the neighboring tables turn to look at them.

"Oh, Christ, now what?" Art said, absently pushing his chicken cordon bleu around his plate.

"Let me think for a minute. I still can't believe it. I mean she told me how much she had hated me, how much she had cried when I left her, and then again when she was the first one fired, she was humiliated, and I did it all to her, Art. I did it. I have some responsibility in this."

"Enough to go to jail, or to be put to death for? That is what she set you up to get. Stop with the feelings of guilt and think about this. This woman wanted you to be hurt like you had hurt her, and she wanted you to be hurt bad. And she almost succeeded. Are you listening to me?" Michael did not answer. "Well, I have to take this news to the police, Mike. I have no choice. You understand that, don't you?"

"I want some time with her first. I want to hear it from her lips, Art. I know her. She cannot have done this. Angry with me or not, she could not have done this. I can't explain it, but she can. I am sure that she can. I need to talk to her. Once they get their hands on her I won't be able to find out for sure." His hands were trembling as he tried to take a drink of his scotch.

"And if she runs? She may run right out the door and then what? Can you swear that you will be able to keep her there until the police arrive? You have to remember—you are living with a murderer—a serial killer, Mike!"

Both men sat quietly. "Where does she think you are now?" Art said, finally breaking the quiet.

"At your office. She could be gone by the time I get home."

"Oh, shit. I never thought of that. You better eat and get going. I will give you a half hour to get home and another half hour to talk to her before I tell them where she is. Is that fair?"

"Yes."

"I don't believe this. They even have the maid that talked to her coming up to identify her, plus a waitress at the hotel in Boston who believes that she served her in the restaurant is being brought down. I am so sorry, Mike. Now I will have to prove that you two weren't in this together, you know."

"What? What do you mean 'we were in it together?' Doesn't this clear me?" He ran his hand through his hair.

"No, and when they find out that she has been at your house . . ." he did not finish. He knew Mike understood the implications of it all.

"Oh, my God. Damn, that is why she has no money. She has been using it to follow me. But how did she know where I was going?"

"Your secretary. She called her and told her that she was planning a party for you with Babs. Then later when Suz talked to your wife, she found out that your wife hates . . . hated Wendy, so I guess that Babs knew about her, right?"

"Yes. I had told her about Wendy when I asked for the divorce."

"Man, this shit gets deeper every minute. Eat and go. I will call you later to find out what she said."

"I am not hungry, Art. I'm sorry," Michael said as he got up.

"Mike, when they come to get her, do *not* go with her. I will come up with a reason why she was there, but don't make it worse by going with her." Art Loganthau watched as his client and friend walked out the door, his shoulders slumped, his arms hanging down at his sides. He made a mental note to ease up on his affair with his assistant, Nancy. He did not need a situation like this in his own home.

* * * * *

She was lying on the sofa in the family room watching the animal channel when he walked in. "Hi Mikie, I was wondering when you were coming home." She became quiet when she saw the look on his face and in his brown eyes. "What's the matter?"

He sat down next to her and took her small hands in his. He was not sure if he did that to talk to her more sweetly or to keep her from running away before the cops got there. "This morning when we were talking, you told me how much you hate me for the things that had happened to you because of me."

"Hated, Mikie, past tense. I don't hate you any more—actually never really hated you. I was just very angry," she said smiling up at him.

"Don't interrupt. Just listen to me, okay?" His palms were very sweaty and his knees felt weak.

"Okay," she said, not sure what was happening, but she felt a chill like she had the day that he had told her good-bye. She was praying that that was not it.

"I want to know several things. First of all, what did you spend your money on? I know you had stocks, bonds, savings, the house. What did you spend the money on?"

"I lost most of it in the divorce, of course," she answered.

"Do not lie to me on these questions. I will call your ex-husband if I have to."

"Hey, what is this about? What's going on with you?" she asked, pulling her hands away from him and getting up from the sofa.

"Did you follow me around the country?" There he had asked it. Her look changed first from anger to sweetness and then to shock at him knowing that.

"Why? Is that against the law?" She picked up her purse and he was ready to grab her, but she took out a pack of cigarettes and lit one.

"Oh, you smoke now, too. But actually, following a person around *is* against the law. It is called stalking! Answer my question, Wendy, please. Were you following me around on my trips?"

"Yes."

"Why? Why in heavens name were you doing that? Did you hate me so much that you would follow me around and . . . and . . ."

"And what? I followed you around at first because I thought maybe if we talked, if we had some time together again, that we could fix our relationship and maybe get back together. I loved you more than life itself. I had to take the chance."

"What did you mean when you said 'at first' you followed me around to try to talk to me?" There were police sirens off in the distance. Michael began to sweat. He wanted to scream for her to run. Or hide her…but where?

"Well, the first day that I followed you to North Carolina, I was watching you, trying to figure out the best time to try to talk to you . . ." The sirens were much louder and he was panicking.

"Why did you kill those women? Were you setting me up?" he blurted out.

"What? What are you talking about? Mike . . ." There was a banging on the front door.

"Answer me! Did you kill those women to get even with me?"

"What women? I didn't kill any women. I didn't kill anyone. Mike?" Now she was terrified. The look on his face, the police pounding on the front door yelling 'Police!'" He took her into his arms and held her tightly. He was shaking so bad that he could barely breathe. She could feel it all as he held her. "Mikie? What's happening?"

"It's open," he yelled to the police.

"Michael? Please. What's happening?" She began to cry.

He hugged her tightly, and then quickly let her go and stepped back away from her.

~Chapter 28~

"You expect us to believe all this, Ms. Westlake?" Corelli asked her gruffly?

"Yes! It's the truth! Look I have told you everything you have asked me. I am tired. I have cooperated with you to the fullest. So you bring your witnesses here and if they say it was me they are out and out lying. Can I leave now?"

"That's enough, guys. Ms. Westlake, unless these fine detectives are going to arrest you, let's go. That's enough," Art Loganthau said, coming into the interrogation room. He looked from Corelli to Bennedetto.

"Don't disappear this time, Ms. Westlake. I am sure that you will need to answer more questions," Corelli told her as she was getting up from the chair that she had sat in for over two hours. "I guess you were both in this together, huh? You even have the same attorney."

"I am only representing Ms. Westlake until she has the time to secure her own attorney, so don't go jumping the gun or you will shoot yourself in the ass."

As they were going outside the building, she asked the attorney who he was and who had called him. "I am Art Loganthau, and for the time being, I have been retained as your attorney until we find you one, as per Michael Bannagan, and that is where you are going as soon as we meet him for dinner."

"No! He turned me in to the cops! I am not going back there." She stopped walking down the steps to the sidewalk, turned and stood with her hands on her small hips, glaring at the attorney.

"Young lady, this is no time to be a jackass. He had no choice. They were looking for you everywhere. He did not want to tell me that you were at his house. I told the police, not him. Now shut up and let's go eat. That man is in enough trouble, and between the three of us, maybe we can figure this all out," he said in his towering intimidating way, his face right in front of hers.

When they got to the restaurant, Michael was waiting. He stood as they approached. Wendy barely glanced at him. "How did it go?" he asked Loganthau.

"I don't know yet, as this young lady is not cooperating with me by telling me what she told them. I think that she needs her own attorney as fast as possible, Mike. She is a hostile witness for us, not to mention that it looks like you are both in these murders together."

"I didn't kill anyone, damn it!" she said vehemently. "I do not know what the fuck is going on here, but I am being shafted is all I know!" she hissed across the table so no one else could hear her.

"I am the one being shafted, Wendy. Someone is killing women wherever I go and leaving some form of my DNA at each killing so that it looks like I had done it and I have no idea why or who. So now, let's start from the beginning and find out what you know and then maybe we can find out who is doing this. Okay?" Michael asked her sweetly, his hand over hers on the table.

She took in a big amount of air and then let out a big sigh. "Okay. After my divorce and the selling of my house, I turned everything I had into cash. I found that horrible place in Trenton in order to keep the money for traveling. The only chance I had of getting you back was to be wherever you were and hopefully be able to talk to you and maybe we could find a way that Barbara could not find out. I was willing to take whatever time I could get from you. I love you Michael, so much that it hurts me until I can't breathe; so much so that I can't think of anything else."

The waitress came over to the table for their drink order. They gave her their choices and then went to the menus in order to find what they wanted to eat. Wendy was not hungry, but the men made her pick something so that she could keep up her strength to get through all of what was about to take place. After the drinks were there on the table, and the dinner orders were taken, Michael once again took her hand, which Art made him release in case anyone was watching them.

"Go on, Wendy, please," Michael asked her.

She shifted a little in her chair, and then leaning forward said, "Okay, where was I? Oh yeah. North Carolina. I tried to get your attention several times, but it seemed that some other girl always had possession of you. I was so jealous!"

"Jealous enough to kill that tourist?" Art asked her before taking a sip of his Manhattan.

"I told you. I did not kill anyone!!"

"Okay, okay. So then what did you do?"

"I decided that I would sit in the lobby and wait until I saw that woman leave and then I would knock on your door. Plain and simple." She took a sip of her Mai Tai, moving the little umbrella to the side of the glass. "I had to go to the ladies' room and when I got back I did not know if she had left or not, so I went up to your floor, and when the elevator doors opened, Barbara was right by your door with her ear against your suite door; she jumped and stood up and turned to see who was on the elevator and it was me. I was so shocked at seeing her there, listening by your door, that I just stood there in the elevator until the doors closed again."

"Barbara? Are you sure it was her?" Michael asked her, unable to contain his surprise. "I can't picture her outside my door listening. And, of course, I had company. Oh, my God," he said, and downed his scotch and water. He motioned for the drink waitress to bring everyone another round. "Oh, my God. Are you sure that it was her?"

"Of course, I am sure. I know what *she* looks like and although we met, it was only that one time, I was sure that she did not recognize me. But I was shaking at that point. I did not know what I should do; should I go home and try again the next month or just forget it and try to accept not having you in my life? But you *were* my life! That was the night that the tourist woman was killed in the elevator. Again I was shocked. It could have been *me* in that elevator alone. I decided the next day to check out and go home. Nothing was going right and I had had too many shocks already for that trip."

"But the newspaper clipping? You had it pinned to your wall. Why?" Loganthau asked her.

"Oh, that. How did you know that I had clippings on my wall?"

"Never mind, that is another story, Ms. Westlake. So, please, continue," Loganthau said.

"Well, I got the paper the next morning to read on the train. When I saw the article on the first page about the murder, I cut it out as a reminder to take heed when I travel alone. That woman never expected to get killed. Plus it would remind me that Michael had another woman besides his wife and that he always would; did I want to live the rest of my life knowing or wondering who else was with him. The clipping was to be a reminder of a bad trip."

The drink waitress came with another fresh round of drinks and the food waitress came with their dinners. While they were there, Michael stared at Wendy who was staring down at the tablecloth. Loganthau watched them both. *Was she on the level,* he wondered. *It was a bit far-fetched, and that was probably why the detectives hadn't bought it, either. But people in love do take chances and do weird and stupid things. He would have the detective agency see if they could verify what she was telling them.*

"That's it?" Michael asked her.

"For North Carolina anyway." She picked up her fork and knife and cut a small piece of stuffed shrimp.

"What do you mean for 'North Carolina anyway?' So, you *did* follow me around on my schedule?" he asked her, beginning to get upset about being followed, no matter what the reasons.

"Yes, Mikie, I did. I even sent you a bouquet of my favorite flowers trying to let you know that I was near, but you never came looking for me. I figured for sure that you would know what they meant. How many people do you know who love Bird of Paradise flowers as their number one favorite?" She sat chewing her shrimp watching him as the light in his eyes came on and she knew that he suddenly understood. "You never even thought about me, did you? That is why the flowers did not even ring a bell, huh? Oh, my God, how stupid am I? What a fool I made of myself in the name of *love*. Not to mention that it took all the money I had. Oh Christ, I am so embarrassed." She began to cry. She jumped up and ran to the ladies room.

Michael sat there, stunned. She was right—he never even thought about her much less connected the flowers to her.

"Um, Mike, I think you better go see if she is okay," Loganthau said to him.

"And say what? *'You're right, Wendy, I never thought about you. I'm sorry?'*"

"How about anything so that she does not skip out on us? What do you think, huh?" Loganthau leaned his chin on his right fist, his elbow on the table, the other fist on his left hip.

Michael Bannagan jumped up, almost knocking his chair over and dashed for the ladies' room without actually running. "Miss? My friend went into the ladies room and she was upset. Could you see if she is okay," he asked one of the waitresses.

The waitress came out a minute or two later and told him that there was no one in there. He asked her if she was sure, and she had laughed and said that the bathroom was not big enough for her to hide in. He looked all around the lounge, the restaurant, but no Wendy anywhere. He went back to the table and sat down heavily.

"Couldn't find her, huh?" Art asked him rhetorically. When Bannagan just looked at him, he said loudly, "Waitress!" When the drink waitress came over to their table he ordered a double round of drinks for the two of them and requested that her meal be taken away.

"Today is as good as any other to get drunk, wouldn't you say?" he said to Bannagan.

"Fuck!"

~Chapter 29~

"What the fuck? It's three thirty-five in the morning. Who the fuck is coming to his house at this hour in a taxi?" Officer Wendall said as both officers stretched their necks. "I'm going to take a look." He turned off the interior light so that it would not go on and quietly opened the car door. He walked softly around the bushes and up the driveway just far enough so that he could see the entrance to the house. A woman was pushing the doorbell and the cab was still sitting there so maybe she wasn't planning on staying. Finally the upstairs light went on and Bannagan peeked out. Then he opened the window and asked quietly who was there.

"It's me. Please open the door."

Bannagan opened the front door without turning on the hall or front porch lights and the woman went into the darkness. The drapes were then pulled shut before lights were turned on. The officer walked back to the car.

"Some chick. At this hour maybe a hooker. He must need some pussy," Wendall said.

"So he expects a hooker and he is *sleeping*? Not a hooker. I'm calling it in." As the officer was calling in the activity, the cab pulled out of the driveway and passed the two stake-out officers.

* * * * *

"We need to talk," he said shortly, tying his robe at his waist.

"No shit," she snapped back.

He grabbed her by the upper arm and walked her to the family room. "First of all, don't you realize that this house is being watched 24/7? I am sure by now that they have called in that you are here at my house again."

"I can leave," she said starting to stand up, but he yanked her back down onto the couch.

"The damage is already done, so sit still." He ran his hand through his hair. "Want something to drink?"

"You having something?" she asked politely.

"Yes. Coffee. My attorney and I decided after you split on us, to go ahead and get drunker than hell. I mean, what else could go wrong? So now, I have a terrible headache, my stomach is not sitting too good, and you show up in the wee hours of the morning to give the outside shit brigade something to wonder about. You want coffee or something else?" He had his hand against the wall and was leaning on it.

"Just a glass of water. I did not want to wreck your life when I came to you a few weeks ago. I came here after I finally got up the nerve to, after I heard that Barbara was dead. I did not know if you would see me; or how you would feel when you finally saw me. But I couldn't help myself. I had to try. My feelings overrode my brain. But I had no idea that the police were looking for me because they thought I killed someone. Just for your sake, and your peace of mind, I never killed any of those women. You believe me, don't you?"

He handed her the glass of water and then sat down on the chair across from the couch and stared at her. "Yes, I guess that I do. So, why did you follow me to South Carolina? I mean I am assuming that you did, right?

"Yes. Same reason. Plus I wanted to see if Barbara followed you, too. I found it quite curious that she was there, and listening by your door. I wonder if she did that to us, too. You think?"

"I have no idea. I am shocked that she did it in North Carolina. That explains why she was never home when I was on the road. She would call me back about a day or two before I came home, and always had an excuse as to where she had been. I never even thought in the beginning that she was having an affair. It was in Georgia that I thought maybe she was seeing someone else. I figured if she was, then I would learn about it sooner or later. That kind of stuff always comes out one way or another. Like with us. She thought that there was someone else, but she had no idea that it was so serious until I asked for a divorce." He sipped some more coffee and stared at the carpet.

"You really did love me, then," she said matter-of-factly. "But you never even attempted to see me, or talk to me, or anything."

"I figured that she had hired a private detective to see if I was still seeing you. She gave me one meeting with you to get it resolved and then that would be the end of it—or else. I'm so sorry that I put my money and possessions ahead of you. But sometimes without the money and the power, women have a habit of slowly disappearing. Women get off on having a powerful and wealthy man who everyone seems to know. They want that prestige. And so I dissolved the relationship, and even though it damn near killed me to not be with you, I took no chances. I guess I doubted your sincerity and love for me if I stood alone, naked with nothing to offer you."

Wendy stood up, walked over to him and sat by his legs. "I can't believe that you doubted my love. I loved *you*, not what you had. Whatever we lost, we could make again—together. I told you that, Mikie." She laid her head against his knees. He stroked her hair—hair that was soft, shiny and clean smelling, not untouchable hair like Barbara had. *But then Barbara had had shiny and soft hair when they were first married, and he could run his hands through it. Why did they change?* he wondered.

* * * * *

"Westlake is at Bannagan's again. The cops on stake out said that a woman fitting her description showed up at his door in a cab," Bennedetto told his partner.

"You woke me up to tell me that?" Corelli asked him, somewhat angry. He looked at the clock on the nightstand. "Shit, Bennie, it's four fifteen in the fucking morning. It will wait until tomorrow. She's not going to go anywhere. She has an attorney now so there is nothing we can do. When we have enough on her, then we can pick her up again. At least we will know where she is. Now go the fuck back to sleep," he said firmly and hung up the phone.

* * * * *

"Let's go to bed and get some sleep. We will talk some more tomorrow and we will find you a good attorney. Art is going to call us early and tell us who to contact and to see if I found you." He stood up, staggering a little, leaned down and pulled her gently to her feet.

"But you didn't come looking for me last night, did you?"

He put his long arm around her. "Honey, if I had seen you standing in front of me on a deserted street and naked, I would not have known it was you, I was so drunk." He kissed her lightly on the lips. "Bedtime before I fall down. I am too old for these long hours, especially with all the alcohol in me. I need to sleep some of it off."

They walked up the stairs, arms around each other's waist. No matter what happened now, she knew that she was home.

~Chapter 30~

Bright and early the next morning, Art Loganthau called to see if Bannagan had found Wendy. After learning that she was at Bannagan's house again, he told Mike that they were to stay right there, that he had a lawyer for her and they would both be by the house around ten o'clock. Now as the four of them sat in the dining room, Angelica brought in a tray of coffee, cups, saucers, sugar, creamer and fresh hot, homemade cinnamon buns.

It didn't take long for Wendy to bring her new attorney up-to-date on everything up to her North Carolina trip and that murder. They soon learned that it had been the same scenarios in Louisville, Mississippi and Atlanta, Georgia. Each time that Bannagan had gone to another place to work, Wendy would follow, and so would Barbara. Wendy explained that she had started clipping the articles out of the paper whenever there was a murder when they were in that state. And there was always another murder. Only the victim's were different.

Her attorney, Brent Collins, said that it was strange that it kept occurring when the same three people were close by. "And you were checked into each of the hotels under the name of Wilma White?" he asked her, sizing her up, listening to every word she said. He had to determine if she was telling the truth or bull-shitting him from the get-go.

"What? Not me. I couldn't afford to stay where Michael did. I always slept at the YMCA or a hostel. I could barely feed myself as it was, if you can call living on Krystal hamburgers or the cheapest hot dogs I could find, feeding myself. I had to keep my money for planes, trains and traveling. I could go hungry if I had to, and I could sleep anywhere, but I had to be able to *get* there. At first I thought that Barbara was just following him to get evidence of his playing around, you know, other women and affairs in order to get a divorce." She frowned at Bannagan. "But then with the murders, I did not know what to think or to expect. Then, I began to suspect that maybe she was killing all the women he was having affairs with. I certainly never had any idea that she was killing women just to plant stuff from Michael to set him up for jail! Had I known that I would have gone to him the first time it all happened and warned him."

"So? Why did you not at least warn him that his wife was following him?" Collins asked her.

She was quiet for a while staring at Bannagan until she finally said, "Because I figured with all the women that he was sleeping around with that he deserved whatever she had in store for him, but I still never figured on murder. I was angry by then. I loved him, too, and he was cheating on me, also. He told me that he could not see me anymore because if his wife found out he was still playing around, she was going to take him for everything. So he stopped seeing me and would not even talk to me. Was I supposed to protect someone who would not even take a call from me but continued to mess around with everyone else?" Again she glared at Michael. He was staring down at the table.

"Does that explain why there were darts found on the floor beneath a picture of Mike on the wall in your apartment?" When she didn't answer, he said, "I guess that is a yes." He closed his Day-Timer where he had been taking notes and said, "Well, you are going with me down to the police station, young lady, as there are two witnesses there waiting and you must stand in a line-up and see if you are identified."

"What? Why?" she asked, horrified, turning to look at Michael as if he could stop what was about to happen. "Michael, are you coming with me?"

"Michael can't do that," Loganthau answered. "It is bad enough that they have connected you two together, but they do not need to think of you both as a couple. In fact you should not even be staying here, but I guess it is too late to change that now. Any damage is already done, and as you no longer have a place to live, it might as well be here."

"She is only staying here until she can find a job and get back on her feet and get a place," Michael said, finally speaking. He saw her staring at him out of the corner of her eye, and he knew that she was really angry. "Can I at least drive her down there and wait in the car for her? What damage can that possibly do?"

"I will bring her back here," Collins said.

"I have things to go over with you, Mike, so you need to stay here with me. Brent will bring her back when they are done." They watched Wendy and her attorney leave for the police station before Loganthau lit into him. "Are you out of your mind? Why did you bring her here, and worse, why are you letting her stay here with you? She could be a cold-blooded murderer, Mike! For Christ's sake, what are you thinking? You are going to blow your own case or did you forget that *you* are the one who is charged with multiple murders?"

"I care about her, Art. I mean I really care about her. I have for a few years now. How can I let her live in that raunchy apartment with no money, no clothes, no nothing, and all because of me? How do you think that makes me feel?"

"Guilty? Then you should not have fired her."

"Now how the fuck was I to know that all that happened to her was going to happen? That her husband was going to divorce her, and in fact did because of her affair with me? I owe her." He ran his hand through his hair.

"Do you owe her your life? Cause that is what you are gambling here—your life. And what do you think is going to happen when they think that you are with her and probably have been all along, and that you two murdered your wife so you could finally be together? That is what it looks like. You two had been having an affair, she was jealous when you went on trips and had other women, so she killed those women out of anger and frustration. Then, you two love-birds made up after Barbara was killed and now you are free to be out in the open with your love affair. I am willing to bet that the police already have all the info on your previous affair. Oh, Jesus, what a mess."

* * * * *

"The woman I saw was older and had longer red hair. And Freckles," the one witness had said, "she had freckles."

"That's not her. The woman I spoke to was a redhead with shoulder length hair, had blue eyes, and seemed older than any of these women," the second woman had said.

Wendy Westlake had been released to go, no charges pending as yet.

* * * * *

Michael sat quietly in his kitchen nook, sipping hot coffee. The first of many trials was about to commence in Boston. On Monday he had to appear in court as they started the process of picking a jury. Art Loganthau had placed a call to Robert Cole requesting that a two-bedroom suite be reserved and then he would call the hotel or the landlord, depending on what they found for him, and put it under his name so as to keep Michael under raps and away from the reporters, as well as any hecklers who had anything to say. Art had told Mike to pack a large suitcase and to wear his expensive conservative suits, shirts and ties as if he was going to a wedding in a large church.

Next he had gone over behavior and image with Michael explaining that he was to keep his cool in the courtroom, no matter what was said about him or anyone close to him. Art explained that the prosecuting attorney was going to say a lot of things that were partially true and partially assumptions he had come up with to make Michael look bad in the eyes of the jurors. Michael was to sit like a gentleman and look as sweet as possible. And on and on the instructions went. Now as he sat alone in his own kitchen, wondering if he would ever be able to do this again, and if he could hold up under the pressure, he remembered that this was just the first of five trials that he would have to go through. He laid his head down on his arms and sobbed with fear.

~Chapter 31~

After Art Loganthau had called him to let him know that Wendy had passed the line-ups and that she had been set free, Michael wandered around his house from one room to another, thinking. Walking into his office he automatically turned on his computer. He had stopped looking at it; there would be no news from his company because it was no longer his company, he guessed; his friends had left him high and dry as if they would somehow be associated with him by the police and they did not want that at all.

"You have mail," the automated voice said. He ignored it. *It was probably just junk mail*, Michael thought. He picked up some of his drawing tablets, figuring that he would at least sketch out some programs. *Maybe he would come up with a great program and then he could have the money he got from it put away until he came out of jail—if he ever came out of jail.* He threw the tablets across the room in frustration. *What if he didn't ever come out of jail? What if they gave him the death penalty?*

"You have mail," the voice said again, as if demanding that he open his mail. He sat down and clicked on the mailbox. There were three messages, each marked Janice. He sat there staring at them in disbelief. *Was he imagining the emails? Was it someone's idea of a joke?* He clicked on the oldest email, sent about two weeks prior.

"Michael, I need to talk to you. It is urgent. I have so much to tell you. Please get back to me as soon as you can. Now you have my email address. Janice"

Oh sure, now *I have your God-damned email address, you bitch,* he thought to himself. Now *you want to talk. Why? Did you find out that your fucking cunt friend is dead?* He clicked on the next message. "Michael, please. I am sure that you are mad at me, and maybe by now you know what Babs and I did, but you at least need to hear my side of this story. Please, Michael, talk to me. Here is my telephone number: 617-555-1778. Please call me. I have so much to tell you. Janice" *I bet you do, bitch, but I do not want to hear it. All of a sudden you give me your email address, then your phone number. You know what you and my wife did and now guilt has you by your short hairs.*

His hands were shaking. Did he want to read the last one? He decided that he did and he clicked on it. "Okay, you obviously have no intention of getting back to me, so what else can I do? I know that you did not kill that girl because I know who did. I saw her do it just as I was getting into the elevator, but it was too late to stop it, so I just kept going down. When I reached the bottom floor, I waited in the lobby for her to come down, but after twenty minutes, the police showed up and so I left. I called and told her that I wanted to tell you, but she said no. She just didn't know that I saw her kill that whore. If you want to call me, fine; if not, it's your life—literally. Good-bye, Michael. Janice"

Saw her? Saw who? Saw the killer who killed Gloria? Oh my God!

He ran downstairs, called Art Loganthau to get his ass over there right away, his witness had showed up on computer and that he was going to call her as soon as he made himself a large scotch. Loganthau told him that he was not to call her back until he got there and that was an order. Michael made himself his drink and went into his family room and clicked on the TV to take his mind off of the messages. He couldn't stop shaking. Was his luck about to change?

* * * * *

"Can you believe that?" Corelli asked his partner. "Neither one identified her and they were our only fucking witnesses. Now what? If he really didn't do it, which I do not believe for an instant, and this chick didn't do it, then who? He has to be working with someone else."

"You two better get a move on. Loganthau just called and said for you both to meet him at Bannagan's house right away and to bring a telephone tap with you with a listening device," Paul Carrolle, the lead officer in New Jersey said, putting on his lightweight jacket.

"Where are you going?" Bennedetto asked him.

"With you. You are still in New Jersey, which is *my* territory, and I have my own homicide involved in this case, so you can move your Italian asses or stay here. It's up to you." He grabbed the phone tap out of the supply cabinet and headed for the door with Corelli and Bennedetto close behind him.

* * * * *

"What the fuck is going on here, Art?" Bannagan snapped at his attorney when he saw the detectives pulling up and getting out of their car.

"Calm down. This may be your out of this problem if she tells that you were with her that night, *and* if she saw who did it. Christ, Mike, this may be finished everywhere. Don't you want it all over with?" he hissed at Michael as the detectives walked up to them. "The detectives are going to tap your telephone and hopefully, she really did see who did it and we can all go home and sleep like babies. Right, guys? Do it to it, fellows. Anyone want a drink besides me?" Loganthau walked into the family room and up to the bar.

"I'll have a double scotch and water, no water," Michael said.

"And how many of those have you already had before we got here?"

"Well, you should have gotten here sooner. I'll have a scotch and water, okay, Daddy?" Michael said sarcastically to Loganthau.

"Look, Mike. You have to have your head together. You have to get her to admit that you were with her that night, that she saw that victim in the hall, and that she saw who killed that hooker. I need you to stay alert and on the ball. This is only your whole damn life!"

"We're ready when you guys are," Paul Carrolle said, getting up from where they had sat preparing the telephones. "Now I'll have a cola if you have one."

Although Michael was hesitant about speaking to Janice or Beverly, whoever she really was, with the detectives listening in, he made the call. He really had no choice. As Art had said, it meant his life, and he knew that he had no choice but to do as they said. He was partially disappointed and partially relieved, when he got her voicemail message instead of her. He looked over at Corelli who was listening in, and the detective gave him the go ahead motion.

"Janice, this is Michael. I just saw your email messages and I would really like to talk to you. I have missed you and there are so many questions with no answers. I pray that you can help me or I am going to jail, and maybe to the gas chamber. Please call me as soon as you receive this message. *Please*, Janice. My number is 609-555-1892. I will be waiting for your call." He did not know why he had given her the telephone number when he knew that her being best friends with his wife, that she would have had the number. Maybe he shouldn't have given it to her, and then he would really know if they had been talking on the phone.

Just as Michael was hanging up the phone, the door opened and Wendy Westlake was standing there, surprise written all over her face, and fear brightening her hazel eyes as she realized that the police were there. "What's happening here?" she asked, watching Corelli take off the headphones. "Michael?"

Before Michael could speak, Loganthau jumped in and said, "Wendy, we are tapping Mike's phone. He is getting threatening phone calls and mail. We are trying to find out who it is. How about if we all decide what we want to eat for dinner? I don't know about the rest of you, but I am getting pretty hungry and we have no idea how long this will take."

Wendy was staring at Michael as if to get confirmation about what the attorney had said. He smiled weakly at her. He had totally forgotten about her staying there, but he knew from what Loganthau had just told her that he did not want her to know what was really going on. He just did not understand why not. *Was she still a suspect,* he wondered, *or was he worried about her getting into it. But how was he to get rid of her without hurting her feelings.*

Again, it was Loganthau who came to the rescue. "Wendy, would you be a doll and go get us all some food? We have to stay here in case the caller tries to reach Mike again. Would you do that for us? Now that you are free of this case, you are the only one that is available to run this errand. We have to protect Mike until we can prove *his* innocence. Okay?"

"Sure," she said seeming to relax a little. "Is he in danger? I mean *real* danger?"

"We don't know if the threats are real or not," Corelli said. "I could go for Chinese food." He looked at Bennedetto and a look passed between them—a look that took many years for partners to cultivate between them; a look that needed no words. "And you can use my car. Just be sure to come back with it." They all laughed—everyone except Michael Bannagan.

"Well, if Wendy doesn't mind making more than one trip, I could sure go for Italian," Bennedetto said.

Art Loganthau caught on and requested Kentucky Fried Chicken and biscuits—if she didn't mind. Carrolle said to just surprise him and bring back whatever.

Wendy laughed. "No, I don't mind making a million stops. Michael? What would you like?"

"Actually I am not hungry." He was twisting his hands, and then he went to running them through his hair.

"You need to eat something, Mike. How about some fast food? A hamburger and fries, maybe?" He looked at Michael and gave him a stare that told Michael to follow what he was saying.

"Sure, that would work, I guess. Wendy, honey, you sure you don't mind so many stops?"

"No, not at all as long as I'm not paying," she said, laughing again. "But I don't promise that the food is going to be still hot by the time I get back. I am going to be gone for quite a while." She got a pad from the desk and a pen, and wrote down what everyone wanted from each place.

Loganthau gave her the money for everyone's dinner, his treat, told Wendy to get whatever she wanted, and thanked her again as she was leaving. Once she was gone, all the men exhaled. Corelli turned on the big screen TV, asking Bannagan if he minded, as he never got a chance to watch one so large.

"So, what do you think, Bennie? Think my old lady will buy me a TV like this for Christmas? Especially if I offer to do the dishes for a month?" Corelli asked his partner.

"You already have an automatic dishwasher."

"Why do you think I made the deal?" Corelli doubled over with laughter.

They all sat back to wait.

* * * * *

As she drove the detective's SUV, Wendy Westlake tried to put two and two together. Something didn't seem to be right about what was going on in that house. She noticed the shock on their faces when she had walked in. Like they had forgotten all about her, which was really okay with her. She was out of that mess once and for all. *That's what you think, you dumb bitch,* the voice in her head said. *You think that his whole world is wrapped around you? If that was the case, why did he not just tell you the truth instead of sending you out on a food run? Surely, you don't believe what they just told you.*

"Shut the fuck up," Wendy said to the empty car. "He loves me."

Yeah, right. Like he loved you two years ago? Like he loved you enough to leave his cunt wife? Like he tried to call you after you broke up, or answer your telephone calls back then? And now you find out that he was having other affairs on his wife after you, just not with you. I wonder how many other women he had affairs with after you while he was traveling. And what were you doing? Crying your heart out, day after day, stuck in a rat- and roach-infested room as big as your old bathroom, while he went about living his wonderful two-sided life of the wife and home, and his traveling and women.

"I said shut the fuck up! Do you hear me? I am not joking. I will run this fucking car into a tree or a light pole and that will shut your God-damned mouth once and for all, now won't it?"

Okay, have it your way, you jerk, but when he is curled up with you tonight, running his dirty hands all over you, think about those other women. And while you're at it, why not ask him about them and see if he tells you the truth. You and I will know if he is lying or laying it out straight for you, wanting an honest relationship now. What do you say? Do you really want to know the truth? Remember, the truth will set you free. That horrible laugh followed—that tinkling, sadistic, hollow laugh.

"Don't worry, I will. I am sure that he will tell me the truth. As soon as we get rid of those asshole cops and that fucking stupid attorney, he will tell me everything. You just wait and see."

No, he won't. He does not know that you know all about everything now, so he will only fess up to what he is sure that you do know. You dumb fuck!

~Chapter 32~

Janice finally called about twenty minutes after Wendy had left to go get the food. "I am so sorry about what is happening to you, Michael."

"Felt so bad, that it took you months to get in touch with me? Felt so bad that you still haven't stepped forward and told the police that I had been with you that night? That it was *you* that I was having sex with, that the maid had heard, *not* Gloria?" His rage was bubbling to the top and Loganthau put his hand on Mike's arm. Michael sighed a deep sigh. "What difference does it all make now, I guess?"

"No. I *am* going to the police, but I wanted to call you first and talk to you about it."

"Why? So you could tell *me* the truth first?"

"Yes. There is much to tell you. Are you alone?"

Michael looked around the room at the men sitting there and who were staring back at him. "Yes. But let me help you with the truth. Your name is really Beverly, you went to school with Barbara and have been good friends ever since. So you both got together to set me up,"

Michael said, talking faster and faster, "am I getting warm?"

There was dead silence on the phone.

"Cat got your tongue, *Beverly*? Look, just tell me why. Tell me why, when I trusted you, that you would do this to me. You know that I did not kill anyone, so why did you two do this?" He ran his hand through his hair and then over his face.

"Babs wanted a divorce," she finally said quietly, "and she needed proof of your affairs, so she asked me to help her. But I *swear* I knew nothing about anyone getting murdered or that she would make you out to be the killer when she was."

Michael Bannagan froze. "She was what?" He was holding onto his friend's arm.

"The person who was doing the killings. I swear, Michael, she never told me that I would get involved in anything like that. In fact, she never even told me about the murders until I saw her kill that hooker that night at your hotel. You have to believe me!"

Mike stared at his attorney, shock written all over his face, which had turned a cloudy white. He felt as if he was going to pass out. Corelli gave a thumb's up to everyone.

"Did you just say you *saw* her do that?" Michael asked her softly, barely able to swallow. His chest was pounding, his throat was dry, and his hands shook. "I can't believe this. I had no idea that she hated me so much that she would kill those women and make it look as if I had done it." He motioned to Art that his throat was dry and the attorney got up and went to the bar to make Mike a drink. He decided that his friend really needed one right now.

"I was just supposed to make it look like we were having an affair and then the private investigator could take pictures. That's it. That was all that she asked me to do. I swear, Michael. I could never be a part of anything that had to do with physically hurting anyone, let alone killing them. But then things changed. You were not the ogre that she told me that you were, and when I looked into your eyes, watched every move you made, listened to everything that you said. You were so handsome and so intelligent, and of course, so passionate, that I forgot what I was supposed to do. Babs had a fit when she found out that we had gone to bed together. I tried to get in touch with her for the past month but whenever I called no one answered except your voice machine, and I decided that I could not wait anymore to talk to her or the police will find out about me and think I did it."

"Oh, so that is why you are now willing to call the police—to cover your own ass, not to save mine." He was let down—again. "Well, the reason she has not been answering the phone is because she is dead, Janice . . . Bev . . . *whoever* you are," he said, angry now and turning sarcastic. "She has been dead about six weeks now."

There was silence on the phone again. Detective Bennedetto's cell was vibrating and he looked at the message. He motioned to his partner by tapping his wristwatch. The telephone company had traced the call and had the address that she was calling from. Michael still did not say anything more, even when Corelli was motioning him to say something. He did not know what else to say. He was hurt, embarrassed and felt like the fool, especially with the cops listening in and taping the call so that everyone could hear what she had to say about him and their affair.

"Michael? Are you still there?" she asked softly.

He knew that she was crying. Loganthau handed him a pad and a pen. On the pad he had written, 'address?' "Are you going to give me your address this time or are we still going to play these childish games?" he said barely audible. After she had given him her address, he asked her when she intended on going to the police.

"Oh, I can't do that now!"

"What? Why not? I thought that was why you called me," he said, looking over at Corelli who was on the extension. Corelli was writing something to Bennedetto on a small tablet.

"Because now that Babs is dead, I have no way of proving my innocence. She is dead and they will think that I was in on all this. Maybe they will even think that I killed her! Oh, God, Michael, I don't know what to do." She was really crying now.

"Will you meet with me?" he asked after reading the note on the tablet that Bennedetto was holding in front of him. "Can we have dinner or a drink maybe? We need to think this through and see what we should do next. How about if I fly up there tomorrow and I will meet you at the Sheppard's Pie? Can you get away from your husband?"

"Michael, I am not married. It was just the excuse that Babs and I came up with so that I could not tell you how to reach me and where to find me. Oh, damn, this all sounds so stupid and immature now," she said sobbing. She blew her nose, but she was truly getting hysterical.

"Then at least now you can meet me or I will come up to your house. You owe me that much, Janice . . . Bev . . ."

"Beverly. Beverly Tempre," she said before going back to blowing her nose again. "Okay. I will meet you.

But not at my home in case you are followed. I do not want the cops to know where I am until we discuss all this." She began to cry again.

"Sheppard's Pie tomorrow, right? What time?" he asked her. Corelli gave him a thumbs up.

"How about seven tomorrow night?" she asked him.

"Beverly, you'll be there, right? If you are going to play me for a fool again, then don't. Please. I have been through enough, don't you think?" he said.

"I'll be there. Good-night, Michael."

"Honey, I'm home," Wendy yelled coming into the family room just as Michael and Detective Corelli were hanging up the telephones. She stood still for a moment and then said, "Did I miss something important?"

~Chapter 33~

After the detectives had assured Wendy that she had not missed anything except that the person who was threatening Mike had called, and that he had to go up to Boston in the morning to meet with the person. They asked her to please stay at the house tomorrow to take any messages in case the person called back; that they were going to set up a sting to capture this person and by the time that Michael came home, it should, hopefully, all be over. They did not want her to know about Beverly Tempre and what was really happening.

Wendy said that she would be happy to help but, unfortunately she had an appointment for a job interview and that she could not miss it, and then had pushed her way into sitting next to Michael. The detectives said that that was okay, wished her good luck on her interview and explained that they had to get a move on, and thanked Wendy for picking up the food. They each took their dinner with them when they left.

Now as Michael was sitting in the back of the cab winding its way through the busy streets of Boston heading for the hotel that the detectives had arranged for him under an alias, he was planning what he would say and do when he saw Beverly Tempre at dinner. Corelli had told him not to look for them, but that he would be well in view, just in case this was a set-up, which Bannagan did not believe for an instant.

They had had to make reservations for him at a hotel where he hopefully would not be recognized, and was given a different name to check in under. There was not a hotel in the city that would have allowed him to stay there if they knew that he was Michael Bannagan, a/k/a Lady Killer. He was thinking of taking that name as a screen name on the computer, but he was sure that the name was already taken and that he would have to pick a number to go with it, and with as many men that would have the screen name of Lady Killer, he laughed to himself that he would probably have to be LadyKiller666. But then using a name like that would remind him for the rest of his life that he had gone through all of this and he would sooner forget it if he ever got out of all of this mess that he was in.

He had just barely put his suitcase down and tipped the bellboy when the telephone rang. It was Corelli letting him know that they would be up to his room soon. He was told to get something to eat, take a nap, then a shower upon rising and that he should be completely dried by the time that they got there as they were going to wire him before he met Bev for dinner. When he asked if all that was necessary, that he felt that he could handle her no matter what, he was advised that they needed to be his witnesses and to have proof of his innocence. He had misgivings about all of it, but he did as Loganthau had advised, and he cooperated.

As he lay there, he could not help but think about her and all that had happened between them before. He still could not believe that she had gone along with the plans that Babs had come up with for a divorce, but what if Loganthau was right? What if *Beverly* was the murderer? She *had* left his room that night and met Gloria in the hallway. Suppose she had killed her? But then, for what reason? It wasn't as if he had really met her on the Internet like he had originally thought until he learned that she had known Babs. But yes, Art and the detectives could be right—maybe she was just a wacko, and maybe she had known or still knew Babs, but that did not mean that Babs knew that her friend was a wacko. Or she could have and that was *why* Babs had used Beverly—because she *was* a wacko.

Maybe Babs had not seen her since school, and it was just all coincidence that Michael had met her, of all the people to meet, and that Beverly was the real killer. But then, Babs could have found Beverly on the Internet through one of those "classmate" sites. Maybe she had been stalking him all along and it had absolutely nothing to do with Babs, the divorce or anything else having to do with his wife. Maybe not only had she killed those women at each hotel, but she had even killed Babs when she realized that Michael was married to her old friend. Bannagan had worked up a severe headache trying to figure it all out.

It was all more than he could decipher, and before long Michael Bannagan fell into a restless sleep.

* * * * *

"Listen to this tape, Cap. The bitch is talking to herself in my car. That Wendy Westlake creeps me out," Corelli said, sitting in his captain's office with Bennedetto.

"You still have that recorder in your car? I thought you got rid of that thing years ago." Captain Forrest looked at Bennedetto who merely shrugged.

"My partner is paranoid," Bennie answered.

"Hey, at least my ass is covered. Besides, it helped us out on another case when they didn't know that they were being taped," Corelli shot back in defense. "It just automatically runs when there is a voice-activation and runs as long as it is plugged in and once in a while it costs me for a new tape, so why the hell not have it?"

"Okay, put the damn thing on," Forrest said.

"Shut the fuck up. . . . He loves me. . . . I said shut the fuck up!. . . Do you hear me? . . . I am not joking. . . . I will run this fucking car into a tree or a light pole and that will shut your God-damned mouth once and for all, now won't it?. . . Don't worry, I will. . . . I am sure that he will tell me the truth. . . . As soon as we get rid of those asshole cops and that fucking stupid attorney, he will tell me everything. . . . You just wait and see."

Corelli shut the recorder off. "Do do do do, do do do do, . . ." he sang to the theme of the Twilight Zone series and then laughed.

* * * * *

Bannagan ordered a scotch and water as soon as he sat down in the restaurant. His mouth was dry and his nerves were on edge, not only because he might finally find out the truth about everything, but because he really was excited to see her again. He kept wanting to call her Janice in his mind, but he had to get used to calling her by her real name, Beverly.

Suddenly she appeared, as beautiful as he had remembered, except that this time she was in new designer jeans that looked faded in the front and back of the legs; she had on a pretty thin, pink sweater that not only hugged her beautiful curves, but showed more than it should have, and wore clogs on her small feet. Her hair was pulled back and fastened at the back of her neck with a gold barrette, but this time she was a brunette instead of a blond. When she saw him, she smiled weakly and walked up to the table as confidant as the day he had first seen her. "Hi," she said softly.

"Hi," he said getting up to his feet and pulling out her chair. "How have you been? You okay?"

"I should be asking you that question," she said back.

"See? This time I didn't spill the water. That's an improvement." They both laughed.

The waitress brought them a menu and they were silent as they looked it over. After giving the waitress their order, it was Beverly who broke the heavy silence. "Michael, I am so sorry that I really do not know what to say at this point. I know that you are angry, but I had to come forward." She reached across the table and placed her hand over his. "We have to find a way to fix all this and clear it up. I decided after I talked to you on the telephone yesterday, that no matter what happens to me, I have to help you clear up this horrible mess. I love you, Michael, but even if you never have anything to do with me again, then at least I will have helped to get you out from under this black cloud that I helped put over your head."

Michael stared at her, analyzing what she said and if her body language matched what he was hearing…and it was. She was being sincere, and he hoped that he was reading her right. He really could not take any more and felt that if all of this did not pan out that he would blow his head off with a thirty-eight revolver. "Thank you for that. I see that you dyed your hair brown."

"I know. I didn't want anyone to find me in case . . ." she said and then paused before changing the subject. "I thought that we might as well get it over with after we eat and we will go down to the police precinct and see the detectives that are handling your case. Okay?" She wiped at he corners of her pretty red mouth.

"Okay. Might as well get it over with, huh?" He ate heartily, having not eaten much since this had all started. He felt that maybe now he had a chance to get out from under all this.

* * * * *

See, Asshole? That woman is back. The police lied. Michael lied. And you believed it all, you fucking jerk! the voice said. *Now aren't you glad that you listened to me and took an early flight to Boston or you would have had no way to find him?*

Wendy kept her eyes on the woman, saw her touch Michael's hand, saw the look on her face when she looked at him.

Once a cheater, always a cheater. He cheated on his wife with you and other women, so what made you think that he would be faithful to you, you idiot! And he had not even married you before he started cheating. He knows that you love him, and look how he respects that love. When will you get the message? You are such a fucking asshole, ya know?

Tears ran down Wendy's small oval face. She did not move, but kept her eyes glued on Michael and the girl.

"Are you ready to order," the waiter asked her kindly.

"No, not yet. I am waiting for someone," Wendy replied, not even trying to wipe the tears from her cheeks, as if she didn't even know that tears were flowing.. Her eyes never left the woman's face.

The waiter went back to the counter area. "Poor girl. Somebody has stood her up. She is crying," he told the other waiters and waitresses busy getting orders ready. They all looked over at her.

Wendy saw the stares, but she looked back to Michael and the bimbo he was with.

Nice! Everyone is staring at you. They know, the voice continued. *They see the pain on your face and the tears as they run from your eyes. Now maybe you will get the picture. You are such a fucking jerk!*

She watched as the woman got up and started walking toward the ladies' room. Wendy slowly got up and followed her.

* * * * *

"She is following Tempre into the Ladies Room. Move it, move it!!" Corelli whispered into the walkie-talkie. "Get a female officer in there right away! Move it!"

"We are already on it and Jenny is already in there," Bennedetto said back.

* * * * *

Officer Jenny Daniels washed her hands slowly, keeping an eye on both women. When she caught Wendy watching her, she smiled and said, "I hate eating shellfish. Now my hands will smell like it all night."

Wendy did not answer her. Jenny walked into one of the slatted stalls and watched through the slit in the door. Wendy moved closer to the stall that Beverly was in. As the door opened, there was a soft click and then Beverly went to the sink to wash her hands.

"If you think that he will stay with you and be faithful, he won't be so don't kid yourself," Wendy said sweetly to Beverly.

"Excuse me?" Beverly answered drying her hands on a clean hand towel.

"You heard what I said. He will not be faithful to you, no matter what he says or does. That is just the way he is. I don't think that he can help it. Some men are just like that. They do not really mean anyone any harm they just have to have variety in sex."

"Who are you talking about?" Beverly asked, getting slightly irritated.

"Michael! Michael Bannagan! You know exactly who I am talking about so don't lie to me." Wendy now stood in front of Beverly.

"Look, Miss, I don't know who you are, but I would think that it is none of your business," Beverly responded, getting fearful of the woman in front of her. "Excuse me, I have to go." As she tried to go past the woman, there was a sharp pain in her stomach and her hands grabbed at the pain, but the woman's hand was in the way. Beverly screamed and crumpled to the floor.

Jenny burst out of the stall and grabbed Wendy by the arms and threw her against the tiled wall. "Let's go," she said loudly into her mike to notify the male officers oustide. "Need some EMTs in here, too."

Wendy was struggling, trying to cut the woman who had eaten shellfish and who was now holding her arms tightly behind her back. "Let go of me, you bitch!"

"You are under arrest. You have the right to an attorney . . . .."

"I have to get back to my table and see what is going to happen. Don't you understand? This woman is trying to take my future husband away from me!" Wendy tried to explain. "Do you not understand? I had to do that. She is getting too close to him."

Corelli, Bennedetto, O'Callihan and Captain Forrest all came running through the door just as two women were coming into the bathroom and saw the ruckus going on, and the girl lying on the floor bleeding. "Sorry, ladies. Please try the men's room. This one is busy."

When Michael had noticed the detectives running into the ladies' room, he got up and ran in there. He stooped down to Beverly and tried to compress the stab wound.

"Michael. There you are," Wendy said when she saw him. "Thank God! Tell these people who I am. They don't believe that we are going to get married. Tell them, Michael, please." He just looked up at her. "Michael? Honey? They are hurting me. Please tell them who I am. And tell that voice. She thinks that you are just stringing me along, you know? Michael?"

"It was you who killed all those women wasn't it? he asked her softly, still holding Beverly.

"I had to, Michael, don't you see? They all wanted you, I could tell. I could see it when you passed them and they looked at you with that special look. Besides, I was angry at you. You had dumped me like a hot potato when the wifey said to. We loved each other. You had said so over and over. But when you dumped me, I had no choice but to put you in jail for hurting me. You really did hurt me, you know—in every way possible. You took my money, my home, my husband, my love and you stomped on all of it and laughed! Don't you see?

Please, Michael, they are hurting me. Tell them you still love me."

"I didn't purposely hurt you, Wendy. I loved you."

"See? See, I told you, now take these cuffs off, please," she said to the cop who still held her against the wall.

The paramedics came rushing through the door and ran right over to Beverly. Michael stood up, his hands, shirt and pants all covered in blood. "I am so sorry that all of this happened to you, Wendy, really I am."

"Oh, look, Michael. She got blood all over your clothes. As soon as they let go of me, I will wash them for you, Honey," she said looking at Michael's clothes.

"Come on," Jenny said, pulling Wendy away from the wall. Wendy tried to get closer to Michael but the cop pulled her back and took her out the door as she continued to call out Michael's name.

"How did you know?" Michael asked the detectives who had been just standing there taking in everything as Wendy had babbled on.

"My car told me," Corelli said laughing.

~Chapter 34~

Wendy confessed to everything with the Boston cops, having signed off on the paper giving up her rights to an attorney. She had listened as the cops had explained how she had followed Bannagan everywhere. How she went to his room each day at each place, taking his hair from his bed and from the shower, his glasses from his drinks the night before, and had used them at each crime scene. They had asked her where the red wig was that she must have worn as well as the blue contact lenses, and although she seemed confused as to some of the details, she explained how she had had no choice. She had to protect him long enough to see him rot in jail, but then she would go back to telling everyone how they were going to be married and have a beautiful home in Princeton, New Jersey.

Even though the knife that she had stabbed Beverly with did not match the wounds on the dead women, they had Wendy's confession, and that was all they needed to indict her. Her attorney had finally walked in to stop it, with medical attendants in tow, and they had Wendy taken to Marlboro State Hospital in New Jersey for evaluation and treatment. He would plead her guilty due to mental incompetence. All charges against Michael Bannagan were dropped with apologies from everyone.

Bannagan had just stared at them like they were the ones who were crazy, not Wendy, and then had just walked away after telling them that they would be more sorry when he sued them all.

Michael had gone back to his company and the board had reluctantly given him his position back, and Bill Schmidt was fired. Now Schmidt had lost his wife, his home, his money and his position with the company, and as fate would have it, no other company would hire him.

Michael Bannagan blamed himself for everything that had happened. *Had it not been for his womanizing, none of this would have happened*, he thought to himself. *All those women would be still alive—except Babs.*

He had learned about her affair before the attorneys and the detective agency, and he was no longer going to put up with her crap. He was not about to let her take everything that he had worked so hard for and enjoy it with someone else. Besides, he had already been indicted for the murders of those women whom he had not killed, so what was one more? Was there really any difference? Silently, he thanked Wendy and prayed that she would get well for her own sake.

Well, he thought smiling, *he and Beverly had other plans and she was moving into his home today until they were married in June and he couldn't wait. The only thing that had really changed in his game of life was the players and he wouldn't have it any other way. She would be just like Barbara,* he decided. *They all hated giving up the wealth, the prestige and the power that they got from being his wife. Yes, life was good. Bev was packing to move down to Princeton. Michael had found a great new home for them and she had sold her fabulous house in Boston. It was all working out.*

* * * * *

Not trusting the movers to be careful with her computer, Beverly put it in the backseat of her car. After all, that was how she had talked to Michael for so long. Once Barbara had told her Michael's screen name, it had been easy from then on to find him whenever he was on-line. It had started out as a joke. After talking to him on the computer for several months, she realized that she had fallen deeply in love with him, so when Barbara had asked her to help her get her divorce, Beverly was all for it. And everything had ended up exactly as Beverly had hoped—she now had Michael all to herself.

"You have beautiful red hair," the mailman just passing by commented as Beverly was getting into her car.

She thanked him and looked at herself in the car mirror, fluffing the red curls. After staring at herself for a few minutes, she casually tossed the red wig out the window and it landed on the top of the bags waiting for the garbage men. She pulled her car in behind the moving truck as they started off, and was driving away just as the garbage truck pulled up to her old home.

"Look at all this great stuff that these people are throwing out," the garbage-man said to his buddy. The stack of throw-a-ways was piled high on the Boston sidewalk in front of Beverly's former home. "I bet my wife would like some of this. It's better than the stuff we have at home."

"That's the trouble with these rich people. They have no appreciation for what they have. They get bored with it, buy new stuff and just throw the old stuff away. What jerks," his buddy said as he was going through all the stuff. "But it's good for us!"

An old woman pushing a grocery cart in front of her full of junk that she had collected along the way had stopped and was standing to one side watching the garbage collectors looking through all the stuff on the sidewalk. One of the men noticed her. "Want some of this stuff, dear? There's plenty for the three of us."

The woman cautiously came toward them, peeking at the pile of goodies now spread all over the sidewalk. She smiled an almost toothless smile as she inched closer to the men, picking up items as she walked toward them.

"Look here, sweetie. Here's a beautiful red wig in perfectly great condition! Want it?"

~THE END~